MURDER ON OLYMPUS

MURDER ON OLYMPUS

A PLATO JONES NOVEL

ROBERT B. WARREN

DRAGONFAIRY PRESS
ATLANTA

MURDER ON OLYMPUS

Cover design by Georgina Gibson
www.georginagibson.com

Published by Dragonfairy Press, Atlanta
www.dragonfairypress.com
Dragonfairy Press and the Dragonfairy Press logo are
trademarks of Dragonfairy Press LLC.

First Publication, April 2013
Trade Paperback Edition, April 2013
ISBN: 978-0-9850230-6-5

Published in the United States of America

Library of Congress Control Number: 2012951597

In memory of Alma Thompson.

1

"There's someone here to see you."

Emilie, my secretary, stood in my office doorway. Her brown eyes widened to the size of dinner plates behind a pair of tortoiseshell bifocals.

"Client?" I asked.

"I believe so."

"Mortal?"

She shrugged. "As far as I can tell."

"Hot?"

"It's a man, sir."

"Damn."

I put my submarine sandwich back in its wrapper and dusted stray food from the front of my shirt. Emilie cleared her throat, pointing to the corner of her mouth. I dabbed a napkin at the gob of spicy mustard on my face.

"Send him in."

"Yes, sir."

Emilie left, and shortly after, a thin man with suntanned skin stepped into my office. He wore faded coveralls and an equally faded baseball cap. Something I hoped was dried mud splattered his leather boots, which looked like they'd been beaten to death.

I stood up and shook his damp palm. "Good afternoon."

"Afternoon," he said.

I waved toward the chair in front of my desk. He sat down. His large eyes darted around the room, ricocheting off everything.

"You'll have to excuse the smell," I said. "I was having lunch."

The man shook his head. "I don't mind."

"Plato Jones, private investigator, at your service. And you are?"

"Nicolas Parker."

"Nice to meet you, Nicky." I offered him a sweet from the candy dish on my desk.

"No thanks." Nicolas continued to look around. His eyes never stayed in one place for more than a second.

"You're not from around here, are you?" I asked.

Nicolas gave a nervous grin. His teeth reminded me of candy corn—small and spaced out, with orange and yellow stains. "How'd you know?"

I eyed his coveralls. "Lucky guess."

"I'm a rancher."

"Is this your first visit to New Olympia?"

"No, sir. I come here three, maybe four times a year. Delivery trips."

"So Nicky, what brings you here today? What can I do for you?"

Nicolas's mouth tightened into a line. He laced his fingers in his lap. His foot tapped against the floor. "I have a problem."

"Tell me about it."

"The other week, someone snuck onto my property." He hesitated. I gestured for him to continue. After a moment he added, "They snuck onto my property and stole one of my best gorgons."

I blinked. "Excuse me?"

"My gorgon," Nicolas said. "She was stolen."

"You're a gorgon rancher?"

"Yes, sir." He nodded.

I crossed my arms to mask a shiver. Gorgons were some of the nastiest creatures around, but they were also big business. Their castoff skins were all the rage in the fashion industry. But raising the buggers was hazardous. They were strong and fast, almost impossible to tame, and had a natural aversion toward humans. Most gorgon farmers ended up getting killed by their own livestock.

"Is that a problem?" Nicolas asked.

"No," I lied. Gorgons gave me the creeps with all their hissing, and slithering, and turning people into stone. But the fact that Nicolas raised them for a living meant he had lots of money. Lots of money he'd send my way if I helped him.

Nicolas's posture relaxed, and he leaned back into the chair. "That's good to hear. I was worried. The last detective I spoke with said he didn't deal with gorgons. Said he didn't want to end up a statue."

"Imagine that."

"Do you think you can help?"

"Maybe. First I'll need some more information. Take me back to the day of the theft."

Nicolas nodded. "Well, I woke up and had breakfast, like I always do. Then I went outside to feed the gorgons . . . like I always do. When I got to their enclosure, I noticed the padlock on the gate was broken. I counted them, and one was missing. A female. A big one. I looked all over the property but couldn't find her."

"And you think someone stole her?" I asked.

"That's the only explanation I could come up with."

"Is it possible she got out on her own?"

"I guess, but it's never happened before."

"Did you report the theft to the police?"

"Yeah."

"What'd they say?"

"They'll call me if anything comes up. That was a few weeks ago."

"Have you contacted them since?" I asked.

"Yesterday. They're still looking into it."

"Then why hire a PI?"

"The police aren't working fast enough." Nicolas dropped his gaze to his lap. "What if my gorgon ends up hurting someone, or worse?"

"It wouldn't be your fault. You were robbed."

"I know. But still, I don't want something like that on my conscience."

"I understand."

Nicolas looked up at me, his expression hopeful. "So you'll help me?"

I folded my hands on my desk. "I'm going to be perfectly honest with you, Nicky. I despise gorgons. Hate everything about them. How they're always hissing and slithering around. How they smell like fish and stale woodchips. Everything. But I like you, so I'm going to look into this."

Nicolas beamed. "Thank you, Mr. Jones."

"Don't thank me until I've solved the case."

"What do you need from me to get started?"

"For now, just your address and phone number," I said. "We'll discuss my fee later."

"Of course."

Nicolas gave me the information, and I keyed it into my laptop.

"Boreasville." I grinned. "You *are* a country boy, aren't you?"

4

Nicolas laughed, his hands fidgeting in his lap. Excitement had replaced his nervous energy. "So, what's the next step?"

"Tomorrow morning I'll take a look at the crime scene, see if I can find any clues."

"And then?"

"And then the search begins."

"Do you think you'll be able to find her?" Nicolas asked.

"I'll certainly try."

"Thank you, Mr. Jones, for looking into this."

"No problem." I stood and moved around the desk. "I'll see you tomorrow."

Nicolas rose from his seat, and we shook hands.

"On your way out," I added, "make sure you talk with my secretary about payment options."

"Okay."

"Have a good one."

Nicolas closed the office door behind him. I sat back down. Minutes later, Emilie reappeared in the doorway. In her ankle-length navy dress, with its white floral pattern, puffy sleeves, and frilly lace neckline, she resembled the schoolmarm from a Wild West serial I watched as a kid.

"Problem?" I asked.

"No, sir."

"Is the client still here?"

Emilie shook her head. "No, sir."

"Then what's up?"

"You have a call."

"Who is it?" I asked.

"The caller refuses to give his name, and the number is classified."

I knew who it was. I leaned back, rested my hands behind my head, and propped my feet onto the desk. "Tell him I'm not in."

2

BOREASVILLE WAS FIFTY MILES REMOVED FROM NEW OLYMPIA, an elderly hamlet of farmers and artisans. Humans made up most of the population, with a dash of satyr and cyclops. The town was once the quintessential coffee stain on the map, until the whole health food craze caught on. Now it was the region's number one supplier of organic produce.

I parked in front of Nicolas's three-story ranch house. It sat in the middle of the plains, surrounded by miles of mud and tall grass. The house's classic design, combined with the austere landscape, gave the impression I stood on the set of some low-budget slasher flick.

As I stepped out of my car, the humid air enveloped me. It reeked of manure and rotting hay. Little white flies swarmed around me. I swatted bugs and skipped over mud puddles as I approached the house. That morning I had debated whether to wear a suit. I was glad I hadn't. In a place like this, a T-shirt, jeans, and boots were more appropriate for stomping through muck.

Nicolas waited for me on the porch, wearing the same clothing he'd worn to the consultation. He held a tranquilizer rifle in his hands. I would've preferred a shotgun, or a rocket launcher. But it was better than nothing.

"Afternoon, Mr. Jones," he said.

"Nicky." I gestured at the gun. "I hope that's not for me."

Nicolas glanced at the gun and made an O-shape with his mouth. "Oh, no, no, it's not. This is just . . ."

"Relax, I'm kidding."

He smiled, looking relieved. "Thanks for coming out. I was afraid you wouldn't show."

"You thought the city slicker was going to take your money and run."

His smile widened. "No, nothing like that."

"Glad to hear it. Now where are these gorgons of yours?" I asked.

"About a half mile away, in an enclosure." He gestured northeast with the rifle.

"A half mile." I whistled. "In that case we had better get moving."

"One second." Nicolas reached into the big pocket on the front of his overalls and pulled out a large pair of sunglasses. They were reminiscent of the hideous UV shades companies used to sell on TV.

"I had no idea ranchers were so fashion-forward," I said with a smirk.

Nicolas chuckled. "These are to protect me from the gorgons' stares."

"Oh."

He reached back into his pocket and pulled out another pair, which he handed to me. "When we get to the enclosure, do not, under any circumstance, take off those glasses."

"You don't have to worry about that."

We walked to an open-air barn on the northeast edge of the property. A chain-link enclosure housed seven gorgons, each one larger than the average man. From the waist up, they looked similar to humans, but not quite. Bald heads capped narrow faces, and their gold-green eyes were serpentlike, with slit pupils. Fangs filled their wide mouths. From the waist down, their bodies were those of snakes. Iridescent scales covered them from head to tail. The colors and patterns varied from one gorgon to another.

As we approached the enclosure, the gorgons greeted us with a fanfare of hissing. Though I wore the protective glasses, I still made it a point to avoid eye contact. Better safe than petrified.

"A lovely group of . . ." I paused. "Ladies?"

"Six of them are female," Nicolas informed me. "The other is a male."

"How can you tell which is which?"

"You don't want to know."

"Have you ever been stoned?" I asked.

"Four times. Luckily, the effect is only temporary—unless you get smashed to bits. No coming back after that."

"And why do you do this again?"

Nicolas shrugged. "Money's good. Real good. What about you, Mr. Jones? You ever been stoned?"

"Once, back in college. But there were no gorgons there."

Nicolas led me around the side of the cage to the entrance gate. The gorgons slithered after us, their bodies rubbing against the fence.

"You say this door was open on the morning after the robbery?" I asked.

Nicolas nodded. "The lock was broken."

"What about the other gorgons? Were they still in the enclosure?"

"Yes. Only one female was missing. The others were calm. You know, docile. They didn't hiss or screech or nothing. It was the darndest thing."

"What was wrong with them?"

"I don't know. But after an hour or so, they went back to being aggressive."

"Did you notice anything else?" I asked.

"Nope. Nothing else."

I searched the surrounding area for clues. In the pasture near the barn, I found a shallow furrow in the ground.

"Is this a gorgon track?" I asked.

"Looks to be."

"Let's follow it, see where it takes us."

The gorgon track ended at a two-lane highway on the edge of the property. Beyond lay a stretch of forest. We crossed the road and combed the woods for the next few hours. Not one single track. I wiped the sweat from my brow. The heat I could handle, but the stench was getting to me. I wondered how Nicolas dealt with it on a daily basis. I guessed it was something you had to get used to.

"Looks like our trail has officially gone cold," I said.

"What's that mean?"

"It means we have more work to do."

"What do you need from me?"

"Patience."

"But—"

"Let's explore our options," I said, cutting him off. "Have you considered contacting animal control?"

"Why?" Nicolas asked.

"Because I'm not convinced your gorgon was stolen."

"Then what happened to her?"

"My guess is she escaped on her own," I began, "and went slithering down the highway."

"How can you be so sure?"

"For one thing, there were no signs of a struggle on the scene. I'm no expert on gorgon behavior, but I'm guessing it'd be tough to abduct a full-grown adult without getting a few cuts and bruises—at least."

Nicolas pointed toward the gorgon pen in the distance. "What about the broken lock?"

"Isn't it reasonable that a four-hundred-pound gorgon would be able to smash through a locked gate?"

Nicolas didn't respond.

"And there's still the matter of the track," I continued. "From the looks of it, the gorgon came here of her own volition."

Nicolas sighed and looked away from me. Sometimes the hardest part of being a private investigator was addressing the inconsistencies in a person's story. I wanted to give every client the benefit of the doubt, but that was impossible. Sometimes the client pointed in one direction, while logic and evidence pointed in another.

In this case, there was plenty of evidence on the scene, but none suggested a robbery had taken place. It was possible someone stole the gorgon when she reached the edge of the highway. And it was possible someone stole her directly from the gorgon pen, and nature had already erased the thief's tracks. Gorgons weighed a lot more than the average person, so the gorgon tracks would last longer. But I had to operate on actual, existing evidence. The evidence told me the gorgon had wandered away on her own.

Nicolas looked at me, his expression hopeful. "Maybe someone led her off the property."

"Is that likely?" I asked. "Again, I'm no expert on gorgons, but from what I know of them, they're hardwired to attack anything that doesn't look or smell like another gorgon. A rustler would've had a hard time not getting ripped to shreds."

Nicolas opened his mouth to speak, but caught himself. His furrowed brow told me he had stumbled upon the gaping hole in his logic.

"She might have chased off the thief after he opened the gate," Nicolas said after a time.

The poor guy was grasping at straws. I couldn't help but feel sorry for him. For the past hour, I had done nothing but disagree with him. It couldn't be helped, though. Disagreeing with people was part of the job.

"I doubt it," I said. "Gorgons are as fast as they are ugly. The thief wouldn't have been able to outrun it."

Concern and frustration warred across Nicolas's face. "Is there anything you can do?"

I shook my head. "Unfortunately not. There's just not enough evidence to suggest a robbery."

He lowered his head. This was another part of the job I hated. The desire to please every single client was maddening. But I tried anyway.

"I'm sorry I couldn't be more help," I said.

Nicolas stared down at his boots. "That's alright."

"I can keep an eye out for the gorgon if you'd like," I offered. "No charge."

He nodded, still frowning. "Much obliged."

"What color is your missing gorgon?"

"Green, with flecks of blue here and there."

I made a mental note. "I'll contact you if I find anything out. In the meantime, you should probably call animal control. They're more suited for this type of thing than I am."

"I'll do that."

I patted Nicolas on the shoulder. "Again, I apologize."

"It's alright, Mr. Jones."

3

AT FIRST GLANCE, THE GODS OF OLYMPUS ARE AS DIFFERENT from one another as salt is from sugar. But if you take a closer look, you'll begin to realize that despite their bickering, they're essentially of a single mind. They share a universal bond, a thread of commonality that unites them as one: they're all jerks.

Hermes was no exception. He barged into my office wearing a white pinstripe suit. His long white hair was pulled back into a ponytail. He looked like a catalog model that had gotten lost on his way to a photo shoot. But the same could be said about most of the Gods. He was thousands of years old but looked around the same age as me—thirty-five. Lucky bastard. Seeing him—or any other God—usually made me take stock of my own appearance.

Some women found me attractive. I didn't see it. Growing up, some kids were skinny with big teeth. Others had giant ears. I had the unique privilege of having all three traits, a veritable trifecta of awkwardness. In elementary school, they called me the amazing rat boy, able to cut through steel cable with a single bite. Not a day went by that someone didn't pluck my ears or stuff me in a locker. But that changed once I reached high school, and had grown into my features. By senior year,

I had lost my virginity and was dating a majorette. Not bad for an ugly duckling.

Hermes was the official messenger of Olympus—basically a glorified errand boy. But he was still a God, so dealing with him required a certain level of finesse. Unfortunately, grace wasn't my strong suit.

Hermes took a seat in front of my desk and laced his fingers. A humorless grin stretched across his face. "You think you're clever, don't you?" he asked.

"Excuse me?" I mumbled, my cheeks stuffed with food.

"I sat in your waiting room for over an hour. Your secretary told me you were in a meeting with clients."

I plastered a shocked expression on my face. I put down the roast beef sandwich I had been eating, dialed Emilie's extension, and turned on the speakerphone.

"Yes, sir?" she answered.

I spoke in an overly calm tone, the kind people use when they're pissed off but still want to seem professional. "Emilie, did you tell Hermes that I was in a meeting with clients?"

"Yes, sir."

"You're fired."

"Yes, sir."

I ended the call and offered Hermes an apologetic smile. His light-blue eyes betrayed a hint of annoyance. My little ploy had failed. He shook his head and I dropped the act.

I called the front desk again. "Emilie?"

"Yes, sir?"

"Sorry about before," I said. "You're not fired."

"Thank you, sir."

I ended the call.

Hermes's smile had fallen by then. "Why do you insist on wasting my time?"

"If time is a priority, then maybe you should have called and set up an appointment before showing up at my office."

"I did call. Repeatedly, in fact. You were always conveniently unavailable. Either out of the office or speaking with clients."

Hermes plucked a piece of peppermint from the candy dish. He let the wrapper fall to the floor.

I wanted to ask him to pick it up and put it in the wastebasket. Not because I wanted to keep my office clean, but because I knew it would irritate him. With effort, I managed to suppress the urge. I had already antagonized him more than I probably should have. Best not to press my luck. Besides, the sooner I found out what he wanted, the sooner he'd leave.

"How can I help you?" I asked.

"The Gods are in need of your services."

"Why would the Gods need a private investigator? Did someone on Olympus lose a sock?"

For a moment, Hermes didn't answer. He crunched loudly into his peppermint. "Eileithyia was found dead in her home this morning."

This had to be a bad joke. I searched Hermes expression, waiting for the punch line. It never came.

I leaned back in my chair, my mind blown. "A Goddess? Dead? Is that even possible?"

"Apparently so," Hermes said. "We want you on the investigation."

I shook my head. "No way. You guys have your own private task force. They should be the ones looking into this. Not me."

"They're already on it. But we need you."

"And why is that?"

"Because some would say you were our best agent. Your methods were . . . unorthodox to say the least, but you got the job done."

"Was that a compliment from a God?" I narrowed my eyes, incredulous. "Are you feeling alright, Hermes?"

His brows gathered into a scowl.

"Come to think of it, you are looking paler than usual. Did you eat something that didn't agree with you?" I reached for my speakerphone. "Just sit tight. I'll have Emilie bring you a glass of ginger ale and a handful of saltines."

"Damn it, Jones!" Hermes shot upright and slammed his fist on the desk. The wood cracked down the middle. "Do you think this is some kind of game?"

Fear stabbed my gut. It had been so long; I had forgotten how strong the Gods were. If he hadn't held back, Hermes could have broken my desk in half.

He dusted off his hands and sat back down. "Tell me. How is this little private investigation venture going for you?"

"It's coming along."

But we both knew the truth. I had hit a dry spell. More like a drought. My last high-profile case was nearly two years ago. Since then I had worked a number of small assignments. I couldn't brag about the money. In fact, it was barely enough to pay the bills.

"Have you ever considered begging Zeus for your old job back?" Hermes asked.

"Just the other night, actually. The next day I woke up with a hangover."

Hermes laughed. "Joke all you like, but I know you miss your old life. The security. The money."

"The money wasn't that great."

Hermes's eyes narrowed. "Do you realize how fortunate you were? You were a government agent, chosen by Zeus himself. Few mortals ever get such an opportunity."

He was right about that. Zeus had founded the Olympic World Council after defeating the Titans. For centuries, only Gods were allowed membership. Then fifty years ago, he offered government jobs to a handful of mortals. It was Zeus's way of throwing mankind a bone.

After that, all sorts of arguments surfaced. Would Zeus ever step down as president? Could a human become president? Could a human become a God? Questions like those always seemed to get lost on the way to Mount Olympus. Big surprise.

I tried to come up with a rejoinder, but couldn't. What could I say? Hermes had made a valid point. Most mortals idolized the Gods and would have killed for the chance to work alongside them. There was a time when even I admired them. That was before I started working with them, before I saw them without their makeup, so to speak. I found out what was behind all the glitz and glamour, and I wasn't impressed. I'm still not.

"I have to admit," I said, "seeing you here, pleading for help, it warms my heart. But the answer's still no."

Hermes frowned. "And why is that?"

"I have my reasons."

"If money is your concern, I can assure you that you'll be well compensated."

"Money isn't the issue."

"Then tell me, Mr. Jones." Hermes leaned forward slightly. "Exactly what is the issue?"

"If this killer of yours is powerful enough to slay a Goddess, what chance would I have against him?"

"Slim to none, I'd say." Hermes helped himself to another piece of candy. An Atomic Fireball. He pursed his lips the instant he popped it into his mouth. He spit the candy back into its wrapper and returned it to the dish.

I grabbed the candy dish and emptied it into the wastebasket.

"But it doesn't matter what I think," Hermes continued. "Zeus has faith in your abilities. His opinion is the only one that matters."

"Spoken like a true lackey."

"He knew you'd play hard to get."

"Who's playing?"

"Let's be reasonable," Hermes said calmly, as if speaking to a child. "This business of yours is slowly going under. A government contract could put it back on track. Find out who's behind the murder, and I promise we'll make it worth your while."

The desperation in his voice tinkled like music to my ears. The smug bastard had never been fond of me, and the feeling was mutual. Most Gods believed that mortals, humans in particular, were inferior to them. Hermes's ideology went beyond that. He'd just as soon enslave humanity as coexist with it. Fortunately, Zeus was around to keep him, and others like him, in line. That he was being forced to play nice almost brought a smile to my face. Almost. I'm a professional, after all.

"There's nothing you can offer that would change my mind." I stood up and strode toward the door. "Tell Zeus he can find someone else to do his dirty work. Now, if you don't mind, I have another client to meet with."

Hermes clenched his jaw. He looked like he wanted to strangle me.

I knew he wouldn't. Despite his power and hatred toward mankind, Hermes was too much of a pretty boy to get his hands dirty. I crossed my arms and waited for him to leave.

"You're a stubborn one," he said.

"That's what they say."

"Are you sure you won't reconsider?"

I opened the office door.

Hermes got up and smoothed the wrinkles in his jacket. "Zeus will not be pleased."

"What a shame."

"This isn't over." Hermes plucked a pair of designer sunglasses from his coat pocket and put them on. He crossed the office to stand in front of me. We were nearly touching. He stared at me. Behind the dark lenses, his eyes flickered with anger.

I stared right back. God or not, he wasn't going to bully me in my own office. I jerked my head toward the open door.

"When this little business of yours fails, you'll be back on Olympus, throwing yourself at Zeus's feet," Hermes spat.

I smiled politely. "Thank you for thinking of the Plato Jones Detective Agency."

Hermes took a step back. "You're making a mistake."

"It wouldn't be the first time."

He slowly shook his head. "It's not wise to insult the Gods. We could make your life a lot harder than it already is."

I laughed. "Yeah, good luck with that."

"Goodbye, Mr. Jones," Hermes said. "I'll be in touch." He straightened his tie and left.

I slammed the door behind him. The conversation had left me feeling drained. Interacting with the Gods usually had that effect on me. I was ready to go home and relax. But before that, I had to meet with a client.

I grabbed a few items from my desk: my cell phone, my reading glasses, and my Desert Eagle. The gun was a souvenir from my days as an OBI agent—the Olympic Bureau of Investigation. I had been one of thirty highly trained special agents. Handpicked by Zeus, we answered only to him, executing his orders without question or prejudice. That was the theory anyway.

I was the first human to join the OBI—which had mostly included Demigods, satyrs, and minotaurs. Before that, I was an army officer. I enlisted just a year out of high school. My family couldn't afford to send me to college, so I figured the army was the answer. After I graduated from college on a military scholarship, an OBI recruiter approached me. He asked if I'd be interested in better serving my nation. I told him I was already doing a pretty good job. Then he mentioned a boatload of money. Needless to say, I was sold.

I checked the gun. The clip held eight osmium rounds, with one more in the chamber. Osmium is effective against most nonhuman creatures—hydras, vampires, and such. A well-placed shot can even slow down a God. Though no amount of bullets, osmium or otherwise, can kill one. Nothing could. At least that's what I'd thought, until today.

I flipped off the lights and walked out of my office. Emilie sat at her desk, filing her nails. She glanced at me over the rims of her bifocals.

"Going out, sir?"

"Meeting with a client," I said. "After that I'll be heading home. Lock up before you leave."

"Have a nice evening, sir."

"You too, Emilie."

4

I cruised down a street in the Gales, a ritzy suburb of New Olympia. Houses started at five hundred thousand a pop, and soared into the millions. Every lawn was immaculately manicured, with flowerbeds, bird fountains, and luxury cars parked in every garage. The streets looked freshly paved, and no trash littered the sidewalks or gutters. It was the ideal place to settle down and raise a family.

My '67 Thunderbird, with its flaking cream paint, cracked windshield, and dented bumper, turned more than a few heads. Dads watering their lawns, moms planting flowers, and kids riding their bikes all stopped to look at me. The way they stared, I might as well have been riding a flying saucer, shouting "take me to your leader."

The Stone residence—a three-story mansion behind an ornate iron gate—sat at the end of a cul-de-sac. A wall of vines, blooming with purple flowers, covered half the house. My client waited for me just outside the front door.

Looking at her made me wish I had dressed a bit nicer, though I wore my best suit. It was a gray number with a maroon button-up. I bought the outfit from a consignment shop about three years ago. Quality cost money, but spending six hundred credits for a jacket at a department store, and another four hundred for a pair of slacks, never made much sense to me. On the other hand, some people thought that buying a TV for two thousand credits didn't make a whole lot of sense either. But hey, we all have our priorities.

Bellanca Stone's petite hourglass figure reminded me of the kind on cartoons and in comic books. Black hair fell in thick curls down either side of her face, framing shadowed brown eyes, a slightly large but attractive nose, and full lips. Her bronze-colored skin glowed in the sunlight. To say that she was beautiful seemed an insulting understatement.

"Mr. Jones?" Bellanca said with a heavy Spanish accent.

"That's me. You must be Mrs. Stone."

Her skin was incredibly soft when we shook hands. I had to tell myself that she was a married woman. If I hadn't, I'm sure the massive diamond on her finger would have reminded me.

"Please, come in." She moved aside to let me pass. Inside the house, black and white covered almost every surface. The walls were white, the floors checkered. A black railing ran along the side of the staircase. White roses filled black vases atop white pedestals. The whole place had a disorienting effect.

Bellanca showed me to the living room. The ceiling soared high above my head. Sunlight poured through a vast skylight, reflecting off the white walls. The rug and drapes were black, but the leather sectional couch and loveseat were red. Fire engine red. *Finally*, I thought, *some color.* I sat on the sectional. A 72-inch flat-screen TV hung above the fireplace, playing the news. Bellanca grabbed the remote off the coffee table and muted the sound.

"Thanks for coming," she said.

"Not a problem."

"Can I get you something to drink? Water? Soda?"

I shrugged. "Soda's good."

As Bellanca walked into the kitchen, I resisted the urge to glance at her ass. While she was gone, I got up and took a stroll around the living room. A large display case occupied the corner, filled with snow globes and crystalline figures. Hanging on the wall behind the couch was a large cubist painting, with black, white, and gray shapes arranged to look like what I could only assume to be a man sitting on a toilet. Rich people baffled me.

I sat back down. Bellanca returned from the kitchen carrying a glass of ice filled with a clear, carbonated beverage.

"Here you are." She handed me the soda. "Sprite."

"Thanks." I leaned back into the sofa cushions. "So, Mrs. Stone, what can I do for you?"

Bellanca sat across from me on the loveseat and crossed her legs. The bottom of her short white dress rode up, revealing a smooth expanse of thigh. I looked away to keep from staring.

"I need you to follow someone," she said.

I raised an eyebrow. "Who?"

"My husband, Collin. I think he's cheating on me."

"Sounds simple enough." I sipped my soda, put it on the coffee table, and then took out my pad and pen. "Why do you think he's cheating on you?"

"The past few months, he's been acting strangely. Collin used to be very affectionate. I couldn't take three steps without him coming after me. Now he barely looks at me."

"That is strange," I commented, still trying not to stare at her legs.

Bellanca blushed. "That's not the only problem. He comes home late. I'm usually in bed by the time he gets here. Whenever I ask him where he's been, he gives me the same excuse: 'I was at the office, finishing up a project.'"

"What does your husband do for a living?"

"He used to be a Major League pitcher, but a shoulder injury ended his career. Now he works at Minos Advertising."

I raised an eyebrow. "A former pro athlete . . . I can see why you're suspicious."

"I've asked him a million times if he's cheating on me. He tells me I'm being paranoid, but I know he's lying. I just can't prove it. Can you help me?" She crossed her arms tightly, and her breathing was shallow. I could tell she was holding back tears.

I held up my hand. "Don't worry, Mrs. Stone, I handle this sort of thing all the time."

"Call me Bellanca."

"Bellanca," I said. "Do you have a picture of Collin I could hold onto?"

She nodded and hurried out of the living room, her high heels clacking against the tile floor. This time I ditched the chivalry and took a peek at her backside. Perfect.

She came back with a wallet-size snapshot. I examined the picture. Caucasian. Mid-fifties. Graying brown hair. Brown eyes. No distinguishing features.

"The picture's a bit old, but it's his most recent one." Bellanca sat back down and crossed her long legs again. "Collin's been a little camera shy as of late."

"Why's that?"

She pushed a few strands of loose hair out of her face. "There was an incident several months ago. It left a scar on his right cheek."

"What sort of incident?"

"He said he was mugged."

Mugged. Right. I'd seen this a dozen times before. Guy cheats on wife with mistress. Mistress gets tired of being a mistress. Wants to marry guy. Tries to convince guy to leave his wife. Guy refuses. He and mistress argue. Mistress gets pissed and goes after guy with a butcher knife . . . And scene. Cut and print.

"That's unfortunate." I slipped the photograph into my wallet.

"Is there anything else I can do?" Bellanca asked.

"Yes. I need to know a little more about Collin. Where he works. What time he leaves for work. The names of places he likes to go. You know."

"Of course." She gave me the information, and I scribbled it down.

"Thanks."

Bellanca let out a deep breath. Her hands trembled. Light reflected off her diamond ring, splintering into multicolored shards.

"You alright?" I asked.

She flashed me a nervous smile and nodded. "Yes, I'm fine. Just a little nervous. That's all."

"Don't be. The truth is nothing to be afraid of."

Bellanca was quiet for a time. Then she said, "Mr. Jones . . ."

"Plato," I corrected her.

"Plato. You said you do this all the time?"

I put the notepad and pen back into my pocket. "Yes."

"Does it usually end badly?"

"Depends on your definition of badly."

Bellanca's smile died, and some of the light faded from her eyes. I should have said something, but I was terrible at cheering people up. Still, I couldn't stand to see a woman look so sad, especially one with a pretty face, a tight bottom, and a great rack.

"Don't worry about it too much," I said. "This could all be a big misunderstanding. Happens all the time."

Some of the light returned to her eyes. "Really?"

"Sure."

She smiled at me. "I hope you're right."

For a long moment we sat in awkward silence, not looking at one another.

"I should probably get going," I said.

25

"Of course." Bellanca leapt to her feet.

I raised the half-full glass of Sprite. "Thanks for the soda."

"You're welcome."

She walked me to the front door.

"I'll call you when I find something," I said, stepping across the threshold.

Bellanca nodded. "It was nice meeting you, Mr. Jones."

"Believe me, the pleasure was all mine."

5

I WAITED IN MY CAR, ACROSS FROM THE STONE RESIDENCE. It was eight in the morning. I had been there since before sunrise.

Stakeouts are, without a doubt, my least favorite part of detective work. The long hours and boredom can drive me insane. A survival kit is essential. Today, mine included an assortment of magazines—*Sports Illustrated*, *Gun Digest*, *Time*—a six-pack of bottled water, a bag of premium beef jerky, and my trusty laptop.

I've met a lot of PIs who claim to enjoy stakeouts. They say the solitude gives them a chance to think, to be alone with their thoughts. Personally, I try not to spend too much time in my own head. A detective's brain is his most important tool, but like any tool, it can be worn down by overuse. Being overly reflective can dull the senses, make a detective less aware of what's going on around him. In my line of work, that can mean the difference between solving a case and getting dropped from it.

Collin came out of the house at 8:15, dressed for work in a charcoal suit and black loafers, and carrying a portfolio and a briefcase. He walked to the end of the driveway, with all the speed and rigidness of a corporate stooge, and climbed into his red BMW Z4. In my opinion, the car was too cool for him. I imagined he had bought it on a whim, in the midst of a midlife crisis. I'd probably do the same thing in a few years.

Bellanca appeared in the doorway behind him. She wore a short, white bathrobe. The partially open front revealed some nice cleavage. A matching towel wrapped her hair. She waved at Collin. He raised his index finger and pulled out of the driveway.

I started my engine and prepared to follow. He drove north out of the neighborhood, and then turned left onto Larken Street. With no police around, he leaned on the accelerator, but a red light at the intersection forced him to brake hard.

As we waited for the light to change, Collin answered his cell phone. I was betting his mistress was on the other end.

The light turned green and Collin sped forward. He took the first exit onto the highway, into bumper-to-bumper traffic. It took us over an hour to reach the downtown connecter. From there, I followed several cars behind him to Minos Advertising, housed in a fifty-story structure with brown-tinted windows. I pulled into the parking lot and killed the engine. Collin remained in his car for several minutes, still talking on the phone. Eventually, he ended the call and got out. He disappeared into the building.

More employees arrived. All wearing suits and dresses. All carrying briefcases and portfolios. They filed into the building like lemmings, one after the other. By ten o'clock, cars filled the quiet the parking lot. Now it was time to play the waiting game.

I read two magazines and then listened to the radio. At noon, Collin came outside and hopped into his car. I trailed him to a nearby café and parked in an adjacent lot.

I turned on my dashboard camera as he entered the café. He sat at a table near the window. The woman waiting for him sported a white tank top and blue jeans. A dark-green baseball cap and sunglasses shielded her face. As Collin sat down, she waved at him with a muscular arm, almost manly compared to Bellanca.

Collin and the mystery woman smiled at each other the whole time they talked. After about a minute, a waitress came to their table. As she took their orders, my cell phone rang. The caller ID displayed Hercules's number.

Herc was the son of Zeus and stepson of Hera. He was also my best friend and an all-around swell guy—Demigod or not. We met twelve years ago, when I was still an OBI agent. One of the perks of being with the bureau was having access to their special training facility. As it happened, Herc used to work out there too. It was the only place adapted for his special fitness needs. I guess I bit off more than I could chew while doing chest presses. My arms gave out during a rep, and the bar landed on my chest. It knocked the wind out of me and pinned me to the bench.

Herc picked up the barbell as if it were made of paper-mache, and helped me to my feet. My chest throbbed and it hurt to breathe. When he asked if I was okay, I lied and told him I was fine, and thanked him for helping out. After he walked away, I gave myself a few minutes to recover, and then resumed working out.

I tried to do another set, but my ego was stronger than my arms. The bar fell yet again. Herc offered to spot me. I told him it wasn't necessary, but he insisted, so I wised up and agreed. Afterward, we chatted about college football and instantly clicked. We've been pals ever since.

"Herc," I said.

"Hey, Jones. You busy?"

"Spying on a mark. How about you?"

"Just sitting on the couch. Watching some TV. Trying not to have a mental breakdown."

"Uh oh," I said. "What is it this time?"

"Hebe. She wants to remodel the kitchen. Again."

Hebe was Herc's wife and the Goddess of Youth. Herc introduced me to her a couple months after the gym incident. At six-two, the blond-haired beauty had legs like a supermodel. Unfortunately, she had all the bearing of a 1980s valley girl. I never heard the word *like* spoken so many times in a single sentence.

"Oh no," I gasped. "Not . . . the kitchen. I can understand the bathroom or the living room. But the kitchen? That wife of yours has gone too far this time."

"Ha ha, very funny. This is serious. You know how much it costs to remodel a kitchen?"

"I never really considered it."

"A lot, that's how much. I don't get it, Jonesy. Hebe just remodeled the kitchen two years ago. It looks fine. Looks great, in fact. Heck, the paint hasn't even dried yet. That's fifty-credits-per-gallon paint, mind you. Why can't she ever leave well enough alone?" Herc went silent.

"Feel better?" I asked.

"Much. Anyway, I'm going to the Night Owl this weekend. You coming?"

"Of course. I'm always up for a little late-night revelry."

"Great, great. Look, Jonesy, I gotta go. Gonna try to talk Hebe out of this remodeling nonsense. Call you later."

"Alright. Try not to have a heart attack between now and then."

"Shut up."

I laughed. "Later, Herc."

"Yeah, whatever."

A few minutes later, Collin and the mystery woman finished their entrees. They talked until the check came. Collin handled it, and both of them stood up. They hugged. Collin's hands didn't wander, but the embrace was tight and lasted about twenty seconds. It struck me as being more than friendly.

The two of them stepped outside, hugged once more, and went their separate ways. I turned off the camera and started the engine as Collin got into his car. He went back to work and didn't resurface until shortly after five o' clock.

I was sure that Collin would lead me to a seedy motel on the edge of town, or to the mystery woman's place, but he drove straight home. After he'd gone inside the house, I parked on the curb and waited to see if he was going to come out again. A half hour later, I assumed he was in for the night. I put my car in gear, did a U-turn, and headed out of the neighborhood.

The first day of the investigation had ended, and unfortunately, things didn't go as well as I hoped. The footage of Collin and the mystery woman was only slightly incriminating. Not enough to expose him as a cheater.

I needed something a bit more concrete.

6

APPREHENSION KNOTTED IN MY STOMACH AT THE THOUGHT of going to the office the next day. I just knew Hermes would pop in for another round of negotiations. Gods were nothing if not persistent. But to my surprise, he never showed.

The day was quiet—so quiet that I decided to leave thirty minutes early. I could avoid some of the evening rush. Traffic often turned what should be a ten-minute drive home into an hour-long journey. On the plus side, it gave me plenty of time to admire the city's glossy veneer. New Olympia, Greece, was one of the most beautiful cities in the world, an amalgamation of new and old, where futuristic skyscrapers rose alongside ancient ruins. The city was a melting pot of races and cultures, a paradise on the surface. But it had a dark side. I had seen it firsthand.

My cramped one-bedroom apartment was on the west side of town. A uniform beige color covered the walls and carpet, and my living room window graced me with a breathtaking view of the parking lot. For the most part, the place was pretty sparse in terms of decorations. I wanted my home to look cool and unique, but I failed at interior design.

My mom once offered to spice up the place for me. Despite my apprehension, I've never been able to say no to my mother.

I agreed to let her redo the kitchen. Big mistake. She ended up designing the entire space around a ceramic chicken wearing a chef's hat.

As soon as I stepped inside the apartment, a sour odor invaded my nostrils. I flipped the light switch.

Liquid had soaked into a spot of the carpet near the coffee table. Shards of glass gleamed on the kitchen floor, the remnants of a fishbowl I had bought the previous week. My goldfish, Gills, was missing-in-action.

The neighbor's cat lounged on the mantle above the fireplace, licking its chops. Its orange fur had splotches of brown and white. A red collar encircled its neck, from which hung a heart-shaped metal tag. The cat acknowledged me with a bland expression, as if to say, "What are *you* doing here?"

This wasn't the first time the little creep had broken into my place. To save money during summer months, I opened my windows instead of running the air conditioner. Whenever I did this, I risked a fifty-fifty chance of a feline home invasion. Even if I opened it only a crack, the fur ball would squeeze through. That ended today. Today it was him or me.

I smiled and took slow, measured steps toward the fireplace. The cat stopped grooming itself and followed me with its eyes.

"Good kitty," I said softly. "I'm not going to kill you. I'm just going to maim you a little."

I walked around the coffee table and came to halt. The cat sat up. Our eyes locked. Then I charged.

The cat sprang off the mantle, barely avoiding my clutches, then took a bounding leap onto the windowsill. It narrowed its gaze, daring me to come after it.

I rose to the bait.

The cat waited until I was nice and close. Then it leapt through the window. It balanced on the ledge and vanished around the side of the building.

Damn pest.

Defeated, I slammed the window shut and grabbed a bottle of peroxide from the bathroom medicine cabinet. I poured some over the wet spot on the carpet—a urine stain, courtesy of my feline friend—and threw a towel over it. Then I grabbed a broom and dustpan from the closet and began cleaning up the shattered fishbowl. *Alas, poor Gills. I knew thee well.*

When I finally had a chance to sit down and relax, my cell phone rang. I considered ignoring it, but after the eighth ring, I gave in. "Hello?"

"Plato? I've been trying to reach you all day."

It was my ex-wife. I suddenly regretted answering the phone. "Alexis. Isn't this a wonderful surprise!" I got up and trudged to the kitchen to grab a beer. I was going to need it.

"Cut the act, Plato," Alexis said. "You know why I'm calling."

"I might have an idea," I said, opening the fridge. No beer. Great.

"This is getting really old, Plato."

I sank into the recliner and tried to get comfortable. Conversations with my ex tended to last longer than I'd like. Alexis had a habit of rephrasing the same arguments over and over.

"I agree," I said. "That hairstyle of yours is so last Thursday."

"Will you be serious for one minute?"

"I suppose I can do that." I glanced at the clock. "You have exactly one minute. Go."

"I need you to come by the house this weekend and pick up the rest of your things. They're cluttering up the basement."

I sucked air through my teeth. "Sorry, but I already have plans."

"What kind of plans?"

"I'm hanging out with Herc this weekend, so I won't be able to make it over there. Maybe next week."

"That's what you said last week. And the week before that. And the week before that. Enough is enough. Listen. Calais wants to the turn the basement into a game room. But he can't do that with all your junk lying around."

"Calais?" I smirked. "So that's his name."

"Yes, it is. What's the matter? Are you jealous that I've moved on?"

It did bother me that Alexis had a new man, but I wouldn't say that I was *jealous*. My biggest grievance was that her loser boyfriend lived in my house, the house I paid for.

"On the contrary, I couldn't be happier," I lied. "I hope you and Callus have a wonderful life together."

"His name is Calais. And I know you don't mean any of that. You never let go of things easily. You know, you should really get out there and start dating."

I pulled the phone away from my ear and glared at it. The conversation was taking an uncomfortable turn. It was probably best to end it before things got awkward.

"Well, I've enjoyed our little talk, but now I have to go."

"Not so fast," Alexis said quickly, before I could hang up. "You're not getting off the hook that easily. I still have something I want to ask you."

I fought the urge to curse. "And what would that be?"

"Calais's nephew just moved to town. He was wondering if you could set him up with a job at your agency. Maybe you could put him on as a personal assistant or something."

I sat motionless for a moment, gazing at the ceiling. That beer would've come in handy right about now.

"I seem to remember you calling my agency a waste of time and money," I reminded her.

"Hey, don't bite my head off!" Alexis shot back. "This is Calais's idea, not mine. I told him about the agency, and he thought you might be able to help his nephew. Will you at least consider it?"

"Sorry."

Alexis sighed heavily into the phone. "I should have known better than to ask."

She probably thought I refused out of spite, which was only partially true. It was more about money. Financially, my agency was teetering on the ropes, and I simply didn't have the funds to hire more staff.

"It's just business," I said.

"Right."

"Ask me again in a few months." This was assuming I'd still be in business.

"Just forget it."

"Okay."

There was silence on the other end. I had the feeling Alexis's anger was approaching critical mass.

"I tried to be cordial, Plato, I really did. But if you insist on acting like a child, I'll treat you like one. If your junk isn't out of here by Sunday, I'm putting it on the curb."

I grinned. This wasn't the first time Alexis had threatened to trash my stuff. She'd done it numerous times over the past year. Even though she was bluffing, it was hard not to play along.

"W-wait a minute," I purposely stuttered. "Let's not be too hasty. I'm sure we can come to some kind of agreement."

"Goodbye, Plato." And she hung up.

I set down the phone and laughed. Alexis wasn't as cunning as she thought. I was wise to her little scheme. The stuff in the basement wasn't the issue. It had never been the issue. She wanted me to stop by the house, so she could flaunt her new boy toy. Forget that. I may be a lot of things, but stupid isn't one of them.

7

THE NEXT MORNING I RETURNED TO THE STONE RESIDENCE. Collin came out of the house at 8:30 dressed in his work clothes, carrying his portfolio and briefcase. I followed him to his workplace and waited in the parking lot until noon, when he took his lunch break.

Collin went to the same café he'd gone to the other day, but the mystery woman wasn't there. He seemed neither disappointed nor surprised. He took a table near the window, ate his food, and returned to work.

When five o'clock rolled around, Collin resurfaced, talking on his cell phone. The way he smiled and laughed let me know it wasn't Bellanca he was talking to. He folded himself into his tiny sports car, hauled ass out of the parking lot, and hit the freeway. For a while it seemed he might head home. But he skipped the exit that would've taken him to the Gales, and took the next one. I followed him down a long stretch of road bordered by shopping centers.

Collin pulled into one of the centers and drove around back, to a movie theater. Red and purple neon lights spelled out the name, Olympus 18 Cinemas, above the main entrance. Cars filled the parking lot. Vans and SUVs lined the curb, dropping off groups of overexcited preteens.

Collin parked his car and got out, no longer on the phone. I parked a few cars away, making sure I had a clear view of the entrance. As he made his way to the ticket booth, I shut off the engine and activated my dashboard camera.

He bought two tickets at the booth and sat down outside on a nearby bench.

Shortly, an orange Hummer H2 pulled into the parking lot, and out stepped the mystery woman from the day before. Her tight, black tank top and camouflage pants clung to some impressive curves—though they weren't nearly as impressive as Bellanca's. The cap and shades were the same ones she had worn to the café. She didn't carry a purse.

She and Collin hugged, exchanged words, and then entered the theater. On the way in, Collin gave her a playful slap on the ass. What a gentleman.

Two hours later, a crowd of people spilled out of the theater, laughing and talking excitedly. Collin and the mystery woman were among them. They hung out near the main entrance for a while, chatting.

At first the exchange seemed to be going well. Both of them were smiling. And at one point, the mystery woman burst into laughter and gently slapped Collin on the shoulder. Then things turned sour. Collin said something that caused the mystery woman to sneer and walk off. He called after her. When she didn't stop or look back, he followed and grabbed her by the wrist.

The woman snatched her arm free and glared at him. She stood completely still, her muscles tense. For a second I thought she would to take a swing at him. But Collin raised his hands in surrender. He said something and she calmed down a bit.

Collin continued to talk, his hands still raised. As the conversation progressed, the anger in the mystery woman's face drained away, and she began to cry.

Collin embraced her. He rubbed her back in slow circles while whispering in her ear. When he pulled away, the mystery woman had regained her composure and was smiling again. He wiped the tears from her face with his thumb and gave her a peck on the lips. Her smile broadened, and she lowered her head. Collin lifted her chin with his finger. They talked for several minutes more. Then they kissed again and went their separate ways.

Collin went straight home after leaving the theater.

Things had gone fairly well. I had enough evidence to get Collin into some serious trouble. But it wasn't enough.

The footage proved that Collin was dating another woman, not that he was actually screwing her. A lot of PIs would have turned in the evidence and called it a day. Not me. I had never left a job half-done, and I wasn't about to start today.

8

HERMES STOPPED BY MY OFFICE THE NEXT DAY, WEARING A gray suit. In his hand he carried a matching fedora. He didn't strike me as a hat person. It would muss his hair.

"Good morning, Mr. Jones." Hermes set his fedora on my desk and took a seat.

"Hermes," I said with a wide, fake smile. "Back for another round of negotiations?"

He shrugged. "Why else would I be here?"

"The answer is still no."

Hermes reached for the candy dish, which had been re-filled since his last visit. I snatched it away before he could get anything, and hid it in my desk drawer.

"How long do you intend to keep this up?" he asked.

"Until the Gods learn how to clean up after themselves."

"I wasn't talking about the candy."

"Neither was I."

Hermes furrowed his brow. "This is a very serious matter, Mr. Jones. One that affects national security."

"I realize that."

"Then why won't you help us?"

I rubbed my chin, pretending to think. "Because I don't feel like it."

Hermes sat still. Nothing moved except his jawbone, a clear sign that he was losing patience with me. "If not for Olympus, you'd be just another worthless mortal working a dead-end job. You owe us."

I chuckled and leaned back in my chair.

"What's so funny?" Hermes asked. His eyes narrowed.

I shook my head. "Just remembering something that happened a long time ago. When I was nine, the one thing I wanted more than anything else in the world was a Dr. Powers junior magician's kit. But it was a hundred credits, and my family wasn't very well off. I asked my dad to buy me one, even though I knew he was going to say no. I—"

"Is there a point to this story," Hermes cut in, "or are you purposely trying to annoy me?"

I ignore him and continued. "As I was saying, I figured there was no harm in asking, right? To my surprise, he actually said yes. 'Yes, son, I'll get you your magic kit . . . if you get all As on your next report card.'"

"So you got all As," Hermes said, dryly.

"For the next few months, I studied my ass off, and at the end of the semester, I came home with straight As. My dad was ecstatic. I can still see the look on his face. But more than that, I remember how excited I was. Soon, I, Plato Jones, would be the proud owner of a brand new Dr. Powers junior magician's kit. Wow."

"Yes, wow." Hermes's face was expressionless.

"Anyway, I asked my dad if we could pick one up. And you know what he said? 'Sorry, sport. I don't have the money right now.' When I tell you I was pissed, you'd best believe I was pissed. I said to him, 'That's not fair! I lived up to my part of the deal. You have to live up to yours!' Or something to that effect."

"Are we getting to the point now?" Hermes asked.

"Just about."

Hermes sighed and rolled his eyes skyward.

"Anyway," I continued. "My dad apologized and said he'd get me one for Christmas, but I didn't feel like waiting that long. So I decided to buy it myself. I mowed lawns, washed cars, did whatever needed to be done. By the end of the summer, I had earned enough money to buy that magic kit. It was one of the happiest days of my life."

"I fail to see the significance of this story."

"I figured as much," I said. "What I'm getting at is this: the world doesn't owe you any favors."

We stared at each other, our eyes narrow and unblinking. A duel of wills.

Finally, Hermes smiled that sly smile of his.

"I see now that talking is useless." He took a check from his coat pocket and put it on my desk. "Perhaps this will help influence your decision."

I picked it up and gave a low whistle. "That's a lot of money."

"Yes, it is."

"This would get my agency back on track."

"Indeed."

"And I'd have a good bit left over."

"You would."

"I could buy a new car, or move into a better apartment." I stared at all those delicious zeros.

"Whatever you'd like."

I sighed and put the check back on my desk. "You know, why don't you hold onto this?"

Hermes raised his eyebrows. "What?"

"I told you before." I handed the check back to him. "I don't want your money."

Hermes stared at me, apparently at a loss.

"You look surprised," I said. "Sorry to burst your bubble, but not all mortals are money-grubbing idiots. Some of us are just regular idiots."

Hermes slipped the check back into his pocket, frowning. "Why do you insist on being so difficult?"

I rose from my chair and walked to the door. "I'm not being difficult. As chief proprietor of this agency, I reserve the right to decline service to anyone. Right now I'm exercising that right."

I opened the door.

Hermes stood and put on his fedora. It looked cooler on him than I'd thought it would. I wondered if it would look just as slick on me. Maybe I'd buy one and find out. Then I'd look like one of those hard-boiled PIs from the old days. I already had a trench coat somewhere in my closet.

"I grow tired of these games, Mr. Jones," Hermes said.

"That makes two of us."

"Expect to see me again soon."

"How soon?"

"Very." Hermes swept past me and through the doorway.

"Thanks for stopping by," I called after him.

9

THAT EVENING, I SAT ON THE COUCH, WATCHING *ANIMAL Cops* on my 50-inch, 1080p flat-screen. My TV was my baby, and the focal point of my living room. Housed in a glass entertainment center, it was the first thing visitors would notice when stepping into my apartment, and the thing they remembered most after they left. I couldn't count how many hours Herc and I had spent seated in front of this monster, watching football and tossing back beers. Good times.

As the show went to a commercial break, my cell phone rang. I grabbed it from the end table and glanced at the caller ID. It was Alexis. Probably calling to pester me about the junk in the basement again.

I answered the call. "Plato's Guns and Ammo. How can I help you?"

"Cut the funny business. I'm not in the mood."

"You sound crankier than usual. What's wrong? Did you and Caesar have a fight?"

"His name is Calais," she snapped.

"Sorry. I don't how I keep forgetting his name."

"Of course you don't."

I flipped through the TV channels. Everything seemed to be on a commercial break. I settled on an infomercial. An old guy in a suit was hocking steam cleaners, while the woman next to him pretended to be amazed.

"Listen, Plato," Alexis began. "There's something I need to talk to you about."

"If this is about me coming over to get my stuff, don't worry."

"Plato—"

I cut her off. "I'm working day and night to fit it into my schedule—"

"Plato—"

"It may not be next week, or even next month, but eventually I'll get around to—"

"Plato!" Alexis shouted.

"Yes?"

"This isn't about your stuff."

"It isn't?"

"No. I threw it out months ago."

I put down the remote and sat forward. "Wait. You threw out my stuff?"

"Donated it, actually. To a thrift store."

"All of it?"

"Every bit. But hey, you can always buy it back."

I waited for her to tell me she was joking. She remained silent. A swell of grief built inside of me. "But my vintage beer steins. My Andy Gibb records. My commemorative coin collection."

"All gone."

"You heartless fiend," I cried.

"Oh, don't be so dramatic. If that junk was so important to you, you would've come and picked it up years ago."

"Easy for you to say. Your stuff didn't get trashed."

"Plato, I didn't call you to argue."

I sneered at the phone. Of course she didn't want to argue, now that she had gotten me into a fighting mood. Memories of my beloved junk cycled through my brain like photographic slides.

"Then why'd you call, Alexis?"

"There's something I need to tell you."

"What? Is it about Sparky? He's dead, isn't he? I knew I shouldn't have let you keep him."

"The dog is fine, Plato. I just . . ." Alexis paused for a moment. Then she blurted, "Calais and I are getting married."

My mind went blank, as if someone had flipped a switch in my head. An instant later I was standing. I couldn't remember getting up.

"Married?" The word sounded oddly foreign as it left my mouth.

"I wanted to tell you in person," Alexis said, sounding apologetic. "That's why I lied about the stuff in the basement. So you'd come over."

I stared out the window, clueless about how I should feel, how I should react. My brain refused to work.

"Aren't you going to say something?" Alexis asked.

"What do you want me to say?"

"I don't know. Congratulations? Burn in Hades? Something."

"We'll go with congratulations," I said.

"Are you angry?"

"No."

Alexis sighed. "I was afraid of this."

"Afraid of what?" I asked, my tone unintentionally aggressive.

"Afraid you'd get all jealous on me."

"Jealous? Me?" I cringed at how high-pitched my voice had gotten.

"Yes, you," she said. "Are you going to be all right?"

"Why wouldn't I be?"

"I'm not sure."

After an interval of silence, Alexis said, "Well anyway, that's all I wanted to tell you. I guess I'll let you go now."

"Talk to you later."

"Bye, Plato."

We hung up. I sat down in my recliner and gazed at the ceiling. Alexis was getting married. I shouldn't have been surprised. She was a good woman. It was only natural that someone would come along and scoop her up. Besides, she and I would've never worked out. We were too similar.

My body suddenly sagged, like I had swallowed a handful of sleeping pills. I got up and walked to the window. The neighbor's cat strolled through the parking lot. It stopped and looked up at me.

I glared at it. "Somehow this is your fault."

10

AFTER THE BOMB ALEXIS HAD DROPPED ON ME, I WAS IN NO mood to go to work the next day. But I did anyway. Bellanca Stone had paid me to uncover the truth about her husband, and she would get her money's worth.

I followed Collin from his house to his place of work and parked in a public lot across the street. Like the previous day, he came out of the office at lunchtime and drove to the same café. He took the same window seat and ordered some kind of sandwich. The mystery woman was nowhere in sight. Collin didn't seem concerned. He didn't shoot glances toward the door the way I'd expect him to do if he were waiting for her. He finished his food and returned to work.

Collin didn't resurface until a few minutes before five. He hastened across the parking lot to his car, glancing at his wristwatch. Something was about to go down. I started my engine and followed him onto the highway.

He drove north for almost an hour, and then hit an exit. It emptied us onto a long road flanked by high-end clothing stores and expensive restaurants. Cop cars idled near the roadside. The officers inside held speed detection guns.

Collin drove just below the speed limit. We went through four intersections and turned left onto another street. Several miles up the road, the stores and eateries gave way to condominiums and gated communities.

Traffic was becoming sparse. I eased up on the accelerator and fell behind a little, so Collin wouldn't get suspicious. At length, he turned into a neighborhood that had been built on a sprawling golf course. Mansions towered on either side of the street—dwarfing those of the Gales—some behind wrought iron gates, and others at the end of long tree-lined driveways. I couldn't help wondering if the occupants ever got lost in their own homes.

Collin drove deep into the neighborhood and pulled into the driveway of a massive four-story mansion. I continued driving and parked on the adjacent street, across from two houses. The gap between them gave me a clear view of the front door. I turned on my dashboard camera and took a bite of beef jerky. Things were about to get very interesting.

Collin rang the doorbell. A muscular woman answered. Her red hair was in a buzz cut. Makeup plastered her face, black lipstick and lots of dark eye shadow. Her white tank top and baggy gray sweatpants did little to emphasize the fact that she was female. Her build told me it was the same woman from the café and the movie theater.

Seeing her this time, I had the feeling that I recognized her. Then it hit me. I had briefly met her during my time as an OBI agent. She was Enyo, a daughter of Zeus and Hera. A Goddess of Olympus. *She* was the mystery woman?

Enyo and Collin might have exchanged two words before she grabbed the back of his head and pulled him into a fierce kiss. Her other hand fondled his crotch. When she released him, he swayed in place. She seized him by the wrist and yanked him inside the mansion. The door slammed shut behind them.

My eyes remained glued to the door, struggling to process what I had just seen. Collin was cheating on his wife with

Enyo. I leaned back in my chair, shaking my head. That a human was dating an immortal wasn't shocking. It happened all the time—usually when the Gods got bored with screwing one another. Zeus and Aphrodite were notorious for having legions of human lovers.

What confused me was the couple itself.

Enyo was a notorious party girl. She was also the Goddess of War, counterpart to Ares, and a fighter by nature. What someone like her could ever see in a corporate stiff like Collin Stone, I'd never know.

But while Enyo's motivations were shrouded in ambiguity, Collin's were as clear as day. There was no question why he was interested in her. She brought excitement to his life. Danger. Everything he was missing at home. Also, Gods were rumored to be devils in bed. As a man, I could see the appeal. But that didn't excuse his actions.

Ten minutes later, Collin stumbled outside, looking like he'd just lost a fight. His clothes and hair were rumpled, and his left eye was swollen shut. *Ten minutes.* Suddenly, I understood why he drove such a flashy car.

Enyo came outside as well. She walked him to his car, and the two of them shared a lengthy kiss. Their hands stayed busy the entire time, rubbing and groping. Watching them made me feel dirty. I could only imagine how poor Bellanca was going to feel.

After the make-out session, Collin got into his car and drove off. Enyo waited until his car had disappeared around the corner before going back inside the house. I turned off the camera. I now had enough evidence to prove that Collin was a cheater, and a minute man. But I wanted more, one more smidgen of proof. I realized it was unnecessary. But I really wanted to stick it to this creep.

Bellanca deserved better than him.

11

NEW OLYMPIA CAME ALIVE AT NIGHT. DOZENS OF BARS AND nightclubs lit up throughout the city, but the real action took place on Siren Strip. It stretched for nearly two miles through the center of downtown, a river of neon lights. Traffic was at a standstill.

Herc was waiting for me at the side of a coffee shop, where the lights were low. A black shirt, jeans, and a baseball cap covered most of his oversize frame. Dark shades concealed his eyes. This was his idea of a disguise. The fact that he was seven feet tall with biceps as big as watermelons kind of ruined the effect.

I crossed the street and joined him in the alleyway. "How's it going?"

"Were you followed?"

"Of course not. Stealth is my middle name. Plato Stealth Jones."

"Gotta good feeling about this new disguise, Jonesy." Herc grinned nervously. "The hat and the sunglasses cost five credits apiece, but I plan on getting a refund first thing tomorrow."

I took a closer look at the sunglasses and noticed the sticker was still on them. "I don't think your adoring public will appreciate being deceived like this."

"Screw the public!" Herc poked his head out of the alley for a split second—to see if anyone had heard him—then dipped back into the shadows. "This is crazy. I can't take a piss in my own house without it ending up in the tabloid. 'Hercules, taking a piss in his own house. Is he really taking a piss? Or is he secretly cheating on his wife? Does he stuff his pants? We've got the truth.' Don't they have anything better to do than pester me?"

The Gods and Demigods of Olympus are worldwide celebrities. Wherever they go, fans and paparazzi follow close behind.

I chuckled softly. You'd think that after years of being in the public eye, Herc would have gotten used to the attention by now. "Scandal of the century," I said.

Herc opened his mouth to respond, but was interrupted by the sound of approaching footsteps. He sank deeper into the shadows and froze as a pair of college girls in bright makeup and glittery dresses passed the alley.

Once they had gone, he released a pent-up breath. "That was close," he whispered. "By the way, Geno's hanging out with us tonight."

"The more the merrier. Where is he?"

"Probably waiting for us at the Night Owl."

"Well, let's not keep him waiting."

Herc peeked around the corner. "We move on three. One . . . two . . ."

We slipped out of the alley and scurried down the sidewalk. Herc tugged his hat down and tried to look inconspicuous. A group of passersby stopped to look at him. It wasn't a good sign.

We hadn't been walking for very long when someone shouted, "It's Hercules!"

Light flashed on the edge of my vision, and voices erupted as a gang of paparazzi appeared. I had no idea where they came from. It was like they had materialized out of thin air. Hera's doing?

Herc covered his face and walked faster. I did the same. The paparazzi followed us, taking snapshots. Hanging out with a Demigod meant that my face occasionally graced the covers of tabloids, where I was known not as Plato Jones, crack detective, but as Hercules's servant, that guy who hangs out with Hercules, or Hercules's gay lover. I'd called the reporter for a retraction on that last one, but he never returned my calls.

I couldn't figure out why the press had never bothered to find out who I was. Maybe it was because I wasn't a celebrity. Or maybe I just didn't look that interesting. I guess it didn't really matter. The idea of fame never appealed to me. Now fortune, that's a different story.

By the time Herc and I reached the end of the block, the group of photographers had evolved into a mob. Fortunately, the bar was around the corner.

It was little more than a hole in the wall, squeezed between an Italian bistro and a place that claimed to have the best Buffalo wings in town. White neon lights spelled out "Night Owl."

Napoleon, the bouncer, stood with his arms crossed beside the door. Brown fur covered his body, topped with smoky-gray horns on his head. He was a minotaur. His black T-shirt had the word SECURITY written on it in bold white lettering. How he managed to fit those horns through the neck hole was a question only he could answer. I wasn't about to ask him.

The photographers gathered around us and continued to snap pictures. But all maintained a distance from the eight-foot-tall minotaur.

"Napoleon," I said. "How's life treating you?"

He returned the minotaur equivalent of a smile. It looked more like a grimace. "I can't complain." His voice came out low and scratchy. "Why don't you fellows go on in? I'll keep the vultures at bay."

"I owe you one, Napoleon," Herc said.

"Anytime."

As we stepped inside, the sounds of the city fell silent, replaced by laughter and the clink of beer bottles. In a cloud of cigarette smoke, thirty-somethings like me packed the tables and dance floor. A jazz band played on a stage at the back of the room, bathed in red light. Scores of memorabilia decorated the walls: clocks, paintings, beer signs, sports jerseys, and photos of various celebrities who had stopped by over the years. One of the photos was of Herc hiding his face from the camera. In the background, I was waving drunkenly at the photographer.

"Hey guys!" a voice called out from across the room.

The voice belonged to Geno Crowne, a lawyer and a satyr. He was another friend I had met while working for the Gods. He used to work in Zeus's legal department, until he decided to quit and start his own firm. From the waist up, he was strictly professional. Expertly cut blond hair framed a smooth and unblemished face. His blazer and dress shirt looked expensive, tailored to his body.

From the waist down, he was a goat.

A bipedal goat with black hooves, a stubby tail . . . and no pants.

But pants or no pants, his fashion sense still put mine to shame. My clothes looked like they had been dipped in a bucket of wrinkles. I'd rolled up the sleeves of my white dress shirt nearly to my elbows. Not because I thought it was fashionable, but because earlier I spilled coffee on the left cuff. My pants were too long in the leg, causing the hems to drag on the ground, which had gradually frayed them over time. They were literally unraveling at the seams. That's what I got for never trying on clothes before I bought them. My former job required me to wear a suit every day. Clean and pressed. Since the day I quit, I hadn't so much as glanced at an iron.

"Good evening, gentlemen," Geno said, tipping a half-full martini glass toward us. His alert blue eyes shined brightly.

"How many of those have you had so far?" I asked.

"This is my third."

"Impressive."

As far as satyrs and drinking went, Geno was a heavyweight. Most satyrs were out cold after three or four rounds, but Geno could hang with the most seasoned of boozers and winos. It was an incredible talent.

Herc took a seat at the bar.

I sat between him and Geno. That way, if I passed out, it wouldn't matter if I fell to the right or to the left. In either case, someone familiar would be there to catch me. Now if I happened to fall backward, that might be a problem.

"Hey, buddy," I said to Geno. "It's been a while. How's the lawyer thing going?"

Geno shrugged nonchalantly. "Tedious, filled with paperwork and client conferences, the usual."

I patted him on the shoulder. "My heart weeps for you, buddy."

"You might want to get that checked out." He smirked.

"Probably."

Geno took a sip of his drink. "So what's going on with you?"

"Nothing much. Following around a cheating husband. Getting harassed by the Gods. Oh, and my ex-wife is getting married."

"Don't you mean remarried?" Geno said.

Herc turned on his barstool to face me. He had removed his cap and shades. He looked like the stereotypical football hero. Everything about him screamed strength and power. His head was square-shaped, his features chiseled, and his curly brown hair was cut short. His electric-blue eyes, which he'd inherited from his father, were always intense and rarely wandered. Meeting his gaze without being intimidated by it required practice.

"Hold on, hold on," Herc chimed in. "Alexis is getting married?"

"Yep," I said.

"To you?" Herc asked, pointing at me.

I stared down at the bar. "No, Herc, not to me."

Herc pursed his lips. "But I thought you two still had something going on."

"Something going on? Herc, she's been seeing that guy for the past year and a half. What's his name? Capricorn?"

"Yeah, but she calls you almost every day."

I shrugged. "And your point is?"

"When people divorce, they tend to, I don't know, steer clear of each other. Unless the feelings are still there."

"I promise they're not."

Herc grinned. "Then why haven't you had a girlfriend since the divorce?"

"I've dated other women."

"All one-night stands. I'm talking about something real."

"He brings up an interesting point," Geno cut in.

I glanced back and forth between them. "Guys, guys! This is a boy's night out, not a therapy session. Now can we please get back to the matter at hand? I'd like to get hammered before midnight."

Herc and Geno shrugged.

"Thank you," I said.

I flagged down Harold, the bartender, a tall man with a hook nose and a receding hairline. In all my years of coming to the Night Owl, he and I must have spoken a total of five times on subjects other than drinks. The conversations we had were brief, and far too general to provide any insight into his personality. He always seemed more concerned with doing his job than chatting with customers, which I could respect.

I ordered three shots of ouzo, one for each of us. As I reached for my wallet, Herc raised his hand.

"Save your money," he said. "First round's on me."

Geno and I did a double take.

"What's with the sudden generosity?" I asked.

"Caring is sharing," Herc said. There was a hint of nervousness in his voice. He took a credit card from his wallet and handed it to the bartender.

My investigator senses tingled. Being the son of Zeus, Herc was one of the richest people I knew. He was also one of the stingiest. Clearance items made up his entire wardrobe, and he kept a money clip full of coupons with him at all times. No way was he sponsoring us out of the kindness of his heart. He was definitely up to something. But I didn't press the matter. Far be it from me to pass up free alcohol.

I raised my glass. "In that case, I propose a toast to you, Herc, whose generosity is an inspiration to us all."

12

An hour and six rounds later, Geno and I were considerably toasted. Herc wasn't there yet. Gods and Demigods tended to have extraordinarily high tolerances for alcohol. Some could drink all day and not even get a buzz. At one point during the night, Herc tried to explain the science behind the whole phenomenon. It had something to do with a hyperaccelerated metabolism, and about a dozen other biological factors. I might have retained more of the information if I hadn't been drunk off my ass.

At nine the band stopped playing. The crowd went silent as Abas, the owner of the Night Owl, waddled onto the stage holding a microphone. A squat redhead, he had a face like a cherub. The blue-and-white flannel shirt he wore fit his chest perfectly, but not his belly. The shirt stretched around his stomach, and the lower buttons looked like they were about to pop off. He did a mic check. The speakers squealed. Everyone winced.

"One two, one two," he said. "Hello, ladies and gentlemen. Thanks for coming out tonight. I have something special planned. But before we get to that, I have a question." Dramatic pause. "Who likes karaoke?"

Everyone cheered, even me. Blame it on the alcohol.

"I guess that answers my question." Abas laughed.

He stepped aside as two bouncers carried loads of karaoke equipment onstage.

"My boys need a minute or two to set up," Abas said. "After that, the real fun begins. Who wants to go first?"

I gulped down the last of my drink and raised my hand. "That would be us."

Herc choked on his beer. He looked at me, coughing. "W-what?"

"Come on, big guy." I motioned for him to rise. "Let's go up there and knock 'em dead."

"Are you insane?" Herc shook his head. "No! Absolutely not!"

Geno turned toward him, and nearly fell off his barstool in the process. His eyes were narrow slits, and his cheeks were flushed. He had loosened his tie and undone the first few buttons of his shirt, revealing a nest of thick, curly chest hair.

"Don't be shy," Geno said, his voice slurred. "Your voice can't be any worse than mine."

"See?" I said. "Geno's on board."

Herc shook his head again. "I don't care."

Everyone in the bar stared at us.

"What's it going to be, fellahs?" Abas asked. "You coming up here or not?"

"No, we're not!" Herc said.

"Don't listen to him. He doesn't know what he's talking about!" I swiveled my head in Herc's direction. "Listen, man. If you don't get on that stage right now, I guarantee you'll regret it."

"How's that?"

I gestured for him to lean in closer. "Think about it. A century from now you're going to look back on all this and wonder 'what if.' What if you had listened to Jonesy and gotten on that stage? And I'll say, 'I guess we'll never know.' Is that what you want?"

Herc smirked. "You won't even be alive a century from now."

I could see that logic wasn't going to work, so I resorted to the second most effective form of influence. Begging. "Come on, Herc. Do it for an old pal!"

Herc sighed after a long moment. "Fine, I'll do it. But this had better not end up on the Internet."

I gave him a hearty pat on the back. "That's the spirit!"

Geno and I shambled toward the stage. Herc followed us at a distance. When seated, I didn't realize how drunk I had gotten. But the moment I stood up, the truth became staggeringly apparent. Jumbled colors and muffled sounds filled the world I moved through. People and objects were reduced to hazy representations of what they once were, and each step I took gave me the sense that I was about to walk off the edge of a cliff.

Geno wasn't doing much better. His head rocked from side to side as he walked, and his legs wobbled. His hooves clacked against the tile floor. Somehow, we made it onstage without falling down. The audience cheered.

We picked the song "Fantasy" by Earth, Wind, and Fire. Herc sang lead. Geno and I did backup. We sounded like a trio of drowning cats. We threw bad notes around like confetti. At one point my voice abandoned me, as if it wanted no part in the musical homicide taking place. When the performance ended, I expected a hail of boos from the audience. Instead they all rose to their feet, clapping and hooting.

We bowed—Geno and I nearly toppling over—and left the stage.

On the way back to my seat, I made a beeline for the restroom. My bladder was seconds away from bursting, like a water balloon in my lower abdomen. Every movement caused the liquid within to slosh around. I shouldered the restroom door open and stumbled through.

I clamped my hand over my nose and mouth and hurried to the nearest urinal. The smell clawed at my nostrils. Whoever had been here before me was either on a high-protein diet or in need of serious medical attention. I relieved myself, washed my hands, and then glanced in the mirror to see exactly how bad off I was. As I expected, I looked like crap warmed over. Come to think of it, I didn't look much different than normal. My black hair was a mess, my dark-brown eyes were sleepy and bloodshot, and my five o'clock shadow made me look older than I really was.

I splashed some water on my face and reached blindly for the paper towel dispenser.

"Here you are." Someone handed me a paper towel.

The voice sounded familiar—annoyingly so. I dried my face and took another look in the mirror. Hermes stood beside me. His long white hair hung around his shoulders. It clashed against his jet-black suit.

"Nice performance, Mr. Jones."

"What are you doing here?" I demanded.

"I came to talk."

"We have nothing to talk about." I turned to leave.

Hermes stood on the other side of the bathroom, in front of the door. I never saw him move. "On the contrary. We have much to discuss."

I knew that muscling past him was not an option. Neither was shooting him, though I favored the idea.

"What do you want?" I asked.

"There's been another murder."

My heart jumped. "Who is it this time?"

"Hephaestus."

The Smith God. I had seen him a handful of times, but we never spoke. He used to work for the military, as the director of weapons development, and had fathered countless innovations, like a rifle whose shots could pass through solid matter, and a ray gun that caused enemies to burst into flames. But he felt Zeus wasn't giving him the recognition he deserved, so he decided to quit. He became a recluse, spending most of his time holed up in his estate.

My guess was he was playing mad scientist, creating things just for the sake of creating them but not bothering anyone in the process. I couldn't imagine why anyone would want to kill him—much less how they managed to do it. Not only was Hephaestus immortal—or so I'd thought—but his house was a fortress, filled with all sorts of booby traps.

"He was found dead in his home earlier today," Hermes continued. "We want you to investigate the crime scene."

I shook my head. The movement roused a spell of dizziness. "No way."

"Why not?"

"Because I don't work for the Gods anymore. Now if you'll excuse me, I have important matters to attend to."

Hermes crossed his arms. "How about this? You come with me and look at the scene. Give your opinion of what happened. Afterward, I'll bring you back here, so you can finish getting drunk, wasted, or whatever it is you mortals call it. I'll even pick up the tab. No additional strings attached."

I crossed my arms. "If I do this, will you get lost and let me enjoy the rest of my night?"

Hermes held up his hands as if to show he was unarmed. "You've got my word."

I closed my eyes. "Let's make this quick."

13

HEPHAESTUS'S ESTATE WAS OUT IN THE STICKS, FAR REMOVED from the glitz and glamour of the city. A wrought iron fence enclosed the entire property. A mile-long road stretched through the woods toward the main house. No streetlights illuminated the way, but Hermes—like all Gods—could see in the dark, and drove without the aid of his high beams.

We pulled into the driveway and stopped. There were six unmarked black cars parked near the front door. Their headlights shined brightly, though the vehicles were empty. Two OBI agents in black suits were conversing at the bottom of the steps. One looked human. The other was a satyr. I didn't recognize either of them.

From the outside, Hephaestus's mansion was a looming fortress of gray stone, complete with ramparts and a bell tower. There were no windows, no decorative shrubbery. If those walls could talk, they'd say, "Get lost!"

We got out of the car and approached the front door. The two agents nodded at Hermes as he passed.

"Sir," they said in unison.

He didn't acknowledge them, and continued up the stairs to the door. I followed at a sluggish pace, sweating like a pig in the muggy air. The alcohol in my system was gradually wearing off, and I felt the beginnings of a headache. This was going to be a long night.

The inside of the house was a museum. Everywhere I looked, racks and display cases full of weapons lined the walls—guns and blades from various eras throughout history. Most of them had been crafted by Hephaestus himself.

In keeping with the whole medieval fortress motif, stone and mortar covered just about every surface in the living room. The ceiling was arched, the furniture rustic, and crimson banners hung from the walls, emblazoned with images of gold hammers. The stench of rotting flesh hung in the hot air, sticking to the back of my throat.

Hephaestus was sprawled across the floor in a pool of oxidized blood. His severed head lay a few feet away, near the dead fireplace. Blue eyes stared into oblivion. Deformed since birth, his bearded face resembled a lump of bread dough covered in brown hair. Hera had been so disgusted by his appearance that she once threw him from Mount Olympus. Allegedly.

I borrowed a pair of examiner's gloves from one of the OBI agents and got to work.

From the looks of the body, death had occurred less than twenty-four hours earlier. Visible through the opening in his red-and-black robe, deep gashes laced Hephaestus's body. Some of the cuts exposed white bone. An unopened bottle of wine and two glasses sat on the coffee table.

I asked one of the OBI agents if he knew who had reported the murder. He told me they'd gotten an anonymous tip from an unlisted number. My guess was that the call had been made by the killer via a throwaway cell phone. If that was the case, it meant the sick bastard was trying to send a message.

After examining the body, I checked the mansion for clues. The OBI agents had already done a preliminary sweep. I made sure they hadn't overlooked anything. The upper floors were mazes of interconnecting hallways, doors that led to nowhere, and rooms that were totally empty. Not only that, but most of the areas were identical, which made navigating them a pain in the ass.

Ultimately, my search of the upper floors yielded no clues. I moved downstairs to the basement, where I found Hephaestus's workshop filled with workbenches, tool cabinets, and piles of techno-junk. A giant anvil sat in the middle of the room. Scraps of metal—gold, silver, platinum—littered the anvil and the floor around it. Gemstones of various shapes and colors glittered on a nearby table.

Hephaestus had been working on something prior to his death—probably a sword. An ornate one, considering the high quality materials. In one of the wastebaskets, I found a crumpled receipt. The ink was badly faded, making it nearly illegible. The only information I gathered from it was the name of a store. Marvin's Scrap Heap, an industrial warehouse. The receipt wasn't the case-cracking piece of evidence I had been hoping for, but it was better than nothing.

During my search, I noticed a number of surveillance cameras strategically placed throughout the house. I asked to see the footage from that day. One of the OBI agents told me that the digital memory cards had been removed from the cameras, presumably by the killer. Looking at the victim's computer for clues was also a no-go. Hephaestus didn't have an e-mail account, and his personal files were heavily encrypted. It would take weeks to decipher them. And if that wasn't irritating enough, I couldn't check his phone records because he didn't own a phone. I can respect a person's desire for privacy, but this was ridiculous.

On the whole, my search of the mansion was a bust. There was no indication of forced entry and no missing property except—possibly—the memory cards. The killer might have left behind a couple fingerprints for forensics to discover, but I doubted it. Whoever pulled this off was good. Damn good.

Nearly three hours had passed. I was short on answers and ready to call it quits. I pulled off my examiner's gloves and tossed them in the wastebasket. Most of the OBI agents were outside by now, combing the surrounding area. Those who remained indoors took notes and snapped pictures.

Hermes waited for me in the foyer, looking at his watch.

"Did you find anything?" he asked.

"Not much." I blotted the sweat from my brow. "From the looks of it, Hephaestus was mauled by a large animal."

"You think an animal did this?"

"Nope."

"Then what?"

"I'm not sure," I admitted. "But it's not human."

"What else?" Hermes asked.

"I think Hephaestus knew the killer."

That seemed to interest him. "What makes you say that?"

"He was dressed as if he'd been expecting company. Also, there was a bottle of wine on the coffee table—with two glasses."

Hermes nodded slowly.

"Did Hephaestus have any close friends?" I asked.

"No," Hermes said at once.

"You sound awfully sure about that."

"I am sure."

"Mind telling me why?"

Hermes's lips twitched upward like he wanted to laugh. "Do I even need to explain? Just look at him. Hephaestus was a freak. The Gods wanted nothing to do with him. Why do you think he lived all the way out here by himself?"

I shook my head in disgust. Hephaestus had been brutally murdered, and Hermes, his half-brother, didn't give a crap.

Where I come from, you're obligated to care about your family members, even if you don't get along with them. It's just the right thing to do. In Hermes's case, omnipotence and compassion were as incompatible as oil and water.

"If you hate him so much, then why bother investigating his murder?" I asked.

"Because we must." Hermes looked at me as though I should have already known the answer. "What do you think will happen if the public finds out that Gods can die, that we can be killed?"

I shrugged. "My guess is chaos."

Hermes nodded smartly. "Precisely. So far, we've been able to keep these murders confidential. But if we don't find this killer before he strikes again, things could get ugly."

"Good point."

"So how do you suggest we proceed?"

"First you should make a list of potential suspects," I suggested. "Do you know of anyone or anything powerful enough to kill a God?"

"No."

He answered without hesitation, and there was no deception in his tone, at least none that I could pick up on. But his eyes darted to the side for a split second, and I couldn't shake the feeling he wasn't being completely honest with me.

"Are you sure?" I asked.

Hermes frowned. The Gods hate to repeat themselves. Asking them to do so is often considered an insult. I was too hot and too tired to care.

"Positive," Hermes said.

"Well it sounds like you've got a problem."

"Do you have any *useful* advice?"

I nodded. "Start your search at home."

"At home?"

"Yeah."

Hermes narrowed his eyes. "What are you implying?"

"From what you told me, the Gods weren't too fond of Hephaestus. The killer could be one of your own."

"That's absurd!" Hermes snapped. "We would never murder one of our own—not even a black sheep like Hephaestus. And let me remind you that Eileithyia was well respected on Olympus. If the killer's problem was with Hephaestus, why would he go after her as well?"

He had me there. "I'm not sure. There is one thing that interests me though."

"What's that?"

"The fact that Eileithyia and Hephaestus are both children of Zeus and Hera."

Hermes raised his eyebrows. "Do you think someone is targeting the First Family?"

"It's possible."

"But who would do such a thing?"

"That's for you to figure out. I've done my job. I investigated the crime scene and gave my honest opinion. Now it's time for you to keep your part of the deal."

Hermes didn't argue. He gestured for me to follow him outside. We walked across the front lawn to his car. At some point in history, he had traded in his winged sandals for a white Ferrari Enzo. A nice upgrade, in my opinion. He unlocked the doors and we got in.

"Are you sure you won't help us?" he asked.

"Afraid so."

"Have it your way, Mr. Jones." Hermes started the engine.

14

It was after one o'clock when I got back to the Night Owl. The crowd had thinned out, but not by much. A man in a green Hawaiian shirt was onstage, singing the worst rendition of Mister Mister's "Broken Wings" I had ever heard. The audience cheered him on.

Geno sat at the bar with his head in his hands, snoring. His now-messy hair hung over his face. A beer in his hand, Herc looked no worse than he had several hours ago.

"Where'd you run off to?" he asked me.

I sat on the stool beside him. "I had something I needed to take care of."

Herc remained silent for a time, staring at his beer, his brow furrowed. Then he said, "Can I talk to you?"

"Sure."

"In private?"

"Uh, okay."

We got up and went to the restroom. There was no one inside. Herc paced back and forth for close to a minute. Then he placed his hands on the counter.

"I have a confession to make," he said.

"Let me guess. You still watch cartoons?"

"No. I mean yes. But that's not what I wanted to tell you. Truth is, the whole thing about Hebe wanting to remodel the kitchen, it was a lie. I'm really sorry."

I shook my head as if to say forget about it. "Why lie about something like that?"

Herc returned a guilty smile. "To throw you off."

"I'm afraid I don't follow you."

"I didn't want you to be suspicious."

"Suspicious?" I said. "What in the world are you talking about?"

Herc hesitated. "Jonesy, I have a favor to ask."

"What is it?"

"Did you hear about Eileithyia's murder?"

I already didn't like where this was going. I nodded slowly. "Yeah, what about it?"

"I want you to investigate it."

Son of a . . . I knew he was up to no good. That explained the generosity. And the willingness to get on stage and make a fool of himself. It all made sense now.

"That's a big favor," I said.

Herc raked his fingers through his hair. "Hebe is pretty broken up about losing her sister. She wants justice."

"I'm sensing there's more to this."

Herc nodded again. "Someone out there has the power to kill Gods. Until they're captured, no immortal is safe."

"You're worried about the killer coming after Hebe?"

"Yeah."

I felt obligated to tell him about Hephaestus's death, but decided against it. It would only exacerbate the situation. Besides, I already had that creep, Hermes, breathing down my neck. I didn't need my best friend laying on the pressure as well.

"I just want to keep her safe," Herc said, just above a whisper. "You've got to help."

I shook my head. "Hermes already approached me about this, and I refused. I don't involve myself with Godly matters. You know that. I'm sorry but I can't do it."

Hercules spun toward me, his eyes wide and intense. Though I knew he'd never hurt me, I couldn't help flinching. I fought the urge to look away.

"If you won't do it for the Gods, then do it for me," he pleaded. "I'll even . . . pay you. Whatever you want."

I stared down at my feet. "I don't know, Herc . . ."

"Please! Hebe is everything to me. If someone was out to kill Alexis, wouldn't you want to stop them?"

I chose not to answer that. "Alright, I'll think about it. But I'm not making any promises."

Herc beamed. He pulled me into the grandfather of all bear hugs. I thought he was going to crush my spine.

"Thanks, Jonesy!"

I frantically tapped him on the back, hoping he'd let me go so I could breathe normally again.

"Oh!" He released me.

I fell to the ground, wheezing. Herc hauled me to my feet.

"Remind me never to get on your bad side," I squeezed out.

"Sorry about that." He flashed me a sheepish grin. "Guess I got a little excited."

"Only a little? Y'know, you could make a killing as a chiropractor."

Herc laughed. "Thanks again, Jonesy."

"Don't thank me yet. I said I'd think about it."

Herc seemed not to hear. His grin widened. "Come on. Let's get back to the bar. I'll buy you a drink. Anything you want under five credits. How's that sound?"

I shook my head. "I appreciate the offer, but I think I'm done for the night."

"You heading out?"

"Yep."

Herc's smiled faltered. "Oh, okay. See you later then."

I left without another a word.

15

I woke up before dawn with a hangover. I had a massive headache, and nausea churned in my stomach. My mouth and throat were bone dry. It was as if I had swallowed a cup of sand. But as crappy as I felt, I knew things could've been a lot worse. Investigating the crime scene had burned off some of the alcohol.

I shambled out of my bedroom, exhausted and feeling like I had to throw up. I hadn't been able to get much rest. Two or three hours, if that much. The rest of the time I spent rolling around in the sheets, trying to get comfortable. For some reason, I can never sleep after a night of heavy drinking. Some people are snoring after two or three drinks. But not me.

I fixed myself an Alka-Seltzer and sat down in front of the TV. I tried to watch *Sanford and Son*, but laughing made my headache worse, so I turned to *Iron Chef*. What would today's secret ingredient be?

As I lounged on the recliner, waiting for the secret ingredient to be revealed, my mind wandered. Two Gods had been murdered, children of Zeus and Hera. Who was the killer? What was their angle? And what did they hope to gain out of all this? Those were the questions of the hour.

But they weren't mine to answer.

When the sun came up, I showered, got dressed, and headed over to the Stone residence. Collin didn't work weekends. It was afternoon before he finally came out of the house, wearing a green polo and khaki shorts. A pair of sunglasses hid the black eye Enyo had given him. I wondered how he'd explained the injury to Bellanca. I bet he told her that he'd been mugged again, or that he had fallen down a flight of stairs. Or maybe he went with the ever-popular I-ran-into-a-wall story.

I followed him to Enyo's mansion and parked on the parallel street. I turned on my dashboard camera and waited for the action to start.

Collin rang the bell. Enyo answered the door wearing a black bra and tight red sweatpants. Without so much as a hello, she grabbed Collin by the collar and yanked him into the house. The door slammed shut.

After an hour, the door burst open and Collin ran outside in his boxers. The rest of his clothes were bundled in his arms. Enyo ran out after him, in a pair of black panties and no bra. Her breasts were all but nonexistent. Metal rings flashed in both her nipples. In her hand, she clutched one of Collin's brown loafers. She shouted something and flung it at him.

The shoe struck Collin in the back of the neck and caused him to stumble and fall. The clothes tumbled out of his arms. Picking them up never seemed to cross his mind. He scrambled to his feet and ran like a frill-necked lizard to his car. He started the engine and screeched out of the driveway.

Enyo chased him down the road and out of view of the camera. It would have been nothing for a Goddess to catch up with a speeding car. So when she returned to her driveway without a mangled bumper in hand, I assumed she had let Collin escape. She snatched up Collin's shirt, ripped it in half, and threw the pieces onto the lawn. She then stormed into the house, slamming the door behind her.

I shut off the camera. A grin tugged at the corners of my mouth. Collin's dirt was finally catching up with him. Unfortunately for him, his problems were about to get even worse. It was time to show Bellanca the footage.

16

MONDAY MORNING, I WAS EDITING THE FOOTAGE OF COLLIN in my office when Hermes made another impromptu appearance.

"Good morning, Mr. Jones."

"What do you want now?"

"You should know the answer to that by now." Hermes sat down and crossed his legs. "I told Zeus about your involvement in last weekend's investigation."

"Is that so?"

"Yes. He was pleased. He strongly insists that you reconsider helping us."

I closed my laptop. "Is everyone on Olympus hard of hearing? I am not—I repeat—am not investigating the murders."

"I think you will," Hermes said with a straight face.

"Zeus pays you to think now?" I said. "You do everything your daddy tells you to do?"

Hermes returned a humorless laugh and stood up. He removed his sunglasses and slipped them into his pocket. "At first I found your impertinence to be quite amusing. But now you're starting to piss me off."

I shrugged. "I'm sorry to hear that."

Hermes reached into his jacket and pulled out a pair of black leather gloves. He slid one onto his hand. I felt a twinge of fear in my gut. Inconspicuously, I opened my desk drawer, where I kept my gun.

"You are, as they say, a tough nut to crack." Hermes tugged the other glove onto his hand. "Zeus suggested that I come up with more . . . creative forms of persuasion."

Every muscle in my body tightened. The pulse in my neck throbbed. My hand was poised above the open drawer.

"You think that by roughing me up, I'll agree to help you?" I asked.

"Some individuals only seem to respond to violence."

"I thought you didn't like fighting."

Hermes smiled darkly. "This won't be a fight, Mr. Jones."

We stared at each other for an interval. Motes of dust floated through the sunlight, the only movement in the room. Then I blinked and he was gone.

Terror flooded me. I grabbed my gun and glanced around the office for something to aim at.

Gloved hands appeared out of nowhere and caught my arm in a crushing grip. I thrashed wildly as I was lifted into the air and thrown across the office. I slammed into the wall and crashed hard onto my side. Air burst from my lungs.

I struggled to my feet, coughing and wheezing. The next thing I knew, Hermes was pressing me against the wall. His fingers closed around my throat.

"So, Mr. Jones," he said, still smiling. "Have you started to rethink your position?"

I pressed my gun under his chin. "Go to Hades."

Hermes laughed.

Emilie came into the office wielding a large revolver. "I think you should leave now."

Hermes ignored her.

My voice cracked with fear; it was embarrassing. "Let me go, before I put a bullet in you."

Hermes smirked. "Exactly what would that do, besides make me angry?"

"It'd ruin that snazzy suit of yours," I said.

Hermes tightened his grip on my throat. I grunted.

Emilie cocked her gun.

No one made a move. Everything was silent except the hum of the air conditioner. Should I shoot him? Could I pull the trigger before he crushed my throat? I knew he was fast. But how fast?

"I should kill you right now," Hermes whispered.

"But you won't," I said. "You need me." The words seemed to grind against the inside of my throat.

Hermes's smile widened. He let me go and backed off slowly.

Emilie moved away from the door, her gun still trained on him. "Are you all right, sir?"

I nodded, clutching my throat. "Yeah."

Emilie covered me as I returned to my desk and sat down. My hand shook. The Desert Eagle felt glued to my palm.

"I'll ask you again," Hermes said. "Have you reconsidered? Or shall I resume trying to convince you?"

"Beat me up all you'd like. Answer's still the same."

Hermes removed the gloves and stuffed them into his pocket. "Are you sure this is the route you wish to take?"

"Sure as I'll be," I said.

Hermes reached into his pocket and produced a white business card. He placed it on my desk. "If you change your mind."

"Not gonna happen."

He chuckled and turned to leave. He stopped near the door and glanced over his shoulder. "A word of warning, Mr. Jones. There are consequences for disrespecting the Gods. Grave ones."

I pointed at the door.

"Have a nice day." Hermes tipped an invisible hat and walked out.

Emilie lowered her gun and straightened. She cleared her throat. "Are you sure you're all right, sir?"

"Yeah. Thanks for the assist."

Emilie nodded. "If you don't mind me asking, sir, what was that all about?"

I shook my head, putting my gun back into the drawer. "Nothing. Just Gods being Gods."

"Is there anything I can get you?"

"An icepack would be nice. And some of those little chocolate cookies. The ones with peanut butter in the middle."

"Yes, sir." Emilie left my office.

I let out a long sigh and rubbed the nape of my neck. The adrenaline coursing through my body began to die away, and I suddenly felt tired. My back and throat felt like they were on fire. They'd feel worse tomorrow morning. But none of that bothered me. Physical pain was something I could deal with. What did bother me was the fact that I had gotten roughed up by a guy with plucked eyebrows and manicured hands.

17

AFTER I FINISHED EDITING THE FOOTAGE OF COLLIN, I SWUNG by the Stone residence to review it with Bellanca. She and I sat in the living room across from the big-screen TV. Sunlight poured through the skylight.

Bellanca watched the recording as if in a trance. As bad as I felt for her, I couldn't help cracking a smile during the part where Collin ran out of Enyo's house in his tighty-whities.

When the recording ended, Bellanca said nothing.

"It looks like you were right," I said.

Bellanca continued to stare blankly at the television screen. When she finally spoke, her voice emerged as little more than a whisper. "He cheated on me." There was no emotion in her tone. No sadness or shock or anger. Nothing. "I asked him if he was cheating on me," she continued, "and he said no."

We were sitting next to each other on the red sectional, about a foot apart. I looked at her. She looked back. Her lips parted, as though she wanted to tell me something but couldn't get the words out.

"You okay?" I asked.

Bellanca gave a partial nod. A few seconds passed. Then she started crying. She bent forward and covered her face. Tears squeezed between her fingers, dripping onto the checkered tile. Being a PI, I had seen this type of thing dozens of times, and it always made me feel awkward.

I patted her on the back. It was the only thing I could think to do. She looked up at me. Her face was flushed and mascara ran down her cheeks.

"I loved him," she sobbed. "How could he do this?"

I wanted to say, "Your husband's a selfish asshole, and you should get a divorce ASAP." But I didn't. My job was to give people the truth. What they did with it was up to them.

"I'm sorry," I said, truthfully.

Bellanca threw her arms around me and buried her face in the crook of my neck. I stiffened. Her hair smelled like fresh coconut. A knot of desire formed in my belly.

"He told me he loved me," Bellanca said, her voice muffled.

I rubbed her back. She gave a shuddering sigh as her tears dampened the collar of my shirt. Comforting clients wasn't in my job description, but today I made an exception. I liked Bellanca. I liked being this close to her. She was a beautiful woman in a vulnerable position. But she was also a customer. And Plato Jones, PI, is all about customer service.

Bellanca stopped crying after a while. But she continued to embrace me. Her lips brushed the side of my neck. At first, I dismissed it as an accident. But then it happened again, and this time it was more than a brush.

Bellanca tightened her hold on me and started kissing my neck. My heart raced, and I suddenly felt light-headed. Feeling her warm body against mine, I found it hard not to close my eyes and go with it. But I knew I had to put a stop to this. Hugging a client was fine, if not ethical. But having sex with one, especially a married one, was a line I refused to cross.

"Bellanca," I whispered.

"Hmm?"

"Don't you think you should stop now?"

She ignored the question and kissed me again. Her soft lips searched the bare flesh on my neck. I fought the impulse to her kiss back.

"This has to stop," I said, my voice coming out huskier than I intended.

"No. Not yet." Bellanca leaned forward and tried to kiss me on the mouth. I turned my head. Her lips pressed against my cheek.

"Stop." I pried her arms away and stood up.

Bellanca stared at me, her brown eyes large and dark, her lips flushed. Then she blinked and her sanity seemed to return. She gasped and shot upright. "I am so sorry!"

I shook my head, still light-headed. "Don't worry about it."

Bellanca started crying again. She covered her face and turned away from me.

"I think I should go now," I said.

She didn't respond.

I saw myself out and got into my car. I started the engine, cranked the air conditioner on high, and drove off. *The excitement never stops*, I thought. In less than eight hours, I had been beaten up by a God and molested by a client. I didn't know whether I needed a hot bath or a cold shower.

18

AFTER MY DIVORCE, MY MOM RECLAIMED THE TITLE OF MOST important woman in my life. I paid her a visit at least once a month. She was the nurturing type. Generous, kind, willing to bend over backward for family. She was protective too. Fortunately she never got too crazy with it.

Early Saturday morning, I drove to the docks and took a ferry to Skiathos, an island northwest of Athens. It was a popular tourist spot, with lots of resorts and restaurants. My mom lived in a beachside villa on the southwestern part of the island. I bought her the house after my second year with the OBI. A white one-story with reddish-brown shingles, it was plain as plain could be. I wanted to get her something fancier, but she wouldn't have it. She said I had already spent more than enough money on little ol' her.

I knocked on the door. A minute later, my mom answered, out of breath and wearing a red-and-black salsa dress. Her long gray hair was pulled back in a bun. When she saw me, her brown eyes lit up.

"Hi, Mom." I smiled when I saw her.

"PJ!" She wrapped her arms around me like I was soldier coming home from war. She felt smaller than I remembered. More fragile. I had to be careful not to hug too hard for fear of breaking her.

Mom released me and poked me in the stomach. "You've put on weight."

I looked myself over. "Maybe a little."

"You'd better be careful," she warned me. "Once you get too much on, it's almost impossible to get off."

"Don't worry, I know what I'm doing."

"Famous last words."

I laughed. "So, what's with the getup?"

"What, this?" She glanced down at her dress. "James is teaching me to salsa dance."

I narrowed my eyes. "Who's James?"

"My new friend. Didn't I tell you about him last time we talked?"

"No. You neglected to mention him."

"Well, come on in and meet him," Mom said, pulling me through the door.

I didn't like this. Didn't like it at all. In the past six years, my mom had gone through four boyfriends. The first three were alright. But the fourth was a real ass. A smooth talker with a nice car and lots of cash. He had this cheese-eating grin that grated on my nerves. One time he took my mom skydiving. Another time, the two of them went bungee jumping. When I caught wind of their little escapades, I was royally pissed—so pissed, in fact, that Alexis had to talk me out of going after the guy. What my mom saw in that loser I'll never know.

She led me into the living room. The space had a tropical theme going on. The furniture was wicker, with bright floral cushions. The fan blades were shaped like banana leaves. The patio window looked out onto the Aegean. Salsa music played on an old record player that had belonged to my dad.

James danced by himself near the fireplace. He was tall and dark, with curly gray hair, a thin mustache, and a bad suntan. His build was impressive, for an old guy. He had on a black button-up with long puffy sleeves and a pair of tight black pants. Beneath his partially unbuttoned shirt, his chest looked like it had a family of chinchillas glued to it. The only thing he was missing was a rose clenched between his teeth.

"Eleanor, is this your little boy?" His voice was smooth, but not in a good way. It was that cheesy kind of smooth. The kind that screamed used car salesman.

"Sure is," Mom said, her face bright.

James salsa-danced up to me and shook my hand. He smelled of cologne and aftershave. The combination made my nostrils burn.

"James Hodges," he said.

I offered him a fake smile. "Plato Jones. Good to meet you, Mr. Hodges."

"Please, call me James."

"Sure."

"Your mom has told me a lot about you."

I wish I could say the same. "Nothing too incriminating, I hope."

James grinned. His veneers were too big and too white for his mouth. They reminded me of piano keys.

"You hungry, PJ?" Mom asked.

"Starving."

"Come to the kitchen. I'll fix you something." She glanced at James. "Would you turn off the music, dear?"

Dear? Gods, how serious were they?

"Of course." James walked over to the old record player and turned it off. I felt a thump in my chest. I didn't like the idea of another man touching my dad's stuff. He was dead and couldn't care less, but still.

"Come on, slowpoke." Mom tugged my arm.

Like the living room, the kitchen also had a tropical theme. But with white floors, blue walls, and lime-green cabinets, it more closely resembled something out of *Pee-wee's Playhouse*. Now, don't get me wrong. I love my mom to death, but an interior designer she is not.

I sat down at the kitchen table.

"Is there anything in particular you want?" Mom asked.

"Nah, just whatever you got."

While Mom rummaged through the fridge, I looked around the kitchen. A picture of me and Socrates sat on the bakers rack. I was eleven and he was thirteen. We had our arms around each other's shoulders, like we were best friends or something. That was as far from the truth as you could get. In reality, I couldn't stand my brother. Just hearing his name made me angry.

Our dad died of prostate cancer when I was fourteen. A few days after the funeral, Socrates took off without saying a word. No goodbye note. No nothing. He abandoned me and Mom when we needed him the most.

I heard from him two years ago, and not a word since. He called me out of the blue to "check up" on me. The conversation quickly turned to money. He'd lost his shirt in some failed business venture. If I lent him a couple thousand credits, he'd pay me back twofold. I hung up when he was midsentence.

As far as I was concerned, I had no brother.

My mom didn't mention Socrates much. Not because she was mad at him, but because he'd hurt her with what he'd done. Knowing she was sad because of him made me want to hunt him down and kick the crap out of him.

"What's wrong?" Mom asked, slicing a tomato.

I shook my head and smiled. "Nothing."

"You should know by now that you can't hide anything from me."

"I'm not hiding anything."

"No, you're not. Your troubles are written all over your face."

I didn't like where this was going. It was time to change the subject. "I saw Uncle Magus not too long ago."

"Oh! How is he?"

"He's doing fine. Still running the shop."

"That's good. Tell him if he doesn't call me more often, he's going to be in big trouble."

I gave a thumbs-up. "Will do."

James sauntered into the kitchen and sat across from me. He had ditched the salsa clothes for a white, V-neck T-shirt and pair of cream leisure pants.

"Your mom tells me you're a private eye," he said to me.

"That's right."

"How's that going for you?"

"Business is good."

Mom sighed as she opened a jar of mayo. "I still don't know why you gave up that nice government job to go play detective."

"It wasn't for me."

She shook her head and spread some of the mayo on a slice of bread.

Mom knew I used to work for the OBI. Alexis knew too. What they didn't know was that I was a field agent, involved in covert ops. As far as they were concerned, I used to be a pencil-pusher with a corner office at OBI headquarters. I didn't like lying to them, but telling the truth was too dangerous.

Keeping your workplace identity a secret is the first rule of being an OBI agent. The second is to never share classified information with civilians. Agents who break those rules tend to disappear.

"Working on any interesting cases?" James asked me.

"Nothing special. Say, Jim, what exactly do you do for a living?"

Mom answered for him. "James owns a successful toilet paper company."

95

James smiled broadly.

"How fitting," I said.

Mom brought me a roast beef sandwich with all the trimmings, a humongous slice of baklava, and a tall glass of tea. I bit into the sandwich. The taste hadn't changed since I was a kid. Delicious.

Mom started making sandwiches for her and James—sliced cucumber and eggplant between slices of tofu. I was pretty sure Mom didn't come up with the recipe. She'd never been much of a health nut.

"Have you talked to Alexis lately?" she asked.

"More often than I'd like to," I answered, my mouth full.

"How is she?"

"She's still the same old Alexis. Annoying. Argumentative. Constantly telling me how I should live my life."

"It sounds like she still cares about you."

"Maybe. But I've moved on."

Mom's eyes widened. "Does that mean you've found someone else?"

I shook my head.

She sighed. "Oh, PJ."

"I just haven't found the right woman yet."

"Well, you'd better hurry up and find her. I want to know what it's like to be a grandmother before I kick the bucket."

"Mom!"

"I'm just saying." Mom finished making the sandwiches and brought them to the table.

The three of us ate and chatted. Mom and James kept making eyes at each other. I could sense that they were playing footsie under the table. I wanted to say, "Do you two mind? I'm trying to eat." But I couldn't find it in myself to give them a hard time. After everything Mom had been through—with Dad dying and Socrates running off—she deserved to be happy.

I wasn't too fond of Jim. I didn't like his stupid mustache. Or his super-smooth voice. But if he made Mom happy, I'd make an effort to tolerate him.

"Are you sure you can't stay the night?" Mom asked. "You can stay in the guest room."

I shook my head, smiling. "Sorry, but duty calls."

We said our goodbyes. A hug and kiss for Mom, and a handshake for Jim. As I walked out of the house, I felt lighter despite all the food in my stomach. Seeing Mom always made me feel like a kid again. A big, woman-chasing, booze-pounding kid.

19

THAT NIGHT I AWOKE TO THE SOUND OF SOMEONE POUNDING on the door. Darkness loomed through my bedroom window. I glanced at the digital alarm clock on the nightstand: 5:45. A feeling of dread crept over me. When people come a-knocking in the wee hours of the morning, they usually brought bad news.

"Hang on a second!" I rolled out of bed, my body stiff and aching, and donned a wifebeater. The scuffle with Hermes had left me with multiple bruises. The worst one was on my lower back. I'd used an icepack to reduce the swelling, then slathered it with ointment. But that did little to ease the pain. When I moved too quickly, or tried to bend over, I felt a twinge of agony. Hermes, that bastard. One day I was going to get him back for this.

I lurched to the door and looked through the peephole. Herc stood in the hallway, fidgeting nervously. He wore a white T-shirt and the same baseball cap he had worn to the Night Owl. The sunglasses were missing. He must have gotten a refund for them.

I opened the door. Herc moved past me without saying a word.

"Come on in," I said, shutting the door.

Herc walked to the window and looked out, his hands at his sides. "Sorry about stopping by so early. I wanted to catch you before you went to work. Got some bad news."

"How bad?" I asked.

"Real bad. Dad called. Hephaestus was murdered."

I didn't want to reply. But I knew he'd find out the truth eventually. Best to go ahead and get it over with. "Yeah, I know."

Herc spun toward me, his brow furrowed. "You knew? How?"

I eased onto my recliner. The leather squeaked beneath my body. "Hermes approached me at the Night Owl. He asked me to take a look at the crime scene."

Herc held up his hand. "Hold up. Let me get this straight. You knew Hephaestus was dead all this time, and you didn't bother to tell me? Your best friend?"

I shrugged.

Herc made a choking sound. "You're an asshole, Plato Jones!"

"You were already worried about the killer coming after Hebe," I said. "I didn't want to make things worse."

"Oh, so I should be thanking you?"

"I was only looking out for you."

"Oh yeah? Well next time don't bother." Herc sat down on the couch, looked at me, and shook his head. "I can't believe you."

We sat in silence for a time, not looking at each other. Then I said, "Want a beer?"

"Sure."

I eased out of the chair and went to the kitchen. I grabbed two beers from the fridge and tossed one to Herc. I didn't normally drink this early in the morning. But I figured a little alcohol would help alleviate the tension between us, as well as dull the pain of my bruises.

"Thanks." Herc pried off the cap.

"Don't mention it." I sat back down.

"Sorry about calling you an asshole."

I waved my hand dismissively. "I deserved it."

"Yeah, you kinda did."

I smirked. "You're not supposed to agree with me, you know."

Herc chuckled and took a swig of beer. "You said you investigated the crime scene. Does that mean you're taking the case?"

I shook my head. "What I did for Hermes the other night was just a favor."

"But you're still considering it, right?"

"Maybe." I drank some beer. It hurt to swallow.

Herc put his drink on the coffee table and stood up. He reached into his pocket and took out a wad of money, which he tossed onto the table.

"What's this?" I asked.

"This is the reason I came by. I want you to take me on as a client."

"Herc . . . I can't take your money."

"You can and you will."

I leaned back in my chair and stared at the ceiling, stalling.

"The killer's going after the First Family," Herc said. "That means Hebe is on his list."

"We don't know that for sure."

"I'm not taking any chances."

I could hear the fear in his voice, see it in his eyes. Guilt rose from the pit of my stomach. "If you want me to help keep an eye on Hebe—"

"That's not good enough," Herc said, cutting me off. "Take the case."

"Tell you what." I rose from my chair. "I'll look into it. But I refuse to work with the Gods."

Herc beamed. He stood up and stepped toward me, his arms outstretched.

I held up my hand. "No hugs. I'm still recovering from the last one you gave me."

"Oh, right. Sorry about that."

I put down my beer, picked up the wad of bills, and offered it back to him. "Here."

Herc didn't move.

"What's the matter with you?" I said. "Take the money."

"No."

"Quit being stubborn and take it."

"It's yours," Herc said. "Think of it as an incentive."

"I'm not going to think of it as anything. Now take it."

Herc crossed his arms.

What followed was a standoff of sorts. Herc stared me down. I stared him down. He was grinning. I wasn't. Neither of us moved. The first rays of daylight shone through the window, burning away the shadows, and filling the apartment with golden light. A beeping sound issued from my bedroom. My alarm clock.

"I don't have time for this." I tossed the money back on the table. "I have to get ready for work."

20

COLLIN STONE STRODE INTO MY OFFICE AT THREE IN THE afternoon, wearing a red polo, jeans, and designer sunglasses. He looked bigger up close—about six-four. The twisted scar on his face suggested his wound hadn't healed correctly. Judging by the thick calluses on his knuckles, he'd been in more than a few scuffles over the years.

"You Plato Jones?" he asked, his voice deep and coarse.

"Last I checked."

"We need to talk."

I pretended not to know him. "And you are?"

"Collin Stone." He said it like I was supposed to be impressed.

"Nice to meet you, Mr. Stone." I gestured at the chair in front of my desk.

Collin sat down and took off his sunglasses. The shiner on his eye was healing nicely.

"How can I help you?" I asked.

Collin leaned back and steepled his fingers. He was trying to look powerful and important. He might have succeeded if not for the black eye.

"I understand you were recently hired to follow me," he said.

I smiled politely. "I typically don't comment on what my assignments may or may not be. Confidentiality and all. You understand." I indicated the candy dish. "Candy?"

Collin sneered. "Mr. Jones, my beautiful wife, Bellanca, thinks I've been cheating on her. She claims to have seen a video of me and another woman. A video you provided. I asked to see this supposed video, but she refused to show it to me."

"Sounds like you've got yourself a bit of a problem."

"Don't patronize me, Mr. Jones."

"Didn't realize I was." I definitely was.

Collin glared at me. "Because of this alleged proof, Bellanca's threatening divorce."

"If she cheated on you, wouldn't you do the same?"

"Maybe I would," Collin admitted. "But that's not the point."

This guy hadn't been in my office five minutes, and he was already getting on my nerves. "Exactly why are you here, Mr. Stone?"

"I need your help."

I raised an eyebrow. "My help?"

He nodded. "The footage you collected on me and my . . . friend. I want you tell Bellanca it was doctored."

"Are you serious?"

"Totally."

"I'm afraid I can't do that, Mr. Stone."

Collin's mouth became a hard line. "And why not?"

"Because it's my job to uncover the truth." I leaned back in my chair. "Not to manufacture lies."

"I'm not asking you to manufacture a lie." Collin inclined forward in his seat. "I'm asking you to save my marriage."

"What makes you think that Bellanc—Mrs. Stone—would even believe me?"

Collin grinned. "Mr. Jones, I love my wife. She's a wonderful woman. But she's not the sharpest crayon in the box, if you know what I mean."

Hearing Collin insult Bellanca made me want to blacken his other eye. But I stayed professional. Point for me.

"I'm sorry, Mr. Stone, but I can't help you. What you're asking goes against everything I stand for."

Collin pursed his lips. "You're an honest man. I respect that." He reached in his coat pocket and pulled out his checkbook. "But as my father used to say, 'Everyone has a price.' What's yours?"

That was all I could take. From the time Collin stepped into my office, he'd done nothing but eat away at my patience. He wanted me to sympathize with him. Wanted me to believe that he was a victim of circumstance. And now he thought he could drop a few thousand credits and all his problems would magically go away. That might have worked for him in the past, but not today. His dirt had finally caught up with him.

"I think you should leave."

Collin slipped his checkbook back into his pocket and stood up. He planted his hands on my desk and leaned forward. His wedding band gleamed on his ring finger. Gold with black diamonds. I wondered if he wore it while having sex with Enyo.

"I don't like it when people say no to me, Mr. Jones," he said, his tone low and threatening. "They end up not liking it either."

I sat up and looked him right in the eye. "Listen, pal. I've been threatened by the Gods of Olympus more times than I can count. If you want to intimidate me, you're going to have to try a lot harder."

"Who do you think you're talking to?" Collin hissed through clenched teeth. "You're a small-time PI. A nobody.

I'm a powerful man with powerful connections. Fuck with me and I'll bury you."

"Whatever you say."

Collin's face flushed an angry shade of red. He came around my desk, probably with the intention of roughing me up. I casually opened the desk drawer that contained my Desert Eagle. Collin's eyes latched onto the gun, and he paused. I slowly shook my head.

He cursed under his breath, whirled around, and stormed out of my office, slamming the door behind him.

"Have a nice day," I said.

21

I GOT HOME JUST AS THE STREET LIGHTS CAME ON, AND WENT straight for the fridge. I took out a box of leftover Chinese food—pepper steak and fried rice—emptied it onto a plate, and popped it in the microwave. Two minutes later, the timer went off, and I took my dinner to the kitchen table. No sooner had I sat down than my cell phone rang. I glanced at the caller ID. Alexis. Wonderful.

"Hello?"

"Hi, Plato. How are you?" Alexis's tone was uncharacteristically perky, which made me suspicious. She used this tone only when she wanted something from me, or when she had unpleasant news to deliver. I wasn't up for either.

"I'm good. Couldn't be better. What's up?"

"Nothing. I just called to check on you. I was worried."

She called to check on me? No. I didn't believe it. Alexis never called just to check on me. She definitely had something up her sleeve. "Oh, really?"

"Yes," Alexis said. "I wanted to see where your head is, regarding the whole engagement thing."

I sighed, almost inaudibly. This again. I should've known. "I'm happy for you and Corbin. I thought I expressed that last time we talked."

"His name is Calais. And I didn't believe you. I still don't believe you." There was an undercurrent of annoyance in Alexis's voice. She tried to hide it, but I was on to her.

She hadn't called for my benefit. She'd called to flaunt her engagement in my face some more. She wanted me to get angry. Wanted me to tell her not to get married, to leave her fiancé and come back to me. She wanted to hear me beg. Wanted to know that I was hurting. I wasn't going to give her the satisfaction.

"Sorry to hear that." I took a bite of food. It was scorching hot. Fanning my mouth with my hand, I reached for my drink only to realize that I didn't have one. I got up to get a bottle of water from the fridge.

"Why won't you be honest with me?" she asked.

"I am." I opened the bottle of water and took a sip.

"You know what I mean. If you have a problem with me and Calais getting married, then you should just say so."

"And what would that accomplish?" I asked, sitting back down.

There was a pause on the other end.

"I don't know," Alexis said after a time. "But I'm sure having those feelings out in the open would make everyone feel a lot better about the situation."

"In addition to massaging your ego," I mumbled.

"What was that?"

"Nothing. Look Alexis, I'm right in the middle of dinner. Can we talk about this later?"

"I guess," Alexis said. Then she gasped, and her tone suddenly turned excited. "Oh yeah. There was something else I wanted to tell you. I was at the grocery store earlier today, and guess who I ran into. Hermes! You know, the God."

I frowned, my fork poised over a chunk of green bell pepper. "I'm familiar with him."

"He told me I was beautiful. So beautiful that he just had to stop and introduce himself."

"Was he looking at you or into a mirror?"

"Oh, shut up." Alexis laughed. "Anyway, he seemed really nice. And he said he knew you, which was strange because I didn't even bring up your name. Isn't that exciting?"

My insides turned to ice. "Very. Listen, Alexis. I have to go now."

"Oh. Well, all right. Talk to you later, I guess."

"Bye." I ended the call, took Hermes's business card out of my wallet, and punched in the number. His phone rang five times before going to voice mail. After the tone, I said, "You stay away from Alexis, understand? Leave her out of this. You hear me? Leave her out of this."

I hung up.

22

I WAS GETTING READY FOR WORK THE NEXT MORNING WHEN someone knocked at the door. I was in such a hurry to get dressed that I opened the door without first looking through the peephole. Big mistake. Hermes stood across from me. At once, my annoyance level went from zero to seven digits.

Today, he wore a light-gray suit with a powder-blue shirt underneath. I couldn't help wondering how many suits the guy owned. I had never seen him wear the same thing twice.

"Good morning, Mr. Jones." Hermes's smile was anything but genuine. "I hope you slept well."

I smiled back at him, equally disingenuous. "I'll bet."

We stood there for half a minute, silently smiling at each other, until my cheeks hurt.

Hermes arched his eyebrows. "Aren't you going to invite me in?"

My first instinct was to say no. Hell no. I didn't trust Hermes. Letting him into my home seemed like the antithesis of a good idea. But I didn't have much choice. If I refused, he'd just force his way inside. And my gun was in the bedroom, on the nightstand. I groaned inwardly. Why me?

"Well?" Hermes said.

Reluctantly, I stepped aside.

Hermes nodded appreciatively. He stepped inside and immediately started looking around the apartment, his hands behind his back. Sporadically, he chuckled and shook his head.

"What's so funny?" I asked, closing the door.

"Nothing, Mr. Jones, nothing at all," Hermes answered, grinning.

He took a picture down from the mantel. A photo of my parents, Socrates, and me. We stood on the front lawn of our house. It was summertime. I was five and wearing a sailor suit, the kind with shorts and suspenders. My mom said I looked precious in it. I remember feeling stupid.

"You have a lovely family," Hermes said.

I was so uncomfortable having him in my place, I barely noticed the compliment. Herc was the closest thing to a God that had been inside the apartment. I'd wanted to keep it that way.

"Did you get my message?" I asked.

Hermes returned the picture to the mantle. "I did."

"I know what you're trying to do."

Hermes lifted his brows. "Indeed?"

"She has nothing to do with this. Leave her alone."

"I will, provided you do as we ask."

"Here we go with this again."

Hermes removed a handkerchief from his pocket and dusted off the couch. He sat down and crossed his legs. "Zeus would like to have a word with you. He has a proposition that might interest you."

I crossed my arms and leaned against the door. "Let me guess. I investigate the murder, and you promise not to hurt Alexis."

Hermes shrugged.

I wanted to smash his face. But I had seen what he was capable of, and I wasn't interested in taking a second look. "I should've known you guys would pull something like this."

"You left us no choice. This matter must be resolved as quickly as possible. The stability of Olympus depends on it. So what's it going to be, Mr. Jones?"

What else could I do? Alexis and I weren't on the best terms, but I couldn't let her come to harm because of my feud with the Gods. Playing hero sucks.

"Let me call my secretary and tell her I won't be in today," I said.

"I knew you'd see things our way. Your ex-wife is quite lovely after all—and fragile, very fragile. But I suppose the same can be said about all humans." Hermes smiled, flashing a perfect set of teeth. "Now make yourself presentable. Zeus is waiting."

23

I arrived at Zeus's around 10:00 a.m.

The King of the Gods spent most of his time in his private estate, high atop Mount Olympus. Perched on the edge of a cliff, the main building was accessible only by helicopter. With its clean white exterior and futuristic design, it looked like an alien spaceship on stilts. Rich people had strange tastes.

Hermes and I entered the mansion through a pair of sliding glass doors. The interior was simple but modern, with a lot of solid colors, stainless steel, and rounded corners. Curved walls enclosed the room. The place was impressive to be sure, but it lacked warmth. Literally and figuratively—the air conditioner was cranked up so high I could see my breath.

In all, the estate felt more like an office building than a home.

Hermes showed me to Zeus's office and told me he'd wait outside. Glass made up the entire room. I wished I'd brought along a large rock.

Dressed like a spokesmodel for a Big & Tall suit shop, Zeus sat behind a glass desk at the head of the room. Light winked off the gold and platinum threads woven into the fabric of his charcoal suit. The light-blue tie matched his eyes. Neatly trimmed dark-brown hair and beard emphasized his chiseled features.

Even sitting down, he radiated power. His presence filled the room like an invisible current, washing over me and making the hair on the nape of my neck stand on end. I wasn't sure if he was doing it on purpose or not. Either way, one thing was clear: you don't screw with the King.

Hera, Zeus's wife and Queen of the Gods, stood to the right of her husband. Her tight white dress showed off some fairly nice curves. Diamond jewelry glittered on her wrists, neck, and fingers, and her black hair was pulled into a severe bun. You could slice your finger caressing her razor-sharp features. I wanted to check Zeus's hands for scars.

"Greetings, Mr. Jones," Zeus said, his voice deep and commanding. "It's nice to see you again. Please, have a seat."

I sat on the couch and nodded at Hera. "Ma'am."

She sneered at me. Charming.

"Would you care for something to drink?" Zeus offered.

I shook my head. "No thanks."

He nodded and laced his fingers. "Hermes tells me you were out with my son the other night. How is Hercules? He and I rarely speak nowadays."

"Herc's fine."

Zeus smiled proudly. Hera rolled her eyes.

"With all due respect, Mr. President, can we just get down to business?"

Zeus stood and looked through the glass wall behind his desk, beyond which lay a spectacular view of New Olympia. Then he began to pace back and forth. Hera continued to watch me. Her gold eyes were daggers.

"Where are my manners?" Zeus said. "I haven't even thanked you for coming on such short notice."

"Well you didn't leave me much choice, did you?" I said. My voice showed every bit of the agitation I felt.

"You forget yourself, mortal," Hera snapped. "You are in the presence of Gods. One more outburst, and I'll have the flesh stripped from your bones."

"Calm down, my love," Zeus said. "Mr. Jones can't help us if he's dead, now can he?"

Hera crossed her arms and tilted her chin. Her diamonds flashed in the sunlight. "I suppose not."

I waited until the tension in the room had eased. "There was no need to bring Alexis into this."

"Desperate times call for desperate measures, I'm afraid," Zeus said. "You were my best agent. Quick on your feet, able to find solutions in the most unlikely places. Your talents were invaluable to our organization. We need them again."

"I appreciate the compliments, Mr. President. I really do. But I'm just a modest PI. I don't have the resources to conduct an investigation of this magnitude."

Zeus summoned me forward. He took a check out of his suit pocket and slid it across his desk. I picked it up. It was double his original offer. My jaw nearly dropped when I saw all the zeros.

"Will this be sufficient?" he asked.

"I believe so." I tried to sound nonchalant. I folded the check in half and slipped it into my back pocket.

"In that case, let us move on. The enemy you face has the power to kill Gods. Being mortal places you at a disadvantage. But I have something that might help." He pressed a button on his intercom.

A woman's voice issued from the speaker. "Sir?"

"I need you in my office."

"On my way."

Seconds later, the door opened, and in came Chrysus, Zeus's personal assistant and director of the Treasury. She was also a certifiable bombshell, in a gray skirt suit that showed off a good amount of thigh and breast. Her thick blond hair was pinned back, revealing perfectly applied makeup. The glasses were a nice touch. I've always been a fan of the naughty librarian look.

She bowed her head to Zeus. "What can I do for you, sir?"

"Chrysus." Zeus gestured toward me. "You're familiar with Mr. Jones?"

Chrysus regarded me with a polite smile. "Of course. How are you, Mr. Jones?"

I gave her a thumbs-up. "Super."

"Mr. Jones has agreed to help us," Zeus said. "Go to the Treasury and retrieve Athena's Aegis."

"Yes, sir." Chrysus bowed her head once more and left.

As she walked away, I glanced at her backside from the corner of my eye. If Zeus or Hera noticed, they didn't say anything about it.

Once the office doors had closed, I asked the obvious question. "What's Athena's Aegis?"

The King of the Gods sat back down. "One of the secret treasures of Olympus. Only a select few know of its existence. Whoever wears the Aegis is rendered invulnerable. I'm lending it to you."

I pursed my lips. *Invulnerability? Now we're talking!* "Thank you."

Hera laid a hand on Zeus's shoulder. Her fingernails were painted blood-red. As she spoke to him, her gaze remained fixed on me. "Are you sure that's wise, my love? Handing over such a powerful treasure to a human? You know how untrustworthy they can be. You've seen their reality shows. Backstabbing left and right."

I smiled innocently.

Zeus patted Hera on the hand, and returned his attention to me. "I'll have the Aegis delivered to you once Chrysus retrieves it from the vault and handles the necessary paperwork. You should have it by the middle of next week."

Hera drew her hand back and scowled at me. "You had better be careful with the Aegis."

I held up three fingers. Scout's honor.

"Well if there's nothing else, I suggest you get started." Zeus began sorting through a stack of papers on his desk.

That was my cue to leave. I rejoined Hermes at the front door, and he escorted me back to the helipad.

The S-O-B had a satisfied grin on his face. "How did the meeting go?"

"As well as can be expected."

"I take it you're going to help us then."

"Yep."

"You know Zeus expects quick results?"

"Yep."

"Where will you start your investigation?"

"I haven't a clue."

24

"So the Gods threatened Alexis to get you on the case." Herc shook his head. "That's pretty despicable, even for them."

We were sitting at a table at the Night Owl. It was twenty after four in the afternoon, so the place was essentially a ghost town. Just us, Harold the bartender, and Abas. For the past hour, Abas had been cleaning the men's bathroom. I was drinking gin and tonic. Herc had a rum and Coke.

"The Gods never cease to amaze me. Just when I think they can't get any lower, they pull a stunt like this. At least the money's good. Which reminds me." I took the wad of money Herc had offered me the other day and tossed it on the table.

"What are you doing?" Herc asked.

"I'm giving your money back."

"It's not mine anymore."

"Sure it is." I slid the cash toward him. "Go ahead. Take it."

Herc stared at the cash. His was mouth tight, his eyes unblinking. He reached for it, but stopped himself at the last second. I cocked my eyebrow in surprise.

"No," Herc said, shaking his head defiantly. "I'm your client. This is your fee. That's the way this is gonna work."

"You're not my client, Herc. Zeus is the one who hired me. He's the one footing the bill. Now go ahead and take it." I pushed the money even closer to him. "Buy Hebe a new ring or bracelet or something."

Emotions clashed across Herc's face: guilt, excitement, anxiety, more guilt.

"You really don't want it?" he asked.

"Read my lips. I do not want your money."

"Are you absolutely positive? Beyond a shadow of a doubt?"

"Will you just take the damn money, Herc? Please! Do us both a favor and just take it. Go on. It's okay. If you don't, I'll have no choice but to donate it to the Young Republicans Society."

Herc hesitated a moment. Then a grin stretched across his face. He grabbed the cash and stuffed it into his pocket. I could've sworn I saw money signs flash in his eyes.

"You're alright, Jonesy."

"You sure about that? I can find at least a dozen people who might disagree."

Herc chuckled. "So what's your first move?"

I sipped my drink. "I figure I'll start with the most obvious suspect."

"Who's that?"

"Think about it." I tapped the side of my head with my index finger. "Of all the people Hephaestus knew, who was he closest to?"

Herc looked at me but did not answer. I could tell from the vacant look in his eyes that the gears weren't turning.

"Someone he swore to love and cherish forever," I said.

Herc shrugged.

I sighed. "His wife."

Herc's face lit up. "Oh, yeah." His gaze narrowed. "You think she's the killer?"

"Probably. I don't know. It's too early to say."

"But you intend to find out."

"Bingo."

"Well, good luck with that."

Good luck was right. Aphrodite was the Goddess of Love, Beauty, and Sexuality. Passion incarnate. An infamous party girl who incited lust in those around her and fed off it like a parasite. I had never met her in person, but I'd heard plenty of rumors. Some good. Some bad. All dirty.

One rumor in particular concerned me more than the others. Supposedly, any mortal who had sex with her would instantly lose his mind and become one of her thralls.

A few years back, a man claiming to be Aphrodite's boyfriend cut off his own hand and tried to mail it to her. An act of love, he called it. On his way to the post office, the moron passed out from blood loss, and ended up wrapping his car around a telephone pole. He was rushed to the hospital, where surgeons reattached his hand. From there, it was straight to the loony bin.

The incident had caused a media shitstorm. As it turned out, the moron was actually a famous lawyer. What would make a smart, well-to-do man lop off his own hand? Aphrodite and her reps weren't telling, so the public cooked up their own explanation.

Apparently, Aphrodite's sex is too good for the average mortal to handle. It causes a sensory overload that reduces our brains to Silly Putty. Whether the theory was true or not, I had no idea. And frankly, I didn't care. Aphrodite was a Goddess of Olympus. That was reason enough to be careful around her.

"The OBI's going to interrogate her within the next couple days," I said. "I'll wait until they're done. Then I'll set up a meeting with her."

Herc gave a sly grin. "And *pump her . . .* for information?"

"Good one." I tipped my glass toward him.

"I have my moments."

I took another swig of my drink. "For now, there's another lead I'd like to follow. I found a receipt in Hephaestus's workshop, from an industrial warehouse. He'd been working on some kind of project prior to his death. I want know what that project was."

"You think it has something to do with the murders?" Herc asked.

"I'm not sure. But it's all I've got at the moment."

25

Marvin's Scrap Heap was on the side of the highway between New Olympia and Boreasville, the only noticeable structure for miles. The building was massive. The white exterior and sheet-metal roof glowed in the sunlight. Four tractor-trailers occupied the parking lot. There were no other vehicles around.

I entered through the main entrance.

The cramped reception area smelled vaguely of rubber tires. Various award plaques hung on the walls, and in the corner, four plastic chairs were gathered in front of an old big-screen TV. The screen was coated in dust. Some joker had drawn a smiley face in it.

A squat old man with curly gray hair and thick glasses sat behind the front desk, reading a magazine. His name, Marvin, was stitched onto the pocket of his dark-blue overalls. Through the window behind him, I could see into the warehouse. There were hundreds of huge, wooden crates, all stacked on top of one another. *I'd hate to be stuck inventorying all that.*

When I stepped up to the desk, Marvin put down his magazine and smiled. Most of his teeth were missing. Those that remained were oddly shaped and rotting.

"Welcome to Marvin's Scrap Heap. Can I help you?" His soft, grandfatherly voice instantly put me in a good mood.

"I hope so. My name is Plato Jones. I'm a private investigator." I showed him my PI badge. It was one of those nice, professional-grade numbers, similar to the ones cops carry. Not some flimsy, laminated card.

Marvin inclined his head forward, took a good look at it, and then nodded.

I put the badge back in my pocket. "The Smith God, Hephaestus, hired me to look into a robbery that occurred at his home this past weekend."

Marvin's brow furrowed. "A robbery, you say?"

"Yes, sir."

"Who'd be stupid enough to rob a God?"

"I have no idea," I said. "But with your help I may be able to find out."

"What can I do for you?"

"I'm compiling a list of Hephaestus's most recent purchases. I understand he bought some materials from your warehouse not too long ago."

Marvin nodded. "He did."

"Do you remember what those materials were?"

"Should be in our records." Marvin adjusted his glasses and looked up the information on his computer. "Four units of aluminum, four units of copper, six units of platinum, one unit of gold, five of silver, and one of bronze. He said he was working on a series of projects. Top secret stuff."

It was just as I thought. Hephaestus *had* been working on something. I had no idea what that something was, or how it fit into the murder—if it fit at all—but it gave me another avenue to explore.

"You want a copy of the invoice?" Marvin asked. I was starting to like this guy more and more. Why couldn't all the people I encountered be so helpful?

"Nah. But thanks anyway."

"Is there anything else I can do for you?"

"No, that's it. Thanks for your help." We shook hands.

"No problem."

I turned to leave.

When I reached the door, Marvin called after me. "I hope you catch whoever's responsible."

"You and me both."

26

I CALLED HERC AND ASKED HIM TO DRIVE ME TO MOTORCARS of Olympia, a dealership that specialized in exotic automobiles. Until now, I had been hesitant to spend the money Zeus had given me for taking the case. But considering that I was up against something that could kill Gods, I might not be around for too much longer. It was best to have a little fun while I still could.

Herc showed up at my apartment a little after one o'clock. He drove a lime-green hybrid. It was a subcompact car, ideal for an average-size person like me, but too small for someone like Herc. He looked funny driving it, all hunched up on the wheel. More than once, I'd tried to convince him to upgrade to a larger car. Each time, he gave me the same tired speech on the importance of substance over style, efficiency over flash.

The ride to the lot was torture. Despite the ninety-plus-degree weather, Herc refused to turn on the air conditioner. Said it burned too much gas. Instead, we rode with all four windows down. But the air that blew around us was hot and dry. Sweat streamed down my face, and I could hardly breathe. Herc, on the other hand, was completely comfortable. As a Demigod, he was resistant to extreme temperatures. Lucky bastard.

By the time we reached Motorcars of Olympia, my shirt was drenched with sweat and sticking to my skin. The lot was on Old Grecian Road, a north-south highway that ran through the entire country. It was framed by strip malls, fast food joints, gas stations, and more car dealerships. The farther north you traveled, the prettier and more high-end everything got.

Herc pulled into the lot. We drove past fleets of exotic cars to the main office. The three-story building was painted completely white. In another life it might have been a warehouse. Beyond the showroom window, Lamborghinis, Ferraris, and other exotics sat atop spinning pedestals.

We got out of the car. The sun bore down like a weight, and no breezes blew around us to take the edge off the heat. Still, it was cooler out here than in Herc's pressure-cooker of a car.

"Are you sure you want to do this?" Herc asked.

"For the millionth time, yes." I groaned, wiping the sweat from my forehead.

"Wouldn't you rather settle for something a little less expensive?"

"Nope.

"Do you at least have a budget?"

"Nothing over eighty thousand."

Herc started. "Eighty thousand for a car?"

"Yeah, is something wrong with that?"

"Only that it's a monumental waste of money. Come on, Jonesy. There are so many other options out there. Cheaper ones."

"Maybe you're right, Herc. Maybe I should get something a little more price-friendly. But since we're already here, we might as well look around. Right?"

Herc sighed.

I opened the door and we stepped into the office. The cool air blowing from the overhead vents chilled the sweat on my skin.

A salesman in a slick charcoal suit walked up, his hand extended. His eyes and smile were wide, and his skin was like spray-tanned shrink wrap. I could tell he'd had a lot of work done. If I were him, I'd have asked the doctor for my money back.

"Welcome to Motorcars of Olympia. My name is Kyle." He had a singsong voice, like a game show host.

"Hi, Kyle." I shook his hand. "I'm Plato. This is my friend Herc."

"Oh, I already know who this is." Kyle smiled at Herc. The two of them shook hands. "It's an honor to meet you in person. I'm a big fan."

"Oh really?" Herc said, one eyebrow raised.

"Absolutely. You know, your wife Hebe was here just the other day."

Herc blinked. "What?"

"She was looking to buy a Porsche, but the model she wanted wasn't in stock. We ordered it for her. It should arrive sometime next week, I believe."

"Is that so?" Herc asked, expressionless. "How much did this Porsche cost exactly?"

"A little over a hundred thousand, if I remember correctly."

I sensed the breath go out of Herc. I nudged him with my elbow and said, "That's not too bad. Right, big spender?"

"Of course not," he said through clenched teeth. "Anything for my beautiful wife."

Kyle smiled, his veneers flashing. "So, what can I do for you gentlemen today?"

"I'm looking to buy a new car," I told him. "Something flashy, but not as flashy as Herc's Porsche. Something sexy, but professional. When I drive down the street I want people to say, 'Hey, that guy's got his stuff together.'"

Kyle nodded. "I have just the thing."

Herc and I followed him across the showroom floor to a silver Lotus Elise. The car was just what I was looking for. It was as if Kyle had read my mind. *Had* he read my mind? With all the crazy monsters running around New Olympia, there was no telling.

I opened the driver-side door and slid into the leather seat. It fit me like a glove, and made me feel like James Bond. A less sophisticated, more rumpled version.

"How much?" I asked.

"Fifty-four ninety-nine base."

I nodded and then glanced at Herc. "That's about half the price of your new car, right?"

Herc smiled but said nothing. I could tell by the tightness in his jaw that he was silently cursing.

"Would you like to look around some more?" Kyle asked me.

"No, this'll do."

"Splendid."

I paid for the car in full and took it for a spin. I had invited Herc to ride along, but he said that seeing me spend so much money at one time had worn him out. He went home to take a nap. And—probably—lecture Hebe about the finer points of penny-pinching.

I wanted to put the car through its paces, so I got on Highway 18 toward Boreasville, where there was little traffic and few cops. Nothing to ruin my fun. Riding at eighty miles per hour, I glanced in my rearview mirror and saw a pair of black motorcycles appear behind me. The riders wore black leather and helmets.

They were coming up fast, so I decided to let them by. I switched lanes, and one of the riders zoomed past. The other rode beside my car for the next quarter mile, looking at me through the darkened visor of his helmet.

"Nice bike!" I shouted out the window.

The rider revved his engine and whizzed ahead to join his friend. Then both riders sped up. Within seconds, they had vanished into the distance.

Jerks.

I leaned on the accelerator. The engine purred. Trees and road signs flew by in a haze of color. I turned on the radio. It was preset to a classical station, but I didn't care. I cranked up the volume anyway. My mind wandered back to the case.

Who could kill a God? That was the million-credit question. Even the Gods themselves didn't seem to know the answer—or at least they weren't telling me.

One possibility was that the Titans were responsible. They were once the Gods' enemies. But their hopes of conquering Olympus had been crushed by Zeus eons ago. The chance of their being involved was slim, but not so slim that I'd disregard it. If the Titans were planning to start a war with the Olympians, I didn't want to be around when the shit hit the fan. My days as a soldier were over.

I was trying to come up with more suspects when a black blur zoomed across the street, scant feet away from my fender. My instincts kicked in. I slammed on the brakes and cut the wheel sharply.

The tires screeched in protest, and the car flipped over, going airborne. My stomach dropped as the world barreled out of control. The car landed on the shoulder of the road and tumbled down a steep incline, shedding parts and thrashing me from side to side. Beneath the screams and groans of twisting metal, classical music continued to play from the speakers.

The car crashed into a tree at the bottom of the hill and jerked to a violent stop. The impact smashed my head against the window. I blacked out. When I came to, the music had stopped. I saw nothing but dust and smoke.

27

I SAT IN THE DRIVER SEAT, PARALYZED WITH SHOCK, MY breath coming and going in sharp gasps. Every inch of my body hurt, but as far as I could tell nothing was broken. I wouldn't know for sure until I tried to move. I shifted a bit, wiggled my fingers and toes. Everything seemed to be working.

Someone must have been looking out for me. I doubted it was the Gods of Olympus.

As my nerves settled, the throbbing in my head began to subside. A stream of warm blood ran down my face. Some trickled into my eye, forcing me to blink. I glanced in the fractured rearview mirror and saw the small cut on my forehead. With all the blood, it looked a lot worse than it really was. It might not even need stitches.

I unbuckled my seatbelt and tried to open the door, but it was mangled shut. I scooted into the passenger seat, tucked my knees in, and kicked at the window. The cracked glass shattered into pieces.

I crawled through and crashed onto the ground. Crows cawed in the treetops above, as if laughing at my misfortune. All I could smell was pine mixed with engine coolant. Slowly, I got to my feet.

I leaned against a nearby tree and assessed the damage. My brand new Lotus Elise was now a twisted heap of metal, wrapped around the trunk of the tree, like crumpled silver wrapping paper. Billows of smoke spewed from beneath the crushed hood. I shook my head. The purpose of this little joy ride was so I could break the car in. I guess I had succeeded, just not the way I had intended.

To my right, two figures in black jogged down the leaf-covered incline, headed straight for me. The riders. The blur that had crossed in front of me—it must have been one of them. They'd trashed my car. That little stunt they pulled had probably been their idea of a joke.

The two riders reached the bottom of the hill and picked their way past the wreckage.

As they drew closer to me, I pushed myself away from the tree and walked forward to meet them. "You dickheads nearly killed me!"

The riders said nothing. They came to a stop, reached into their jackets, and pulled out handguns.

My heart jumped into my throat. I whirled on my heel and darted into the woods.

The riders gave chase.

Shots rang out from behind me. Bullets whizzed past me, narrowly missing their mark. Blood from my forehead flowed into my eyes, partially blinding me. The undergrowth was thick, the ground uneven, and stones jutting from the soil threatened to trip me with every step.

I wished I had brought along my gun. At least then I could defend myself. But I had left it back at my apartment. I didn't think I'd need it to go car shopping. Shows what I know.

"Get back here!" shouted one of the riders. Another shot rang out. It grazed the trunk of a tree, inches away from my arm.

I cut left, crashed through a wall of brush, and ran, half-stumbling down a steep hillside. When I reached the bottom

I picked up the pace, my breath rasping in my throat. Behind me, the riders scrambled down the hill.

I couldn't say why they were trying to kill me, but I was betting it had something to do with the case. Someone didn't want me to find out the truth, and they'd hired these goons to make sure I didn't. But who was their employer?

I peeked over my shoulder. I couldn't see my pursuers, but I could hear them crashing through the bushes. I had lengthened the distance between us, and gained myself some breathing room. But I couldn't run forever. Eventually I would tire, and one of their bullets would catch me.

I had two options. I could find a good hiding place, or I could take down my pursuers. After what those two jerks did to my beautiful new car, I was leaning toward the second option.

I veered right and scrambled up a rocky incline. Several feet ahead, I skidded to a sudden halt just in front of a deep chasm. Below was a dry creek bed filled with jagged rocks.

The width of the gap was intimidating enough to make me think twice about trying to jump across it. The fall would almost certainly kill me. But what choice did I have? It was either jump or get shot.

I took several steps back, told myself that everything was going to be fine, and then took a running leap. My heart flew into my stomach as I sailed through the air.

My chest struck the lip of the chasm. The impact knocked the wind out of me. I desperately groped for something to grab onto. My fingers wrapped around an unearthed root. I gritted my teeth and used it to hoist myself over the edge.

I collapsed on the grass, gasping. My chest felt like it was on fire, but it could have been worse. Had the lip of the chasm been made of stone instead of dirt, I might've ended up with a fractured sternum, or worse.

I pushed myself off the ground and stumbled away, cradling my chest. On impulse, I glanced over my shoulder. Through the foliage, I could see that one of the riders had made it over the gap. The other was still on the far side, preparing to jump.

I ran faster. As I fought though a web of brush, a scream rose up behind me, punctuated by a dull smack.

"Damn!" shouted the rider who had cleared the gap. His friend, I assumed, must not have been as lucky.

I hoped the remaining rider—after seeing his pal fall to his doom—would give up chasing me and leave. But I wasn't betting on it. If anything, he was probably more determined than ever to put a bullet in my head.

At this point, I figured it was either going to be him or me, and it sure as hell wasn't going to be me. Not without a fight anyway.

I hid behind a tree and attempted to catch my breath. Sweat and blood poured down my face, and my legs burned with fatigue.

Frantically, I scanned the area for anything I could use to defend myself with. A big piece of wood lay close by. As long and thick as a two-by-four. I picked it up, taking it into both hands like a baseball bat. It wasn't my Desert Eagle, but it was nice and sturdy. A well-placed blow could do some serious damage.

I could hear the rider fast approaching my location. Leaves crunched loudly beneath his footfalls. I bent down, picked up a rock, and tossed it across from me, into the neighboring bushes. The rider halted briefly. He crept over to where the rock had landed.

With his back to me, I broke cover and ran straight at him. He heard me coming, a second too late. I swung the stick just as he turned toward me. My blow caught him on the side of the head. His helmet flew off, and he stumbled off balance.

Before he could recover, I brought the stick down on his forearm, forcing him to drop the gun. The rider fell to his knees, screaming and cradling his arm at the elbow. His forearm was bent at a funny angle.

I tossed aside the stick, grabbed the rider's gun from the ground, and pointed it at him.

His screams of agony dwindled to a series of breathless groans. He glared up at me with cold blue eyes. They had no light in them. They were the eyes of a man who had seen and done unspeakable things. A man desensitized to violence. The rest of his features made me think ex-military, from his gray buzz cut and strong jaw, to his rough, suntanned skin.

"I should kill you for what you did to my poor car," I said. "But I'm willing to give you a chance to save yourself." I moved the gun closer to his face. "Why were you trying to kill me?"

The rider gave no response.

"Answer me!" I yelled.

He grinned. His face had turned red, and a large vein throbbed in the center of his forehead. His breaths came hard and fast. Droplets of spit flew from his mouth with each exhalation.

"If you don't start talking, I *will* end you," I warned. "Do you understand?"

The rider chuckled. "You're not going to kill me."

"You sure about that?"

"Yeah. I can see it in your eyes. You're no killer."

That was where he was wrong. I had killed during my time as an OBI agent. In those days, it was my job to track down dangerous criminals and bring them to justice. Most suspects surrendered without too much of a fight. But every now and then, I'd come across some psycho who'd rather shoot it out with me and my squad than come along quietly. Once they'd gone down that road, all bets were off.

I wasn't proud of things I had done, but I knew they were necessary. Some people—people who thrive on the fear and suffering of others—needed to be put in their places. All the same, I couldn't shoot a defenseless opponent in cold blood, even if he deserved it. I was a killer. But I wasn't a murderer.

"Are you willing to risk it?" I asked the rider.

He smiled and said nothing.

I did the dramatic gun-cock that action heroes always do when they mean business, hoping that would loosen his tongue. He continued to grin, unimpressed.

I could see I was going to have to try another approach. I reared back and swung my foot upward. The tip of my shoe struck the rider's injured arm.

He screamed and fell onto his side, gripping his forearm. "You bastard!"

"Ready to talk yet?" I asked.

"Screw you!"

I stepped on his broken forearm, pinning it beneath my foot. "Look, pops. You're starting to get on my nerves. Tell me what I want to know, and we can end all this drama. Why did you try to kill me?"

"Because killing is what I do." The rider groaned and writhed in the dirt.

"Let me rephrase the question: Who sent you?"

The rider let out a wheezing laugh. His face contorted with pain. "Like I'm gonna tell you."

I eased more of my weight onto his forearm. He grimaced.

"Who was it?" I demanded, enunciating each word.

"I don't know!" the rider hissed. "I've only ever talked to him over the phone."

Him? So his boss was a man.

"Why did he want me dead?"

"Wouldn't you like to know?"

I ground my heel into his forearm. He cried out.

"Why did he want me dead?" I repeated.

"He said you needed to learn your place!" the rider shouted.

"What did he mean by that?"

"I don't know. I didn't bother asking either. A client's motives are their own damn business. Got nothing to do with me."

I removed my foot from his arm and stepped back, the gun still trained on him.

Gradually, he got to his knees. Sweat poured down his face.

I couldn't tell if he'd been lying to me or not, and I didn't have the energy to keep interrogating him. I figured it'd be best to turn him over to the OBI. Maybe they could get some answers out of him.

"Get up." I gestured for him to rise.

The man stubbornly remained on his knees. I grabbed the collar of his jacket and hauled him upright. I started to walk, pulling him along with me.

"Where are you taking me?" he asked.

"To the cops."

"I don't think so." The rider rammed his shoulder into me from behind.

The maneuver caught me off guard. I stumbled, tripped over something—probably a rock—and fell.

He bent and yanked up his right pant leg, revealing an ankle holster. As he drew a pistol from it, I rolled onto my back and fired a round from the gun I had confiscated. The bullet struck his broken forearm. He dropped the gun and went down screaming. I rushed over to him, snatched up the pistol, and pointed both guns on him. He laughed as he struggled to sit up. Blood poured from the hole in his arm, spilling onto the fallen leaves.

"S-see," he squeezed out. "I t-told you . . . you . . . you're no killer."

"Shut up!" I kicked him in the face. The blow knocked him out cold. At once, I regretted hitting him. Now I had to carry his unconscious ass all the way back to civilization. This day was getting better and better.

28

DIRTY, TIRED, AND BURNING WITH FATIGUE, I DUMPED THE unconscious man on the edge of the highway and collapsed beside him. The sun had begun to set, staining the sky orange and deepening the surrounding shadows. Getting out of the forest took longer than I had anticipated. Finding a route around the chasm had lengthened the trip by over an hour.

After I had a chance to catch my breath, I called Herc on my cell phone—which, luckily, had been in my pocket—and asked him if he could come pick me up. I would've called him sooner, but I had no idea where I was until I reached the highway. When he asked me what was wrong, I said I'd tell him the whole story once he got here. At the moment, I was too exhausted to hold a conversation.

While I waited for Herc to arrive, I considered everything I knew about the assassin's employer, which wasn't a whole lot. I knew that he was male, and that he had lots of money. Other than that, I was in the dark.

It was possible that he and the God-killer were one and the same. But that theory didn't make a whole lot of sense. Why would the killer single me out as opposed to members of the OBI—especially since I had only recently agreed to take the case? Besides, it wasn't like I was on the brink of uncovering the killer's identity. Hell, I had doubts about whether or not I could even solve this mystery.

Maybe it was Collin Stone. He did threaten me after all. And he definitely had the funds to hire an assassin. Or two, in this case. But I'd been doing this detective thing long enough to know not to jump to conclusions.

The only thing I knew for sure was that someone out there wanted me dead, and I needed to find out whom. The assassins' attempt on my life had ended in failure. But I knew better than to think their employer would give up so easily. Eventually, he'd send more hired guns after me. With any luck, the OBI would find out who he was and arrest him before that happened.

Herc arrived shortly after nightfall. The assassin was still unconscious—he had woken up earlier, but a kick to the head put him back to sleep. Herc parked his hybrid on the shoulder of the road and stepped out. The car's headlights burned through the darkness.

"I got here as fast as I could," Herc said, coming over to me. The blood on my clothes made him pause. "Geez, what happened?"

"I ran into a bit of trouble."

Herc looked around. "Where's your car?"

I shook my head solemnly.

Herc helped me to my feet, then glanced at the rider, who had begun to stir, but was still unconscious. "Who's that?"

"An assassin. He and his buddy tried to kill me."

"Why?"

"Someone hired them to do it."

"Who'd want you dead?"

I shrugged. "Hell if I know."

"You think it has something to do with the case?"

"Maybe. Probably. I don't know."

Herc went silent. "The assassin's employer," he said after a few seconds. "Do you think he's—"

I shushed him before he could finish his question. Though the rider was still unconscious, I still didn't feel comfortable discussing the case around him.

"We'll talk about it later," I said.

Herc inclined his head toward the rider. "What do you want to do about him?"

"Take him to the hospital to get that arm patched up. After that, I'll have the OBI do a pickup. Let them deal with him."

I got in the car and buckled my seatbelt, while Herc loaded the rider into the backseat. My body felt like it'd been put through a meat grinder, but at least I was alive. I wished I could have said the same about my Lotus.

We drove back to New Olympia and headed downtown, to the hospital. The rider woke up about halfway through the ride, but was too weary from blood loss to give us any problems. He mostly stayed quiet in the backseat, drifting in and out of awareness. Even if he was fully aware, I doubt he would have tried anything funny, especially with the seven-foot monster sitting in the driver's seat.

Herc pulled into the emergency room parking lot of Olympia General and carried the rider into the hospital. I stayed in the car and contacted OBI headquarters. I gave them a play-by-play of what had happened. They said they would send someone over immediately. My guess was they were going to interrogate him in the morning. I intended to be there when they did.

I ended the call and put away my cell. My head felt like it was cracking open. Today had definitely not gone the way I planned. I leaned back in the seat and closed my eyes. I hadn't realized I had fallen asleep until the driver-side door opened, and Herc got into the car. The vehicle shifted beneath his weight.

"The doctors are taking care of him," he informed me.

"Good for him," I said, yawning. "I hope whoever hired him covers medical insurance."

"You should get yourself looked at too."

"Nah."

"Jonesy," Herc said, as if talking to a child.

I sighed. After all the excitement I had that day, I wanted nothing more than to go home and go to sleep. But Herc was right. Having a doctor look at me would be the smartest thing to do. I couldn't crash the interrogation if I couldn't get out of bed tomorrow.

We walked inside the hospital. I filled out an information sheet, then took a seat in the crowded waiting room. The chairs were stiff and uncomfortable, the lights bright and disorienting, and the icy air blowing from the overhead vents made my sore body feel even worse.

The doctor saw me after an hour and a half, which translated to a thousand hours hospital-waiting-room time. She was short and cute, with curly brown hair and a big, dimply smile. "My, my, aren't you looking rough?"

She checked me for broken bones and internal bleeding.

"You're pretty bruised up, but other than that, you'll be just fine," she said. "That cut on your head will need stitches."

The doctor left the room, humming to herself. A nurse came in minutes later and sewed three stitches into my head. Fortunately, she didn't have to shave my head—if only fixing my car could have been so simple.

After I got to my apartment, I took a hot shower and slathered a soothing cream all over the bruises forming on my chest, arms, and legs. Then I fell face first onto my bed and drifted off to sleep.

When I woke up it was almost 7:00 a.m. My entire body was sore and tight, as if I had been working out for the past twenty-four hours. I took a couple of aspirin for the pain and grabbed my cell off the kitchen counter. I needed to call OBI headquarters and see when they were planning to question the assassin. I sat down on the sofa and dialed the number of the main office.

The agent who took my call had a low, monotonic voice. He could have been mistaken for one of those automated answering systems. "This is the office of the Olympic Bureau of Investigation. Please identify yourself."

I sighed. Another mandatory ID check. Every call to OBI headquarters began with one. I knew that verifying my identity was an important security measure. But that didn't make the procedure any less tedious or annoying. It was still just red tape. Of all the things I hated about working for the government—long hours, small salary increases, limited career growth—red tape was by far my least favorite. Everything I did, or tried to do, was mired in protocol. I couldn't even take a piss without filing a ten-page report.

I cleared my throat and gave him my information. "Plato Jones. Agent number 1056077714829. My clearance code is HGF920."

Since I wasn't a member of the OBI—not anymore—I didn't have access to their private network. Fortunately, Zeus had made me a temporary profile that would remain active until the case was closed.

"One moment," the agent said. I could hear him typing on a computer. "All right, everything checks out. I apologize for the inconvenience, Mr. Jones. Thank you for calling the office of the Olympic Bureau of Investigation. I'm Agent O'Neil. How can I help you this morning?"

"Hi, Agent O'Neil. I just have a quick question. I called last night to report an assassination attempt on my life. You sent some of your agents to Olympia General to arrest the suspect."

Again, I heard O'Neil typing on his computer. "It says here that at 9:47 p.m. last night, OBI operatives arrested a Mr. Dalen Scott, following a murder attempt on a Mr. Plato Jones. Is that correct?"

I didn't answer right away. Since I didn't catch the assassin's name while he was trying to murder me, I first needed to make sure the OBI hadn't picked up the wrong guy.

"The man you arrested, Dalen Scott," I said, "describe him to me."

O'Neil clacked away on his computer keys. "It says here that Mr. Scott is a white male, six-three, well-built, with gray hair and blue eyes. He had a bruised jaw and multiple injuries to his right forearm, all resulting from a confrontation with Mr. Plato Jones."

Good. They got the right guy.

"Does this sound like the man who attacked you?" O'Neil continued.

"Yeah, that's him. When are you guys are planning to interrogate him?"

"I'm afraid there won't be an interrogation, Mr. Jones."

"What?"

"Mr. Scott was killed last night."

I started. "By whom?"

"By the arresting agents. During his processing at OBI headquarters, Mr. Scott assaulted one of the agents and stole his gun. The other operatives had no choice but to neutralize him."

"Wait. He wrestled a gun away from an OBI agent?"

"Yes, sir."

I laughed. "I'm sorry, Agent O'Neil, but that's a little hard to believe. Scott was barely conscious when I dropped him off at the hospital. Not to mention his arm was busted. How could he have stolen an agent's gun?"

O'Neil offered no explanation. "I could fax you a copy of the report if you'd like."

"No, that won't be necessary. Could you give me the names of the arresting agents? I'd like to speak with them."

"I'm sorry, Mr. Jones, but that information is currently unavailable."

I pursed my lips in suspicion. "When will it be available?"

"I'm afraid I don't have that information," he said. "Is there anything else I can do for you?"

"Yeah. Did your guys find the other assassin?"

O'Neil went silent for a moment. Then he said, "It seems they did. Mr. Noah Salter was found dead in the woods bordering Highway 18. The report says he died of a brain hemorrhage in relation to a fractured skull."

That, I believed.

"Do you have any more questions, Mr. Jones?" O'Neil asked.

"No, that's all. Thanks for your help, Agent."

"You're welcome, Mr. Jones. Have a nice day."

I ended the call and went over to the window. I raised the blind. Morning light shone through the mist-covered glass.

I didn't have to wonder if the OBI was lying to me. The details of Scott's death were too far-fetched to be authentic. For one thing, his wrists and ankles would've been shackled during processing. He would've had a hard enough time walking, let alone fighting a highly trained special agent. Furthermore, why were the names of the arresting agents unavailable? The whole thing stank.

Why were they hiding the truth? What did they have to gain? Were they somehow involved in the assassination plot? If that was the case, it meant Zeus was involved as well, since the OBI answered only to him.

The idea terrified me. What do you do when the King of the Gods has it out for you? What can you do? I couldn't answer either question.

And more importantly, why would Zeus hire me, pay me a bucket of cash, and then try to kill me? It made no sense.

Confronting him directly was out of the question. If he was responsible, he'd likely kill me on the spot. If he wasn't, he'd kill me for insulting him. Either way, I was screwed. For the time being, my best option was to stay quiet and continue the investigation, as if the attempt on my life had never happened. With luck, I'd figure out a way to get myself out of this mess.

29

My appointment with Aphrodite was scheduled for 12:15. We were meeting at Arturo's, an expensive restaurant on Siren Street. I would have preferred to question her somewhere more private, but I let her chose the location. I hoped that mistake wouldn't come back to bite me in the ass.

When I arrived at Arturo's, the door was locked. I peered through the window. The lights were on, but there were no customers. Two waiters chatted at one of the tables, a man with a shaved head and a woman with a blond ponytail. I tapped on the glass. The waiters glanced at me. I waved at them. Both looked annoyed.

They talked for a minute, probably arguing over which of them should get up and deal with me. Eventually, Baldie got up and unlocked the door. He looked me up and down. His top lip curled as if he'd caught a whiff of something foul.

"We're temporarily closed to the public," he said, his voice dry and unfriendly. "Someone's rented us out for the afternoon."

"That someone wouldn't happen to be Aphrodite, would it?"

Baldie's eyes narrowed. "Yes. May I ask your name?"

"Plato Jones."

"Ms. Aphrodite is expecting a Mr. Jones."

"Great." I waited for him to show me inside.

Baldie didn't budge.

"Problem?" I asked.

"I need to see at least three forms of ID." He held out his hand.

"Just three?" I pulled out my wallet. "No blood or urine samples?"

He frowned.

I handed him my driver's license, social security card, and library card. Baldie held them like a hand of playing cards. He glanced at the cards. Then at me. Then at the cards again. After at least a full minute, he gave them back to me.

"I apologize for the delay, Mr. Jones," he said, though he didn't sound very apologetic. "Please, come in."

"Thank you." *Prick.*

The inside of the restaurant was gorgeous, with cream walls, hardwood floors, crystal chandeliers, and the biggest chocolate fountain I had ever seen. Pieces of gold-rimmed china were arranged neatly on each table, and classical music drifted through the air. Nothing looked out of place.

Baldie escorted me to a dining room on the second floor. It was identical to the one downstairs, minus the chocolate fountain. He seated me at a corner table. My seat granted a clear view of the stairwell, so I'd know if someone was trying to eavesdrop on the interrogation.

Baldie held out his hand and cleared his throat. I took a piece of peppermint candy out of my pocket and placed it on his palm. He stared down at it.

I patted him on the shoulder and sat down. "You're welcome."

He sneered and walked off.

Aphrodite arrived ten minutes later. She was short and model-thin, with a narrow face and a pointed nose. Her white camisole clung to small but shapely breasts, and matching pants flowed down lean legs. A big-rimmed sun hat, flip-flops, and large sunglasses completed the outfit.

I had never been able to figure out why the world was so obsessed with her. I realized that she was the Goddess of Love, Sex, and all that good stuff, but she simply didn't do it for me. Don't get me wrong. She was good-enough-looking, just not the bombshell everyone made her out to be. Maybe there was something wrong with me . . . Nah.

I stood up and shook her hand. Her skin was among the softest I had ever touched. I was careful not to squeeze too hard. "I'm Plato Jones."

"Aphrodite. Pleased to meet you." Her voice was deep and breathy—attractive voice, but too big for such a small woman.

I pulled out a chair for her. As she sat down, I caught a whiff of her perfume. It smelled out-of-this-world good. Was it lavender? Rose? Citrus? I couldn't tell.

I sat back down. "Thanks for coming."

Aphrodite nodded. "It's my pleasure." She removed her hat and sunglasses and placed them in an empty chair. The pixie-cut style of her auburn hair struck me as an attempt to look cool and edgy. But any edge she might've gotten from it was dulled by her eyes. They were large and innocent. Doe eyes. Their greenish-blue color reminded me of seawater.

The blond waitress came up the stairs and hurried to our table, her smile huge and bright. A pair of menus trembled in her hands. From the start, all her attention focused on Aphrodite. I might as well have been invisible. But that's alright. Thanks to Herc, I was used to being ignored in the presence of celebrities.

"G-good afternoon." The waitress's voice squeaked, as she placed the menus in front of us. "Ca-can I start you off with s-something to drink?"

"A raspberry tea would be nice," Aphrodite said, examining her fingernails instead of looking at the waitress.

"G-great choice. That's my favorite too, by the way."

Aphrodite smiled. I couldn't tell if it was genuine. The waitress seemed to think so. She giggled like an idiot, then looked at me.

"And for you, sir?"

I could've gone for a stiff drink. But that wasn't an option. Being around the Goddess of Love, I didn't need anything that might lower my inhibitions. Besides, I was on the job.

"Water," I said.

"One raspberry tea and one water." Blondie nodded. "I'll be right back."

She hurried to the bar area and returned moments later with our drinks. She put the glasses on the table and looked to Aphrodite with stars in her eyes. "Are you ready to order?"

"I think so." Aphrodite pointed at something on the menu. "Is the Kobe burger good?"

The waitress returned an eager nod. "It's really good."

"I'll have that, medium rare, with a side of sweet potato fries."

I arched my eyebrows, surprised by Aphrodite's selection. I was sure she was going to order the fanciest item on the menu. Funny, I'd have never pegged her as a meat and potatoes type of girl. Still, it was refreshing to see an Olympian choose something as mundane as a burger—even if it was Kobe beef.

The waitress took out her notepad and scribbled down the order. Then she turned to me. "And you, sir?"

I opened the menu and raised an eyebrow at the prices. "Can I see the kid's menu?"

She blinked. "Um . . . we don't have a . . ."

I held up a hand. "I'm just kidding."

Aphrodite laughed. The sound reminded me of tiny silver bells.

The waitress laughed too. She sounded like a goose that had just smoked a carton of cigarettes.

"You're a funny man, Mr. Jones," Aphrodite said.

"I try." I closed the menu and glanced at Blondie. "I'll have what she's having."

The waitress nodded. "Two Kobe burgers, medium rare, with sweet potato fries. Got it." And she scurried downstairs.

Aphrodite smiled. She had beautiful teeth. Straight and white. "Mortals are so adorable."

"You seem to be in a good mood," I said.

"I am." She reached for her drink. Her fingers wrapped elegantly around the glass, one at a time starting with her pinkie. Her nails were painted red. The color looked nice on her.

"Aren't you the least bit upset over your husband's death?"

She sipped her tea. "I was. But I'm over it."

"That's some fast recovery time."

"I can't change the fact that Hephaestus is gone." She shrugged. "What's the point of worrying about it?"

She made a good argument. I nodded and moved on. "I heard you two were having marital problems."

"Problems?" Aphrodite laughed, her large eyes sparkling. "Oh no, Mr. Jones. There were no problems between us. Hephaestus and I had an . . . understanding."

"I'm afraid I don't follow you."

She smiled at me as if I were a puppy that had just sneezed. "I married Hephaestus on Zeus's order. I never loved him. I had no intention of ever loving him. He understood this. He hated it, but he understood."

"So he let you cheat on him?" I asked.

"He had no choice." Aphrodite took another sip of tea and licked her lips. The wetness made them look softer and fuller.

My throat tightened. I gulped my water. "Where were you on Saturday night?"

"I was at home," she said without hesitation.

"Were you alone?"

Aphrodite shook her head. "I had friends over."

"Would these friends be willing to corroborate your story?"

"Of course."

I was interested in hearing what she and her *friends* had been up to that night, though I already had a pretty good idea. "Can you think of anyone who'd want to kill your husband?"

"No," she said quickly.

"Is it possible that one of your lovers got jealous and decided to take him out?"

Aphrodite giggled. I had no idea why. "It's possible, but very unlikely."

"What about Eileithyia?" I asked. "Anyone have it out for her?"

"Hades was never fond of her."

That made sense. Hades and Eileithyia were polar opposites. He was the God of the Underworld—the personification of death—and she was the Goddess of Childbirth. Their very natures put them at odds.

"When was the last time you spoke with Hades?" I asked.

Aphrodite pursed her lips in thought. She looked like she was puckering up for a kiss. My palms began to sweat. I blotted them on my pants.

"About a hundred years ago," she said.

"So you don't know what he's been up to lately?"

"I'm afraid not. I would suggest you ask him yourself, but I'd hate to see something bad happen to such a handsome man."

The compliment caught me unaware. I grinned like a Cheshire cat. "Thanks for the concern, but being a detective means exploring every avenue, even ones that may lead to dead ends."

"You're a brave man, Mr. Jones." Aphrodite smiled approvingly. "I like that."

30

AFTER LUNCH, APHRODITE AND I STOOD IN THE RESTAURANT lobby, waiting for her limo to arrive. A horde of paparazzi gathered at the main entrance, snapping photos of us though the glass door.

Unlike Herc, Aphrodite embraced her fame. Her image graced the covers of countless magazines and tabloids, and she held the number two spot on *People*'s "25 Most Intriguing," just below Zeus. Big surprise there.

And speaking of the president, I wanted to question Aphrodite about him. Earlier, I had decided to put the matter aside. But my curiosity refused to die. It was trying to drive me into dangerous territory. It urged me to discover the truth, no matter the risk.

Fortunately, common sense intervened before I could open my mouth. I realized there was nothing I could've said, no question I could've asked, that wouldn't have sounded condemning. Aphrodite seemed nice enough. But she was still an Olympian. Any questions I asked, any comments I made around her, would almost certainly reach Zeus's ears. I couldn't risk that happening.

"You seem anxious," she said.

"I get nervous around photographers," I lied.

She smiled. "They probably think you're my new boy toy."

"Fine by me. So long as they don't know what's really going on."

She looked at me with those big sea-green eyes. I could see my reflection in them. "I want to thank you, Mr. Jones."

"For what?"

"Picking up the check. It was very gentlemanly of you."

"Don't mention it."

We were silent for a while. The shouts of the paparazzi filled the silence between us, muffled by the glass door. Aphrodite was looking toward the exit. Sporadically, I found myself glancing at her from the corner of my eye. She had a great profile.

"I understand you used to be an OBI agent," Aphrodite said out of the blue.

I nodded. "Yeah."

"Why did you quit?"

I hesitated. My history with the OBI was not something I liked to talk about, especially with people I didn't know very well. But Aphrodite had given me a suspect in the form of Hades. The least I could do was answer her question.

"A few years back, my team and I were sent to Belgium to locate an Anti-God terrorist cell. Our orders were to capture the leader and his followers. Intelligence reports led us right to their base of operations."

"What happened next?" Aphrodite asked.

I didn't mention how the base of operations was a two-story house in the suburbs, or how the so-called terrorist cell leader was actually Paul Rousseau, a public access radio host, whose only crime was criticizing the government for treating mortals like second-class citizens. His alleged cohorts were his wife and two young daughters.

As Rousseau's show gained more and more popularity, a bunch of pro-human radical groups started popping up throughout the nation. Most of them were nonviolent. But a few took their radicalism to another level, sending threatening letters to government officials and planting car bombs. Whether or not Rousseau was to blame, I'll never know. But the bigwigs on Olympus labeled him a threat to national security, and sent OBI to bring him to justice.

But I didn't tell any of that to Aphrodite—because I didn't know what she'd do with that information.

"We apprehended the terrorist leader. Then we radioed HQ to report our success. We all thought the mission was over, but command told us that there had been a change of plans. We were ordered to eliminate the terrorist and his followers. Murder them in cold blood. I refused. But that didn't matter. My teammates were more than willing to carry out the order. I tried to stop them, but I couldn't. When we got back to New Olympia, I turned in my badge. And here I am."

Aphrodite stared at me, her expression unreadable. Then she smiled and said, "Thank you for sharing that with me."

I nodded. For some reason, I felt as though her opinion of me had changed. But if she thought less of me for disobeying Zeus, that was her problem. What I did in Belgium, I did for the right reason. No one could convince me otherwise.

"I have something for you." She pulled an unmarked envelope from her handbag and gave it to me.

"What's this?"

"A copy of a letter. It's from my husband. I received it the week before he died. It might help in your investigation."

"Did you show this to the OBI?"

Aphrodite nodded. "They couldn't make sense of it. Maybe you'll have better luck."

"Thanks." I opened the envelope and went to pull out the letter.

Aphrodite put her hand over mine to stop me. "Not now," she said. "Let's try to enjoy our time together." Her hand lingered before she pulled it away.

I slipped the letter into my coat pocket.

Again, Aphrodite had surprised me. Before meeting her, I thought she was going to be a sex-crazed lunatic, obsessed with turning me into one of her thralls. But it seemed I was wrong. Maybe there was more to her than just pretty eyes and scandals.

"I may not have loved Hephaestus, but I didn't want him to die," she said. Her eyes glimmered with unshed tears. "Promise me you'll bring his killer to justice."

"I'll do my best."

Outside, a white limo pulled up.

"That's my ride." Aphrodite put on her hat and sunglasses. "I enjoyed meeting you, Mr. Jones, though I wish it could have been under happier circumstances."

I smiled. "Ditto."

"We should do this again sometime."

"Yeah."

She waved goodbye and left the restaurant. The sea of paparazzi made way for her. A million flashbulbs went off.

I watched her as she walked past them and got into the limo. For the Goddess of Love, Sex, and all that, Aphrodite was astonishingly reserved. Nothing like the sexual dynamo featured in the media.

She did have a nice ass though.

31

I WAITED UNTIL THE PAPARAZZI HAD DISPERSED BEFORE leaving the restaurant. I drove to the Ammo Crate, a store located in one of the older parts of town. Squeezed between a barbershop and a hardware store, it specialized in antique weapons. The owner, Magus, was a family friend. After my dad passed away, he assumed the role of father figure. Whenever life had me in a chokehold, I could always count on Uncle Magus to help me out.

I opened the door and went inside. Weapons filled the walls and display cases. An antique cannon sat in the middle of the floor, surrounded by a velvet rope. The sign next to it read, "Do Not Touch. Owner Is Not Responsible for Decapitation." In the corner of the store, swing music crackled from an old record player.

Magus was polishing a revolver behind the counter. He was tall with dark-brown skin and a cul-de-sac of curly gray hair. He wore a white T-shirt covered in oil stains, and a pair of camouflage pants. Despite his age, the muscles in his arms were lean and sinewy and popping with veins. When he noticed me, he put down the revolver and grinned.

"Well, if it isn't PJ."

His deep, husky voice made whatever he said sound big and important. I once suggested he close the shop and do voiceovers for insurance commercials. He laughed and told me to get real.

"In the flesh." I glanced at the revolver. "Nice gun."

"Isn't it?" Magus picked up the gun and handed it to me. "I got this baby from a collector yesterday. Former collector, actually. You see, his new wife has a gun phobia. She's making the poor guy sell his whole collection. It wouldn't be me. That's for damn sure."

I examined the weapon. Smith & Wesson Model No. 3, otherwise known as the Schofield revolver. This one was in excellent condition. Not a scratch on it. I wondered if it had ever been fired.

"They don't make them like this anymore." I handed the revolver back to Magus.

"That's the truth." He put the weapon aside.

"I need to place an order."

"Sure. What do you want?"

"Osmium rounds. Ten boxes."

"No problem." Magus keyed the order into his computer. "I'll call you when they get here."

"Thanks," I said.

Magus inclined forward and rested his elbows on the counter. A sign near his arm advised against leaning on the glass. But when you're the boss, you can break the rules.

"So, what's been going on with you, PJ?" Magus asked. "Staying out of trouble, I hope."

I smirked. "Come on, Uncle Magus. I never look for trouble. You know that."

"It looks for you, right?"

I winked. "Exactly."

Magus chuckled. "I swear. You're still the same little hellraiser I met years ago. You just got bigger and uglier."

"You left out hairier."

"Thanks for reminding me. So, how's your love life going?"

"It's not."

"You're not still caught up on Alexis, are you?"

I shrugged. "Just a little."

Magus swore. "You've been divorced for three years. It's time you got out there and found a nice young woman to settle down with. Preferably one with an attractive grandmother."

"Okay, that's gross."

"I'm serious, PJ."

"So am I. Did my mom put you up to this?"

"What are you talking about?"

"Last time I saw Mom, she got onto me about finding a new girlfriend. And now you're doing the same thing. You two are in cahoots, aren't you? Go ahead. Admit it."

Magus laughed. "You're crazy. Me and Eleanor haven't spoken in months."

I narrowed my eyes. "So you both claim."

Magus gave me an annoyed look. "PJ . . ." He shook his head instead of finishing the sentence.

I sighed and held up my hands. "Alright. You win. I'll take your advice. I'll find a nice girl."

"Now that's what I want to hear."

"A college girl—with huge breasts, a tiny waist, and flexible morals . . . among other things."

Magus laughed "That's the spirit!"

32

THAT NIGHT, A VIOLENT STORM RAGED OVER THE CITY. It had appeared out of nowhere, without warning. The TV weathermen called it a phenomenon and pretended to be baffled. But everyone in New Olympia knew the truth—that somewhere out there, Vice President Poseidon, the mighty God of the Sea, was having a temper tantrum.

Rain pounded against my living room window as I sat at the kitchen table, reading the letter Hephaestus had sent to Aphrodite.

My dearest Aphrodite,
I know you hate me. I know it well. But I need to talk to someone. I've done something terrible. Unforgivable. I despise myself for it. Despite the fact that I was capable of it. But I'm going to make things right. I'm going to redeem myself. I'm going to confess what I've done. Confess to everyone. Starting with you. But I won't do it in this letter. I want to tell you face to face. See the hurt in your eyes. Hear you call me all the terrible things I know I am. I need to see you very soon. Until then, I just want you to know that I'm sorry for everything.
Your husband,
Hephaestus

For a God, Hephaestus had sloppy handwriting. They say that a person's handwriting is a reflection of his character. If that was true, I wondered what the Smith God's handwriting said about him. Now, I'm no graphologist, but if you asked me, I'd say he was a God in motion. Always in a rush. Probably had a million things happening in his head at any given time.

I read the letter once more, and then put it back in the envelope. No wonder the OBI couldn't get anything out of this. The information—being as vague as it was—could have been interpreted a thousand different ways. I needed something more specific.

I swallowed the last of my beer, got another from the fridge, and plopped down on the couch. Outside the window, a flash of lightning illuminated the sky. A second later, a crash of thunder caused my entire apartment to tremble. Poseidon must have been pretty pissed off.

I sipped the beer, my thoughts going back to the letter. What did Hephaestus do that was so awful? Did it have something to do with his secret projects? Was it connected to his and Eileithyia's murders? I was leaning toward yes, to both questions. Problem was I couldn't prove it.

On the plus side, I finally had new suspects to interrogate. Hades was one. Aphrodite's lovers were the others. I'd start with the lovers. To question them all would have taken years, so I narrowed the list down to the big three: Ares, Hermes, and Dionysus. The next step was to decide who to go after first.

Ares passed his time living as a rock star. He had been on tour with his band, Inheritor, when the murders occurred, so I ruled him out as a suspect. That left Hermes and Dionysus. Might as well start with Hermes, since I already had his number. I took out my cell phone and scrolled through my contacts list until I found his number, stored as "Jackass."

I hit send. He picked up on the fourth ring.

"Mr. Jones." Hermes sounded annoyed, as if I had interrupted him in the middle of something. He was probably scrubbing toilets at Zeus's estate. Or sharpening Hera's cheekbones.

"Hello, sunshine," I said.

Hermes sighed. "What can I do for you?"

"I'd like to have a chat with you ASAP."

"Regarding?"

"The case you insisted I investigate."

Silence stretched across the phone line. Then Hermes said, "My schedule for this week is extremely tight, but I suppose I could spare a few minutes. Be at my office at 10:00 a.m. tomorrow."

"Alright."

"Oh, and Mr. Jones," Hermes said. "Try to be punctual."

33

HERMES LIVED IN AN ESTATE ON MOUNT OLYMPUS. IT LOOKED similar to Zeus's place, only smaller and with fewer windows.

Granite double doors opened into his office. Carved into the stone was an image of Hermes, naked and wearing his famous winged sandals. Seeing that jerk in his birthday suit made me grateful I had skipped breakfast.

I knocked on one of the doors. The sound reverberated throughout the hallway. Both panels slowly swung open. Hermes, in a navy blue suit with a pink tie, sat behind a desk at the head of the room, staring at a laptop.

"Come in," he said, without looking up from his work.

I stepped inside, and the doors closed behind me as if by remote. The office was stylish. But it was the type of stylish that seemed too deliberate to be properly admired.

The walls had been painted black, surrounding a gray hardwood floor. The furniture, with its white leather cushions and stainless steel legs, was as cold and angular as Hermes himself. A fully stocked bar occupied the far left corner of the room, and a giant aquarium was built into the wall behind Hermes's desk. Sharks and other exotic fish glided through the glowing blue water.

"You're three minutes late." Hermes's eyes remained glued to the laptop.

"Not according to my watch." I sat in a chair in front his desk. It was as uncomfortable as it looked, forcing me into perfect posture. Mom would have liked it. She was always getting on me about slouching.

"You said you wanted to talk about the case," Hermes said.

I nodded. "I did."

"So talk."

I glanced at the minibar. "Mind if I have a drink first?"

"If you must."

I got up and went to the bar. I suddenly felt like a kid in a candy store. Top-shelf liquors and wines filled the bar. Some of the vintages were hundreds of years old. A few of them I had never even heard of. I poured myself a glass of two-hundred-year-old scotch and sat back down. I took a sip. Its rich, mellow flavor went down easy.

"Mmm." I pointed at the glass. "This is good."

Hermes raised an eyebrow. "I'm a very busy God, Mr. Jones."

"Sorry." I leaned back and crossed my legs. "I have some questions, if that's okay. Shouldn't take more than a few minutes of your time."

"What would you like to know?"

"I want to know about your relationship with Aphrodite."

Hermes looked up from his laptop. His blue eyes narrowed with suspicion. "Aphrodite and I are friends."

"Friends with benefits?"

Hermes smiled. "Yes."

"Did you ever want to be more than friends?"

"Long ago," Hermes admitted, with a hint of longing in his voice. "But I've since gotten past those feelings."

I nodded and took another sip of scotch. The second taste was better than the first—the flavor seemed to build upon itself.

"Were you ever jealous of Hephaestus?" I asked.

Hermes burst into laughter. He finally looked up from his computer and into my face to see if I was joking. When he realized I wasn't, he laughed again, louder.

"Jealous? Of that freak?"

"That *freak* was married to Aphrodite," I reminded him. "The Goddess you were in love with."

Hermes's laughter dwindled to silence, but he continued to smile. He closed his laptop and pushed it aside. Then he laced his fingers and put both hands on his desk. "Mr. Jones, if you're attempting to implicate me in the murders, you're wasting your time."

"You still haven't answered my question. Were you jealous of Hephaestus?"

"No, Mr. Jones, I was not."

"Why not?"

"Hephaestus's marriage to Aphrodite was a joke. He couldn't please her in bed. He wasn't even *potent* enough to give her a child. Why would I be jealous of someone like that?"

I sat silent for an interval, trying to come up with a reason why Hermes might by jealous, while swirling the scotch in my glass. Light reflected off the amber liquid. "I don't know."

Hermes grinned victoriously. "Is there something else I can help you with, Mr. Jones?"

I drank some more scotch. "One more thing. I'd like to know where you were the day of the murder."

Hermes answered at once. "I was here in my office, filing reports, when the OBI contacted me with news of the murder."

"I assume there's some evidence to back up your claim?"

He nodded. "I maintain detailed records of all my schedules."

"The records for this month, I'd like copies of them if you don't mind."

"Of course. I'll fax them to you as soon as possible."

I gave him a thumbs-up. "Great."

"Anything else?" Hermes asked. He opened his laptop again and pulled it toward him.

I thought about it and shook my head. "No, I think I'm good."

"Then I'll have to ask you to leave."

The office doors opened.

I finished the rest of my scotch in one gulp. "Thanks for the drink."

34

When I got back to my apartment, the acrid smell of cat urine greeted me. I hit the lights and glimpsed a flash of orange fur vanishing through the window. Hair covered the couch, and there was a wet spot on the carpet, near the fireplace. *One day*, I thought, *one day, I'm going to catch you. Then your furry ass is history.*

I went through my usual routine of pouring peroxide on the wet spot and covering it with a towel. Then I rolled my vacuum cleaner out of the hall closet, attached the upholstery tool, and vacuumed the couch. Once that was done, I decided to check on Alexis. The Gods had promised not to harm her so long as I danced to their tune. But I wasn't convinced. The Gods had made lying into an art form. A promise from them was about as genuine as a battery-operated Rolex.

I took out my cell phone and dialed Alexis's number. The person who answered said nothing, but I could hear them breathing.

"Alexis?" I said.

Still nothing. Fear seeped into my heart. Had the Gods gotten to her?

"Hello?"

There was a sigh on the other end. Then Alexis said, "You're a creep, you know that?"

Relief washed over me. I had to sit down. "Okay, what did I do this time?"

"It's not about what you *did*. It's about what you *didn't* do. Why didn't you tell me you were seeing someone?"

I raised my eyebrows. "Seeing someone? What are you talking about?"

"Don't play dumb. It's all over the tabloids. Aphrodite and her new boyfriend share a romantic lunch. I didn't know Goddesses were your type."

That instant, confusion gave way to flattery. A grin touched my face. She actually thought that Aphrodite, a Goddess accustomed to dating actors and pro athletes, was interested in a regular Joe like me. And she was angry about it. An evil little voice in my head urged me to play along, but I ignored it. She was already about to give me an earful. No need to add fuel to the fire.

"It's not what you think," I said.

"I'm so sure! The article says she shut down Arturo's for the entire afternoon, so the two of you could have some privacy."

"Okay, that part is true. But the rest of it is a lie."

"You're trying to one-up me, aren't you?"

"Huh?"

"You're jealous of what Calais and I have."

I chuckled, but not at the silliness of the accusation, because the accusation actually held some degree of truth. What got to me was the fact that she felt I was in a better place—relationship-wise—than she was. It made me feel like a little kid at show-and-tell—the kid who had brought the best toy to class.

"You're not listening," I said. "Aphrodite and I are not dating. We're just friends."

"Yeah right. I've heard stories about Aphrodite and her *friends*."

"Those stories have nothing to do with me. My relationship with her is strictly platonic. And even if it wasn't, what does it have to do with you?"

"Nothing." Alexis's tone went abruptly casual. "I don't care who you screw."

"Then why are you so mad?"

She gave a scornful laugh. "I'm not mad."

"Okay."

Agreeing with her somehow made her angrier.

"I don't need this right now," she said. "I have enough on my mind with the wedding. We'll continue this discussion later."

"Sure," I said. "Stay safe."

Alexis mumbled something under her breath and hung up. I closed my cell phone and smiled.

35

DIONYSUS. I HAD SEEN HIM ON THE NEWS AND IN NUMEROUS business publications, but I had never met him in real life. Contrary to his title, the God of Wine and Ecstasy's public image was one of a stiff, no-nonsense businessman. He'd never been featured in the tabloids, never been implicated in any scandals, and frequently donated to charity. You'd be hardpressed to find someone with a cleaner reputation.

The same couldn't be said about the people his businesses catered to. He owned three successful nightclubs, one in New Olympia, one in Miami, and one in Tokyo. Drunken celebrities were regularly seen stumbling out of them.

I looked for Dionysus's home address in the phonebook and online, but it was unlisted. I then called the records office on Mount Olympus. The information they provided led me downtown to N.0.1, the tallest residential tower in the nation. The clear blue sky reflected off the building's mirrored façade.

Dionysus lived in a penthouse. Considering that there were 103 floors, I doubted he ever took the stairs. A long corridor stretched to his apartment. The door was made of opaque glass, and there was an intercom beside it. I rang the doorbell.

After a moment, the glass turned clear—it was smart glass, the kind that turns from opaque to clear with the push of a button. A little old woman stood on the other side of the door, wearing a powder-blue maid's uniform. A net covered her steel-gray hair. I could tell she used to be a looker back in her day.

The woman's voice issued from the intercom.

"May I help you?" she asked, her eyes narrow.

I dredged up my friendliest smile. "Good afternoon, ma'am. My name is Plato Jones. I'm a private investigator." I showed her my badge. "I'm looking for Dionysus."

"Mr. Dionysus isn't here right now."

I cursed silently, but my smile didn't falter. "Do you know when he'll be back?"

The woman shook her head.

"Do you have any idea where I might find him?"

"I don't," she replied. "Would you like to leave a message?"

Now it was my turn to shake my head. "That won't be necessary. Thanks for your time."

The woman pressed a button on the wall beside the door. The glass turned opaque again.

Well, that was a waste of time.

I left the tower and headed down the street to Elysium, one of Dionysus's clubs, in hopes of catching him there. The building bore a futuristic design, similar to Zeus's and Hermes's estates: a white exterior with black windows and rounded edges. A neon sign on the roof spelled out the club's name. At this time of day, the lights were off.

I entered the parking lot and pulled into a space near the main entrance. There were only three other cars in the lot—an Audi and two BMWs. They probably belonged to the employees. Next to them, my ride stuck out like a sore thumb. I missed my Lotus, now more than ever.

I got out of my car and checked the front door. Locked. I knocked on it. No answer. Another bust.

As I returned to my car, I heard voices. I followed them to the side of the building, where two men leaned against the wall, talking and smoking cigarettes. The taller of the pair was skinny, with brown hair and a scraggly beard. The shorter one was stocky, with sandy-blond hair and a goatee. Both men wore black polos and khakis.

"Excuse me," I said.

The men stopped chatting and looked at me.

"You guys work here?" I asked.

The short man nodded. "Yeah."

"My name is Plato Jones. I'm a private investigator." I showed them my PI badge.

They barely glanced at it.

"I'm investigating a recent string of robberies that have been committed against the Gods. I think Dionysus might be next. I'd like to speak with him if possible."

The short man puffed his cigarette. "He's not here."

"Do you know when he'll be in?"

"Nope."

"Do you have an idea of where I might find him?" I asked.

The short man took another drag. He blew the smoke from his nostrils. "Sorry."

This was going well. "When was the last time he came in?"

"About a month ago."

I raised an eyebrow. "He's been missing for a month?"

"Yeah."

"Did he say anything before he left?" I asked.

"Just that he had some business to take care of."

Two Gods murdered in the past month, and Dionysus was nowhere to be found. It was too convenient to be a coincidence. I needed to find him. Fast.

The short man took a long pull from his cigarette and flicked the butt away. "You want us to give him a message or something?"

"Nah." I shook my head. "I'll just come back another day."

"Whatever," the short man said, and he and his coworker resumed their conversation.

36

When I arrived at work the next day, a thick document waited for me on my desk. A sticky note on the first page informed me that it was a copy of Hermes's schedule for the past month. I flipped it open to a random page. Included in the information was a lengthy list of alibis. This was going to take some time.

I poured myself a cup of coffee and got to work. It was a little after 8:00 a.m. when I started. By the time I finished, it was close to 10:00 p.m. My eyes burned, and I had a throbbing headache. I pushed aside the stack of papers and leaned back in my chair.

As far as I could tell, Hermes was innocent of any wrongdoing. His schedule was meticulously detailed, and backed by a slew of eyewitness reports. I called each witness. They all checked out. Considering the evidence, I had no choice but to temporarily eliminate him as a suspect. Imagine my enthusiasm.

With Hermes out of the picture—for now—I had two suspects left: Dionysus and Hades. I decided to go after the latter for now, since I couldn't find Dionysus.

With Dionysus's money and resources, he could have been anywhere in the world. But I wasn't too worried. I had a feeling he'd show up in New Olympia sooner or later, if he was the guilty party. For some reason, criminals can't resist returning to the scene of the crime.

Before going after Hades, I decided to get a little R&R. This case was beating me into the ground. My mind was overworked, tired. A small respite was just what I needed to recharge the ol' batteries.

That night, I threw on some gray sweats and went to karate class. Classes were held once a week at the Warrington Recreation Center, on the north side of town. When I quit the OBI, I knew that if I didn't keep active, I'd end up looking like a manatee. Weightlifting was never really my thing. Neither was basketball or football—I'm better at watching them than playing them. But martial arts were right up my alley.

I was four when my dad enrolled me in my first karate class at the neighborhood community center. The classes were free, but that didn't mean the training was subpar. My shidoshi—teacher—was a master of Shotokan, Judo, and Jiu-jutsu. I trained under him until I went off to military college. He had taught me to follow orders, so adjusting to life in the military was an easy transition.

There were ten other students in class tonight. All men, ranging in age from eighteen to fifty. We were all pretty well acquainted, but I wouldn't exactly call us friends. When we talked, we kept it general. Conversation rarely went beyond sports and women, which was fine with me. I didn't take the classes to make friends.

The rec center had been built back in the '50s. The building was brownstone and shaped like a wedge. A giant mural hanging over the entrance depicted two old-timey boxers with handlebar mustaches, squaring off against each other.

As I pulled up to the curb, I saw my instructor, Caesar Bowden, unloading a duffel bag from the bed of his truck, which was parked a few spaces down from me. His gi—uniform—and belt were worn and tattered—the sign of a seasoned martial artist. He spotted me as I got out of my car and came over, carrying the bag on his shoulder. His six-one, heavyset frame and bald head might be intimidating to someone who didn't know him. He spoke with a heavy Dutch accent. "Mr. Jones, how are you this evening?"

"I can't complain." I gestured for him to give me the duffel bag.

"Thanks." Caesar handed the bag to me. "I'm glad to see you showed up. You missed our last two classes. Me and the other guys were starting to worry."

Somehow I doubted that.

"Sorry," I said, hefting the bag onto my shoulder. "I've been kind of busy lately."

Caesar shook his head as if to say don't worry about it. "All that matters is that you're here now."

"So, you got anything special planned for us tonight?"

"As a matter of fact I do. I'm going to show you guys some special techniques. I may need your help demonstrating them."

"Sounds good."

"Great." Caesar opened the door for me, and we took the stairs to the second floor.

The floors of the dojo were hardwood, and a mirror covered the wall at the head of the room. In the back of the room, an arsenal of Asian weapons sat in wooden racks.

Besides Caesar and me, four other guys had shown up to class that day. Marco was a tall man with red hair and one of the worst suntans I had ever seen. Jim was almost sixty, but you couldn't tell. He was six-one with brown hair and too-white veneers. He had a muscular build, the kind you get from doing hard work in the sun. Paul, the youngest in the class, was a college sophomore. He wore his hair in a short ponytail, a hipster style that suited him. His long arms had hardly any muscle mass. He didn't really have the aptitude for karate. Still, he did the best he could.

And then there was Donovan, the one-upper of the group. One of those guys who always had to outdo everyone around him. The prototypical meathead, he was muscle-bound, with a large head and small features. Judging by his orange skin and rampant acne, I guessed his physique wasn't completely natural. He was always asking me what I thought of his various muscles. Any kind of criticism pissed him off. He probably juiced up when he got home. I made a point to give him only positive feedback. I didn't want him overdosing on steroids because I said his delts needed work.

When I walked in, everyone turned toward me. They were unusually happy to see me, welcoming me with smiles and nods. Even Marco, who rarely showed any kind of emotion, wore a big grin on his face. I didn't know what to make of any of it. Maybe they had seen pictures of my rendezvous with Aphrodite.

I dropped the duffel bag in the right front corner of the room and went to the center of the floor for lineup.

The first thirty minutes of class went as usual. We started off with stretches, followed by punching and kicking drills. Then Caesar called me to the front of the class, to help him demonstrate the new techniques he'd mentioned. That's when things got weird.

"Come on up here, Jones," he said, motioning for me to hurry up. He grabbed an empty plastic water gun from his duffel bag, tossed it to me, and then turned toward the class. "Alright, guys. Tonight I'm going to teach you how to disarm an opponent with a firearm. Now before we get started, know this. In a situation where you're being held at gunpoint, it's best to just do what your attacker says. Only attack if you know, without a doubt, that the attacker's going to pull the trigger. Understood?"

"Sir," the class answered in unison.

Caesar nodded. "Okay, Jones. Point the gun at me."

I did as he asked.

"The first thing you need to do is raise your hands," Caesar said. "The second step is to try to reason with your attacker. Beg for your life. Tell him you have a family. Hell, cry like a little girl if you think it'll help. If that doesn't reach him, and he still wants to kill you, it's time to act."

First he demonstrated the move at regular speed. He stepped out of the line of fire, trapping my arm in a joint lock. Then he used leverage to disarm me. Once he had the gun, he turned it on me and told me get on the ground. I did.

The move was pretty slick, I had to admit. Caesar really knew his stuff. He helped me up and demonstrated the move again, this time in slow motion.

"Did everyone get that?" he asked.

"Sir," the class said.

"Good." Caesar helped me up and handed the gun back to me. "Does anyone want to come up and try?"

"I'll give it a go," Donovan said, and he came up to the front of the class. In the mirror I could see how much bigger he was than me. It was almost scary.

I pointed the water gun at him. Donovan glanced at the ceiling, probably replaying the steps in his head. When he was ready, he stepped out of the line of fire. Moving with all the speed of a rhino dipped in cement, he performed the disarm maneuver. But he twisted my arm a little too hard. A jolt of pain raced from my elbow to my shoulder, taking my breath away, and forcing me to my knees. I grimaced, trying not to cry out, as he tore the gun out of my hand and trained it on me.

"On the ground, scumbag!" he shouted.

I complied, my arm throbbing.

"Good job, Donovan," Caesar said. "Anyone else want to try?"

Jim was next. Then Paul. And finally Marco. Like that lummox Donovan, they all managed to injure me in some way. Jim almost broke my finger trying to disarm me, Paul poked me in the eye with his thumb, and Marco damn near ripped my arm out of its socket. At this rate, I'd end up blind, crippled, and unconscious before the end of class. I was terrified to find out what the next technique was.

"Good job, class," Caesar said. "Now I'm going to show you how to disarm an opponent who's holding a gun to your back."

He turned around. I pressed the gun to his back.

"Watch carefully." Caesar spun toward me, capturing my wrist in the crook of his elbow, while at the same time pretending to strike me in the throat with his forearm. He followed with a fake knee to the stomach and forced the gun out of my hand. He did the move two more times, in slow motion, before calling for volunteers. I swallowed deeply.

Paul came forward, smiling. I had a feeling things were about to get ugly. He turned around. I put the gun to his back.

He whirled around and clumsily trapped my wrist. His elbow missed my throat by a mile and smashed into my nose. A burst of pain exploded in my face. My head whipped back. Paul hit me full force, and he had to have known it. But instead of stopping to check on me, he slammed his knee into my gut. The blow knocked the air out of me, and I doubled over. He awkwardly took control of the water gun and let me go. I fell to all fours, gasping for air.

"Good job, Paul," Caesar said.

"Thank you, sensei." Paul bowed toward Caesar.

No one helped me up. They just watched as I struggled to rise. My nose was bleeding. I pinched the bridge of my nose and tilted my head back.

"You alright?" Caesar asked me.

"I'm good."

"Go to the bathroom and wash up. We still have a few more techniques to go over."

I left the dojo and walked down the hall to the restroom. Inside, I washed away the blood running down my mouth and chin. Then I plugged my nostrils with rolled up bits of toilet paper. Thankfully, Paul hadn't broken my nose. I wanted to kill him for hitting me that hard and not apologizing. What in Hades was his problem? And why did Caesar congratulate him for what he'd done? He was always preaching to us about self-control. I wondered if this was his way of punishing me for missing the past two weeks of class. I couldn't call it. All I knew was that I was ready to go home and put some ice on my nose. I had already gone over my recommended daily allowance of ass-whooping.

After the bleeding stopped, I went back to the dojo to tell everyone I was leaving. When I stepped through the door, Marco, Paul, Donovan, and Jim were lined up across from me. Caesar stood in front of them, his arms crossed, a sly grin on his face.

"How's your nose?" he asked me.

"Fine."

"Glad to hear that. You ready for the next technique?"

"Yeah, about that. Sorry but I gotta run. Something just came up. Maybe next time."

No one said anything.

"Alright then, see you guys later." I turned and opened the door. No sooner had I stepped through than a pair of large hands grabbed me from behind and threw me back into the dojo. I landed rolling, and scrambled back to my feet as Donovan shut the door and locked it.

I turned to Caesar. "What's going on?"

"I think we'll skip the next technique and go straight to sparring," Caesar said. "Full contact."

He nodded and all four students came at me.

37

I ran to the opposite side of the dojo to keep from getting surrounded. Paul ran after me while Caesar and the other three men hung back. Paul's body language told me he was about to throw a right cross. I reacted before he had the chance, back-fisting him in the face. He shuffled backward, clutching his mouth.

"Chill out, Paul," I warned him.

He cursed. Blood trickled down his chin from a busted lip. He planted his feet and threw a roundhouse. The move was sloppy. Easy to counter. I caught his ankle and side-kicked to the groin. He flew backward and crashed to the floor. Groaning and red in the face, he curled up in a ball, his hands between his legs.

I looked at Caesar and the others. "If this is about those classes I missed, I already told you I was sorry."

Caesar glared at me. He nodded at Donovan, who started toward me, smiling and cracking his knuckles. He stopped about five feet away from me and took a fighting stance.

"You don't have to do this," I told him.

Donovan wasn't hearing it. He started throwing punches. With his large, heavy hands, it would've only taken one or two hits to put my lights out. But there wasn't a whole lot of speed behind his power. I dodged the flurry and retaliated with a spinning leg sweep. Donovan's heels went skyward. He hit the ground hard, the back of his head smacking against the floor. He slowly pulled himself up, wobbled in place, and fell over again.

Caesar frowned. He grabbed Marco and Jim by their shirtsleeves and shoved them forward. Both men glanced nervously at each other, then ran to one of the weapons racks. Marco picked up a quarterstaff while Jim grabbed a set of tonfas—wooden batons.

So that's how it's gonna be, I thought. *Well, three can play at that game.* I rushed to the nearest weapon rack. I had to choose between a nunchaku and a kusarigama—a sickle with a ball and chain attached. The kusarigama looked cool and scary but was hard to control, at least for me. I'd probably end up slicing off my own head. The nunchaku on the other hand, while also hard to control, didn't carry the risk of decapitation. I picked it up and spun it around, Bruce Lee-style.

I hoped the show would scare off Marco and Jim. The two men hesitated, keeping their distance. In the mirror at the head of the room, I saw Donovan trying to sneak up on me. I whirled around, swinging the nunchaku horizontally. It cracked him in the jaw and sent him reeling.

I spun back around as Jim thrust his quarterstaff at my head. I slapped it aside with the nunchaku, barely in time. He came back with a wide swing. I ducked beneath the hit and countered. Jim raised his staff to block my attack. But I wasn't going for his head or body. I flicked my wrist. The nunchaku twirled outward, popping him on the hand. He let out a yowl and almost dropped his weapon. I pivoted and followed through with a left roundhouse. My foot smashed into Jim's face. He went limp and collapsed.

Next up was Marco. I swung my nunchaku in fast circles, forcing him to move backward. Wood clacked against wood as he used his tonfas to block my attacks. I had to give him credit: he was pretty good. But he still had a long way to go. I started swinging faster, my nunchaku a blur in the air. One of my attacks slipped through his defense. With a loud pop, the stick struck him on top of the head, opening up a gash in his forehead. Marco stumbled back. Blood poured from his scalp.

I pivoted again and thrust my heel forward, like a battering ram, into Marco's stomach. Marco doubled over and went down to his knees, coughing and wheezing. A voice echoed through the dojo. "Son of a bitch!"

I turned and saw Donovan charging at me. I had been so preoccupied with Marco and Jim that I'd forgotten about him. I swung my nunchaku. It struck him on the shoulder. He didn't seem to feel it. Roid rage must have dulled his senses.

Before I could attack again, Donovan wrapped his huge arms around my waist, trapping me in a bear hug. I grunted and dropped the nunchaku. I threw punches and elbows, hitting him in the eyes and nose. He squeezed harder. The breath rushed out of me. Blood pounded at my temples.

The room started to get brighter. Donovan was growling like an animal. I karate-chopped either side of his head, just below his earlobes. Pressure points. He made a strangling noise, and I felt his hold on me loosen. I brought my right arm up, hooked it around his thick neck, and twisted my body, tossing him over my hip. The floor shook as he hit the ground. Two solid punches to the face finally put him away.

I sucked in a few breaths of air, then stretched my back. Donovan hadn't hurt me too much. But he would have if I hadn't taken him out when I did. I couldn't believe I let him get me in a bear hug. I probably shouldn't have missed those two weeks of classes.

"Not bad," Caesar called out from the other end of the dojo, clapping slowly.

"Thanks. Now, are you going to tell me what's going on, or am I going to have to beat some answers out of you?"

"You think you can take me?" There was a trace of laughter in his voice.

It was a valid question. Caesar was good. But how good? Better than me? Maybe, but probably not. One thing that tipped the scales in my favor was my OBI training. Some of the best fighters in the world were on Zeus's payroll, and I had studied under all of them. Still, that didn't mean this fight was going to be a piece of cake. Any way you looked at it, Caesar was a dangerous man. He was going to make me work for this one.

"Care to find out?" I asked.

Caesar smiled.

We both walked to the middle of the floor and took fighting stances. Caesar circled me, while I stayed motionless, waiting for him to attack. He came at me, throwing open hand strikes. I blocked his hands and returned a quick roundhouse. He sprang back, and my foot barely missed his head. His smile turned into a beam.

I nodded at him, a show of respect for his skills. He nodded back. By now, the other students had dragged themselves off the floor and gathered around us. I caught glimpses of their faces, all glowering at me. I could tell they wanted to jump in, but they wouldn't. This was a one-on-one duel between master and pupil. Interference was forbidden. It'd be like saying their master wasn't strong enough to fight his own battles.

This time I was the aggressor. I let loose a barrage of kicks and punches. He blocked them all and reached for my throat, his fingers curled like claws. I backpedaled, evading his grasp. I smiled. He was even better than I thought. Waves of nervous energy emanated from the other students. Caesar and I smiled at each other. I gestured for him to bring it on.

He threw two punches and some kicks. I blocked the first few attacks, but he eventually saw an opening. He grabbed me and slammed me onto the floor. Before he could stomp me, I grabbed his ankle. He lost his balance and fell. We both scrambled to our feet. I kicked him in the chest as he reared back for a punch. He shuffled back.

He wasn't smiling anymore. I was.

For an instant we stood across from one another, not moving. Like in an old western showdown. It wasn't as cool as it looked on TV. I was exhausted, and I feared what would happen if Caesar landed a solid blow. I needed a second to think, to come up with a game plan.

But there was no time for strategy. Caesar charged me, punching, chopping, and kicking. I weaved and ducked, then rose up with a left hook. The blow caught him squarely on the chin. His hands dropped as his bones turned to jelly. He fell flat on his face and started snoring. Someone cursed. I backed away as the other guys rushed over to check on him.

Paul rolled Caesar over and slapped him on the face a few times, attempting to wake him. "Sensei!"

"He's out cold," Marco said.

"He won't be the only one if you guys don't start talking," I warned.

They glanced at one another. Paul looked as though he wanted to speak. Marco gave him a warning glance.

"Got something to say, Paul?" I asked.

He shook his head.

"Look, if you tell me what's going on, I promise not to call the police."

Again they looked at each other. Marco nodded. Then Jim said, "Okay."

I crossed my arms. Their compliance came as a surprise. But I was relieved that I didn't have to fight anymore.

"A while back, someone came in during one of our classes," Jim said. "He knew you were a student here. He told us to rough you up the next time we saw you. Gave us twenty thousand apiece to do it. I don't know what you did to piss him off, but I wouldn't want to be in your shoes."

"What's his name?" I demanded.

Jim hesitated. "Hermes."

38

EARLY THE NEXT MORNING, I MADE AN UNEXPECTED VISIT to Hermes's estate. The brawl at the dojo had landed him back on my list of suspects, which suited me just fine. I was hoping I'd get the chance to take down that arrogant prick.

Before leaving home, I left Herc a voice mail and told him where I was going, in case I didn't return.

Hermes was at his desk, working on his laptop. His fingers were pale blurs as they rapidly tapped the keys, pounding out what had to have been hundreds of words per minute. I sat down in front of his desk. He didn't acknowledge me, just continued to type away as if I wasn't there. I cleared my throat.

Hermes's voice, when he finally addressed me, was calm and even. His composure made me angrier than I already was. "Good morning, Mr. Jones. What brings you here this morning?"

"You know damn well why I'm here."

"I'm sure I don't know what you're talking about."

"Of course you don't. Well, let me refresh your memory. You paid off my karate class."

"Oh, that." Hermes chuckled, still typing.

I frowned. "You think this is funny?"

"Very much so."

"Why'd you do it?"

Hermes shrugged. "Hera requested it."

I laughed incredulously. "Wait, wait. Did you just say that Hera put you up to this?"

"I did."

I didn't know what to think about that. I knew Hera wasn't the nicest Goddess around, and that she despised mortals. But I was trying to find her children's killer. It made no sense that she would come after me like this, unless there was something she didn't want me to find out.

"A while back, two assassins tried to kill me," I said. "Did she hire them too?"

"She did."

Suddenly, a lot of things made sense. The OBI agents who arrested Dalen Scott—they didn't kill him in self-defense. They killed him because Hera ordered them to. Because he was a liability, one that could expose her master plan, whatever it may be. Considering that, it was probably no coincidence that the names of the arresting agents were being kept secret. Hera didn't want them available for questioning. I wouldn't be surprised if she had them killed as well.

What didn't make sense was why she would try to kill me *now*, when Zeus wanted so badly for me to investigate these murders.

"Does Zeus know about this?" I asked.

Hermes looked up from his computer and anchored his light-blue eyes on me. "No, and he never will."

I got the implication. If I blabbed to Zeus about the conspiracy, Hera would double her efforts to kill me. I had already dodged the bullet twice, but my lucky streak wouldn't last forever. It was safer to stay quiet for now.

"Why is she doing this?" I asked.

"She has her reasons."

"Which are?"

Hermes smiled. I knew this conversation wasn't going to lead anywhere. He was toying with me now, dangling a carrot from a stick. I'd had enough of it.

"You've already threatened my ex-wife. And now Hera's out for my blood. How am I supposed to solve this case with this crap going on?"

"You're the master detective. You figure it out."

I clenched my jaw, wanting to knock that smug grin off his face, knowing he'd kill me if I tried.

"Look at it this way, Jones. In the unlikely event that you solve this case, perhaps the First Lady will decide to leave you alone."

I smiled. "Or will she be more bloodthirsty than ever?"

"I'd watch what I say if I were you, Mr. Jones." Hermes peered down his nose at me.

"It was just a question."

"Don't patronize me, mortal. I know what you're getting at. You think Hera is involved in these murders."

He was right. But I wasn't about to let him know that. "I'm not accusing anyone of anything."

"Smart move. Now, if there's nothing else, I'll ask that you get out of my office. I have a lot of work to do."

There was no point in arguing. It wouldn't have gotten me anywhere. Hermes was done playing ball. He knew why Hera was coming after me. That much was obvious. But he wasn't going to tell me. Whether he was scared of angering the First Lady, or he just liked watching me squirm, I couldn't tell. The only thing I knew was that I was up to my eyeballs in trouble.

As I stood, Hermes said, "Oh, and Mr. Jones. Don't mention any of this to Zeus. For your own sake."

"I won't say a word," I assured him. "But you have to do something for me."

Hermes grinned. We both knew that I was in no position to bargain. But he humored me regardless. "And what would that be?"

"The guys from the dojo. I don't want to them to end up like that assassin. You get what I'm saying?"

Hermes chuckled. "Of course, Mr. Jones. I'll see to it that they're not harmed."

I nodded in appreciation.

Hermes nodded back and returned to his work. He was probably lying to me. But there was nothing I could do about it, except call the guys from class and tell them to watch their backs. Even though I was still mad at them, I didn't want their blood on my hands.

I left Hermes's office and went to the foyer. An elevator behind the staircase took me to the base of Mount Olympus. The doors parted and I stepped into the dim, subterranean parking deck where my Thunderbird waited for me. Not for the first time, I felt guilty about trying to replace the old clunker. No doubt about it, the Lotus had been prettier and more in tune with my style. But the Thunderbird had been there for me through thick and thin. It was like an old friend. An old friend I had wronged. I felt like I should apologize.

I got in the car, started the engine, and drove out of the deck. When I got home, I cracked open a beer and slumped onto the couch. The midday sunlight filtered through the window blinds, staining the floor with bands of white light.

As far as I was concerned, Hera was now my prime suspect. If she was so eager to kill me, it meant she was probably involved in the murders. But why would she kill her own offspring?

Though I didn't have an answer to that question, I was relieved that Hera was after me instead of Zeus. From the beginning, I had doubts about the president's involvement in the attempts on my life. He was the one who hired me after all—and I was friends with his son. There was no explanation as to why he'd want me dead.

Hera, on the other hand, could cook up more than a few reasons to take me out.

Though Zeus knew what his wife was capable of, I'm sure he never expected her to go this far—taking control of the OBI right under his nose. I wanted to tell him the truth. But Hera would kill me if I did. For now, my only option was to continue the investigation, and hope I lived long enough to discover the truth.

39

THE FOLLOWING AFTERNOON I GOT A CALL FROM MAGUS, who told me that my order was ready. After work, I swung by the Ammo Crate to pick up my osmium rounds.

"What's up, Unc?" I asked as I walked through the door.

Magus was behind the counter doing a crossword puzzle. He looked up and smiled. "Hey."

"You've got something for me?"

"I do." Magus reached under the counter and brought up a sealed cardboard box. He sliced it open with his box cutter.

Inside were ten small red boxes, all of them unmarked. I opened one. It was filled with lustrous blue-gray bullets. I nodded and closed it.

"You good?" Magus asked.

"Yep." I handed him my debit card and he rang me up.

"You know, someone else came in here the other day and ordered some osmium bullets," Magus said, giving the card back to me, along with a receipt. "Fifty boxes."

My eyes widened. "Fifty boxes?"

He nodded. "He said he needed them as soon as possible."

"How much did that run him?"

"A little over a quarter million."

"Wow!"

"I asked him why he needed so many. He claimed that he and his friends were going on a chimera hunt. I wasn't convinced."

"Why not?" I asked.

"He was a little too jittery."

"Maybe he was just excited."

"Maybe."

I picked up the cardboard box.

"You're leaving already?" Magus asked.

"Yeah," I said. "I'm meeting someone this evening."

Magus raised an eyebrow. "That someone wouldn't happen to be a woman, would it?"

I smiled. "I wish."

After leaving the Ammo Crate, I drove across town to pay Hades a surprise visit. The last time I'd seen him was about nine years ago, while I was still with the OBI. One of his prized Cerberuses had escaped its cage, and was running amuck all over the city. Hades went to Zeus, who ordered me and the other agents to track down the beast and return it to its owner. Four agents had been eaten and another three wounded before we finally completed the mission.

Hades showed his appreciation by throwing us a lavish party at the New Olympia Civic Center. I couldn't make it because Alexis and I were celebrating our anniversary that night. But it was just as well. I heard things got out of hand, and several people had to be sent to the hospital. No one would tell me exactly what happened. I didn't want to know.

Hades lived in a subterranean complex beneath Mount Olympus. The only way in was by elevator. On my way down, screams of horror issued from the various floors. An indication of things to come? I hoped not.

By the time I reached the bottom level, the screaming had stopped. The elevator doors parted to reveal a magnificent foyer. The floors were marble, the walls cream, and a chandelier sparkled overhead, throwing flecks of gold light. Twin staircases led to a balcony on the second floor.

I stepped out of the elevator and was met by a minotaur with gray fur and black horns. He wore a hunter-green suit and an earpiece.

"Plato Jones?" he said.

"Uh, yes."

"The master is expecting you. Come with me."

The God of the Underworld was expecting me? That couldn't be good.

I followed the minotaur upstairs to Hades's office. The space was large and inviting, with warm colors and sumptuous leather furnishings. It would have been perfect if not for the ghastly paintings on the walls. One depicted a man in a loincloth being impaled on a stake. Another showed a fire-breathing dragon burning a group of people alive. But the worst, by far, was of a woman eating a baby. I don't think I'll ever understand rich people and their fondness for the bizarre.

Hades was practicing his golf swing on an indoor putting green. His light-blue sweater-vest looked like it had been ripped straight out of *Mr. Rogers' Neighborhood*. Khaki slacks and a pair of sensible loafers completed the look. His blond hair was slicked down and parted in the middle. He smiled at me, flashing straight white teeth.

"Good evening, Mr. Jones." His voice was creepily low and gentle.

"Same to you."

Hades put aside his putter and raised the window blinds. On the other side of the glass was a picture of a beautiful countryside. Artificial light flooded the room.

He sat down behind his desk. "Please, sit."

I sat on the couch.

Hades sat in silence for a while, smiling at me. It was a pleasant smile. Unsettlingly pleasant. Like Zeus, he emitted power. But his was different than his brother's. It felt conscious—a dark presence looming behind me, silent and observant.

"Can I offer you something to drink?" he asked.

My first instinct was to say no. But declining the hospitality of a God was never a good idea. Besides, I was in a unique position. Hades normally offered his guests fire, chains, and torment.

I shrugged. "Why not?"

As if on cue, the door opened and Persephone, the Goddess of Spring and Queen of the Underworld, strolled into the office, bringing with her the smell of wildflowers. It might have just been my imagination, but all the potted plants in the room seemed to sway in her direction.

In a white sundress with red flowers, and red heels, she looked like a sixteen-year-old on her way to a picnic. Her blond hair sported a poodle cut, and her makeup was a little too perfect. She carried a pitcher of lemonade in one hand while balancing a tray of cookies in the other.

"Hello, sweetheart," she said cheerily.

"Hello, dear. Are those oatmeal cookies I smell?"

"They sure are."

"Splendid."

These two couldn't be serious. I glanced back and forth between them. They *were* serious.

Persephone set the pitcher and tray on the coffee table. She kissed Hades on the lips and then fetched two glasses from the minibar.

"Dear, you remember Mr. Jones, don't you?" Hades said. "He used to work for my brother a few years back."

"Of course." Persephone poured me a glass of lemonade. Her blue eyes were wide and unblinking. Her smile looked painted on. "How are you, Mr. Jones?"

"Ask me again in a few minutes," I said.

Hades laughed, shaking his finger at me. "Oh, Mr. Jones."

"Have a cookie, Mr. Jones," Persephone offered. "They're to die for."

I'll bet. "Thank you very much."

I picked up a cookie, a small one, and put the whole thing into my mouth. It was grainy and crunchy. All I could taste was sugar. Pure, unbridled sugar. Hades and Persephone went as still as mannequins. They stared at me as I chewed. The intensity in their eyes made swallowing difficult.

"What do you think?" Hades asked.

I returned a shaky smile. "Delicious."

The tension in the room disappeared. Persephone touched her chest and let out a breathless laugh. "I'm so relieved. I was worried you wouldn't like them."

I shook my head vigorously. "Oh no," I lied. "I love exceedingly sweet things." Especially on an empty stomach.

"You simply must try the lemonade next," she said.

I did as she asked. I was afraid not to. The lemonade was like cold corn syrup with a dash of lemon. One sip nearly sent me into diabetic shock.

"Well?" Persephone asked. She stood on tiptoes as if too eager to stay still.

I smiled again, struggling not to wretch. "Best lemonade I've ever had."

Persephone beamed and put her hands on her hips. "Mr. Jones, you've just gone and made my day. How would you like to stay for dinner?"

I smiled apologetically. "Maybe next time."

Persephone stared at me for a long moment, silent and unmoving. It was as if a circuit in her head had blown. Finally she said, "Yes . . . next time."

"Dear," Hades cut in politely. "Do you think you could give us a moment? Mr. Jones and I have important matters to discuss."

"Of course."

"Wonderful."

"I love you," Persephone said.

"I love you too, schnookums."

Persephone turned and literally skipped out of the room. The door closed behind her. I tried not to gape.

Hades jabbed his thumb toward the door. "Great girl, isn't she?"

"Sure."

He took a cigar out of his desk drawer. "Would you like one?"

I shook my head. "No thanks."

He put the cigar in his mouth and searched his pockets for a lighter—but didn't find it. I was about to offer mine when he touched the tip of the cigar with his index finger. The cigar ignited with a tiny spark.

Neat trick.

Hades exhaled a puff of smoke and sank back into his chair.

"How did you know I'd be coming?"

Hades smiled patronizingly.

"Then you also know why I'm here?"

He nodded. "It's a shame what happened to my darling niece and nephew." He took another pull from his cigar, held the smoke in his mouth for several seconds, and then blew it out in a stream. "Are you sure you won't have a cigar?"

"Positive," I said.

"Let me know if you change your mind."

"I'll do that. In the meantime, why don't you tell me a story?" I leaned forward and waited.

"I'm afraid I'm not very good at telling stories," Hades said.

I waited some more. He puffed his cigar.

"What have you been up to this past month?" I asked.

Still smiling, Hades placed his cigar in the ashtray. When he spoke, he sounded more apologetic than insulted. "I know where you're going with this, Mr. Jones, and I'm afraid my answer might disappoint you."

"Try me."

"I've been here."

That answer came as no surprise. Hades was the most reclusive of all the Gods, even more so than Hephaestus had been. He rarely left his estate.

"For the entire month?" I asked anyway.

He nodded. "I've been overseeing the construction of a special project."

"What kind of special project?"

"I was having an arena installed in the dungeon. The missus says it's a waste of money, but I think every male needs his own private getaway, a place where he can be himself. A man-cave, as you mortals call it. Would you like to see it?"

I shook my head decisively.

"Maybe another time then," Hades said.

"Is there anyone besides your wife that can verify your story?"

Hades glanced at the ceiling, pondering. "There's my staff and the construction crew."

"I'd like written statements from each of them."

"Of course. Is there anything else you'd like to know?"

"Yes. After Eileithyia and Hephaestus died, did their souls pass through your realm?"

"I don't believe so, but let me check." Hades logged onto his computer and searched his files. "No, I'm afraid they haven't been to my neck of the woods."

Strange. I thought all departed souls went to Hades. Did that mean immortals don't have souls?

"When was the last time you spoke with the victims?" I asked.

"Eileithyia and I hadn't been on speaking terms in ages. The last time I spoke to Hephaestus was over a month ago. I wanted him to help with the construction effort. I figured the builders could benefit from his expertise."

I waited for Hades to continue. He just looked at me. His blue eyes shone with an eerie emptiness. A chill raced through me.

"What did Hephaestus say?" I asked.

"He said he couldn't help me. That he was preoccupied with an important project of his own."

"Did he mention what this important project was?"

"I'm afraid not."

"Did he mention anything else?"

"Just that he wished Aphrodite loved him as much as he loved her."

I nodded.

"Any more questions?" Hades asked.

"No, I think that's all. Thanks for your time."

"The pleasure was mine."

I shook Hades's hand and left the office. After our conversation, I had doubts about his involvement in the murders. At least *these* murders. But I knew better than to jump to conclusions. Until I confirmed Hades's alibis, he was still in the running.

The minotaur escorted me back to the elevator. I pressed the up button and waited for the doors to open. Nothing happened.

I pressed the button again and crossed my arms. The doors remained closed. I turned to the minotaur, smiling through a clenched jaw. "There seems to be a problem with the elevator."

"It looks all right to me," he said.

I turned back around and hammered the button with my finger. Still nothing. From the corner of my eye, I glimpsed the minotaur pull a thin, metal baton from his coat.

That moment, instinct took over. I drew my gun and spun around. But before I could squeeze off a round, the minotaur lashed out with his baton. The blow caught me on the side of the head. An explosion of pain tore through my brain.

The world turned black.

40

Pain throbbed in my forehead. That was both good and bad. It meant I was still alive. But it also meant that I was in deep shit. I cracked open my eyes and discovered that I lay on my back, in the sand-filled pit of an indoor coliseum. The stone bleachers were empty, and massive lanterns hung from the rafters.

Strangely, I found none of this surprising. I pushed myself to a seated position. The movement made the pain in my head worse. I touched the side of my face and drew back fingers covered in blood. Another concussion. Great.

Hades appeared in the arena's main viewing box. Persephone was with him, cradling a brown Cerberus pup in her arms. The three-headed dog was no bigger than a football, but would one day grow to the size of an elephant. Two of its heads nipped playfully at each other. The third looked to be asleep, its tongue hanging from the side of its mouth. Behind Hades and company stood the minotaur.

"Hello, Mr. Jones." Hades's voice echoed through the arena. "So glad to see you're all right."

"Hi!" Persephone said, making the pup wave at me with one of its little paws.

"What's going on?" I demanded. "Where am I?"

"In my new arena. My man-cave. What do you think of it?" A grin stretched across Hades's face.

"Why am I here?"

"To fight for your life, of course."

My pulse quickened. I planted my hands on the floor and pushed myself to my feet. The world tilted back and forth. I held out my arms for balance. My stomach lurched with nausea. I took a deep breath and regained control.

"Why are you doing this?" I asked.

"To prove a point," Hades said. "I'm sure you've noticed by now that my dear sister Hera isn't very fond of you."

Hera, I thought. *I should've known.* "Yeah, I noticed."

"She wants the investigation to be exclusively under OBI jurisdiction. No outside help, especially from a human. She thinks you're incapable of getting the job done."

"Incapable or unworthy?"

"Take your pick." Hades's eyes twinkling with laughter. "I, on the other hand, happen to disagree. I think you're fully capable of solving this mystery."

"Thanks for the vote of confidence," I said. "But that still doesn't explain why I'm standing in the middle of this pit."

"Hera and I have a wager. You're going to battle one of my minions. If you die, Hera wins, and Zeus will be forced find a more fitting candidate to look into the murders. If you survive, I win. Hera will leave you alone, and the investigation will proceed according to Zeus's plans."

"Something tells me you have more to gain from this wager than the satisfaction of beating Hera."

"You're a sharp one, Mr. Jones." Hades chuckled. "If you survive this trial, Hera will hand Athena's Aegis over to me . . . after the killer has been brought to justice, of course."

"What does the Aegis have to do with this?" I asked.

"Everything," Hades said. "I'm concerned that my brother gave it to you. Whoever wears the Aegis becomes impervious to harm, able to cheat death. Able to cheat *me*. No mortal should ever possess such power."

"Typical," I said under my breath.

Hades must have heard me because his smile broadened. "Only Gods should be able to cheat death. The natural order of things must be preserved. You understand, don't you?"

"Fear is pretty easy to understand."

Hades's smile faltered. "Don't take this personally, Mr. Jones. It's just business."

"Right." That made me feel so much better. The Gods were playing a game, and I was the pawn.

"Now then, let's begin." Hades clapped his hands.

The arena doors boomed open. At first, nothing happened. Then I heard footsteps. Big ones. Growing louder by the second.

I cursed inwardly as a cyclops lumbered through the doorway. He was at least twelve feet tall, grotesquely muscled, and naked except for a fur loincloth. His gray skin reminded me of bleached leather, and was covered in white scar tissue. His hand gripped a stone club as long as my body.

His stench hit me like a baseball to the nose. A vile mixture of musk, blood, and feces. I was betting he ate, slept, and crapped all in the same room.

The cyclops ambled toward me. I reached for my gun. It was missing.

"Looking for this?" Hades called down from the stands.

The minotaur held up my Desert Eagle, dangling it by two fingers. Bastard!

"Throw it here!" I shouted.

"I'm afraid I can't do that," Hades said. "Hera and I agreed. No guns. They would give you too much of an advantage."

"Oh, come on!" I protested. "How do you expect me to beat this guy? Throw sand at him?"

"Of course not." Hades snapped his fingers.

The minotaur drew a knife and tossed it into the arena. It landed in the sand between me and the cyclops.

"A knife." I gaped at it. "Are you kidding me?"

"Give us a good show," Hades said.

"You can do it!" Persephone cheered.

The cyclops halted. His red eye glanced at the knife, and then anchored onto me. A growl oozed from a mouth filled with rotten teeth. He was challenging me to come and get the weapon.

I stayed right where I was. I knew a deathtrap when I saw one. The knife was lying within range of the cyclops's club. There was no way I could grab it without getting squashed into jelly. My best option was to draw him away from it. Fortunately, cyclopses aren't renowned for their intelligence. They are, however, known for their pride.

I laughed maniacally.

The cyclops tilted his head to one side, doglike. "What's so funny?" he demanded. His voice was deep and guttural, like an animal trying to mimic human speech.

"You're a little small for a cyclops, aren't you?" I said.

The cyclops stiffened. "What did you say, human?"

"I said you're small for a cyclops." I glanced at his lower half. "And judging by the size of that loincloth, I'm sure all the female cyclopses would agree."

"Now, Mr. Jones, that wasn't very nice," Hades shouted across the arena, a hint of humor in his voice.

The cyclops roared. Strands of spit flew from his mouth. When his shoulders hunched, I knew he was about to charge. The first step in my plan had worked. The next step required me to stay alive long enough to grab the knife.

I hunkered down. The cyclops charged. I waited until he got nice and close, and then dived out of the way. He rushed past me, his momentum driving him forward.

"Good job, Mr. Jones!" Persephone shouted.

I scrambled to my feet and made a break for the knife. A roar rose up behind me, followed by thunderous footsteps. I didn't look back. Just kept running.

I grasped the knife and spun around to see the cyclops coming toward me. His club came zooming down.

I threw myself sideways. The club smashed into the floor, inches away from my foot. The impact roused a cloud of dust.

"Come here!" the cyclops roared.

He reached for me as I tried to get up. His massive hand closed around my waist and hoisted me into the air. I jammed the knife into his wrist, withdrew it, and then stabbed his forearm. Blood flew, spattering against me, dark as motor oil. The stink was overwhelming.

In the stands, Hades was clapping. The Cerberus pup started to howl. So did I. The cyclops was crushing me—I could feel my body collapsing into itself. I stabbed him again, in the wrist. The blade struck bone. He bellowed and tossed me aside.

I landed flat on my back. The air burst from my lungs. Spots of light momentarily danced before my eyes. I heard the cyclops coming for me. Felt the ground tremor beneath his footfalls. I rolled over and scrambled to my hands and knees. A massive shadow fell over me.

"Squash you!" The cyclops raised his club.

Breathless and dizzy, I did the only thing I could think of. I scooped up a handful of sand from the arena floor and threw it at his head. He grunted and spun away from me, clutching his face.

"A dirty move, Mr. Jones," Hades said.

I drew a deep breath and wrestled to my feet. While the cyclops rubbed his eye, I slashed downward, slicing his Achilles tendon. His leg buckled and he collapsed on the arena floor. Blood gushed from the wound.

Hades's voice rang out. "Brilliant!"

Unable to walk, the cyclops dropped his club and dragged himself toward me. He was squinting, his eye bloodshot. Clumps of wet sand clung to his lashes. I knew he couldn't see me. I kept my distance until he finally gave up and dropped to the sand. He lay prone and still, except for the ragged rise and fall of his breathing.

"Bravo, Mr. Jones, bravo!" Hades said, clapping. He and Persephone rose to their feet. "My faith in you wasn't misplaced. Now, finish off your opponent. Then we'll head upstairs to celebrate."

He turned and started toward the exit, which was marked by a neon EXIT sign.

I dropped the bloody knife. "No."

Hades stopped and turned around. "Excuse me?"

"I'm not going to kill him."

Hades looked as if he might laugh. "Are you refusing me, Mr. Jones?"

"That's exactly what I'm doing," I said, trying to sound braver than I actually felt. "I won't murder someone in cold blood just to amuse you. I did what you wanted. I survived the fight. Let me go."

Hades stared at me for a short time, and then nodded. "Have it your way, Mr. Jones."

He snapped his fingers and the minotaur raised my gun.

I instinctively shut my eyes. A shot fired. The loud bang made my heart leap into my throat. For several seconds, I found it impossible to move. When I finally opened my eyes, I was amazed—pleasantly so—to find myself still alive. I checked myself for bullet holes. I was still in one piece.

Nearby, the cyclops lay motionless on the sand, a smoking hole in the back of his head. A pool of blood was spreading beneath his body. The sight made me angry and sick to my stomach. Whenever the Gods killed, they claimed divine right. It looked like plain old murder to me.

"Well that was fun," Persephone said. "Lemonade, anyone?"

41

After Hades let me out of the arena, the first thing I did was get my gun back. Then I went to the bathroom to wash up. My face and clothes were splattered with the cyclops's blood, and there was lump on the side of my head from where the minotaur had hit me. My entire body ached. But a few scrapes and bruises were a small price to pay to get Hera off my back. I just hoped she lived up to her part of the deal.

Hades and Persephone were waiting for me at the elevator. The God of the Underworld stood with his hands in his pockets. His wife held a pink cardboard cake box.

"It was nice of you to stop by, Mr. Jones," Hades said. "We don't get to many visitors."

I can't imagine why.

We shook hands.

"Are you sure I can't convince you to stay for dinner?" Hades asked.

I shook my head. "Sorry."

"That's disappointing to hear. But I understand. You have a case to solve."

Persephone offered me the box. "Here."

"What's this?"

"A box of my oatmeal cookies. For the road."

I reluctantly accepted the gift. "Uh, thanks."

"Enjoy them," Persephone said. It sounded like a recommendation.

I stepped into the elevator. Hades and Persephone waved and smiled until the doors closed.

I shivered.

42

It was nighttime when I got home. I could tell the cat had been there at some point. The little bastard had clawed up the carpet and covered my couch in hair. Too exhausted to be angry, I put the box of cookies on the coffee table and went to bed.

I woke up around noon the following day, sore and stiff. No surprise there. I swallowed a couple aspirin and took a hot shower.

Afterward, I fixed myself a late breakfast of scrambled eggs and toast. The swelling on my face turned the simple task of eating into a battle of attrition. I fought through the pain and managed to clean my plate. As I dumped my dishes into the sink, my cell phone rang.

I glanced at the caller ID.

"Hey, Alexis," I said.

"What's going on, Plato?" she asked sharply.

"Huh?"

"Some guy in a black suit flagged me down while I was taking my morning jog around the park."

Alarms went off in my head. I sat down on the couch. "What did he want?"

"He told me to give you a message," Alexis said. "You're running out of time."

My breath caught. *Shit.* The Gods were getting impatient.

"Are you in some kind of trouble?" she asked, her tone suspicious.

"No, of course not."

"Are you sure?"

"Positive." I stood and started pacing back and forth in front of the couch. "Listen, Alexis. I need you to stay in the house for a while."

"Plato, will you please tell me what's going on?"

I sighed. "Just do this for me, okay?"

Alexis didn't respond.

"Promise me."

"Fine," she said after a few seconds.

"Thanks. I have to go now. I'll be in touch."

Alexis drew breath to speak. I ended the call before she could get a word out.

43

I WAS IN MY OFFICE, ABOUT TO LEAVE FOR LUNCH, WHEN
Bellanca Stone poked her head through the door. "Hi, Plato.
Do you have a minute?"

A thrill of excitement arose in my stomach. The memory
of our last meeting flashed in my mind.

"Sure," I said.

Bellanca stepped inside, wearing a red tank top and dark-
gray trousers. Her hair was pulled back into a curly ponytail.
She wasn't wearing much makeup, just lip gloss and eyeliner.
The casual look somehow made her even more attractive.

"Sorry for showing up unexpected." She sat down in the
chair across from my desk.

I shook my head. "Don't worry about it."

Her face reddened. "I want to apologize for what happened
back at my place. I let my emotions get the better of me."

"No apologies necessary. What can I do for you?"

"I came to talk about Collin."

"Is he giving you any trouble?"

Bellanca shook her head. "No, I'm just concerned about him."

"Why's that?"

"The other day he left a weird message on my phone."
Bellanca reached into her purse and took out her cell phone.
She played the message on speaker.

Collin's voice filled the office, high and frantic. "Bellanca, when you get this message, call me immediately. I-I'm in trouble. Kind of. I just . . . I just need someone to talk to. Please don't call the police. J-just, ah—I don't know what I'm saying. Never mind. Forget I called. Bye."

The message ended.

Bellanca placed the phone on my desk.

"Did you call him back?" I asked.

"I tried, but he wouldn't pick up."

"Maybe this is some elaborate scheme to get back in your good graces?"

"I don't think so."

I considered telling her that Collin had recently threatened me. But I quickly reconsidered. Bellanca was already overstressed. I didn't want to make things worse.

"What kind of trouble do you think he's in?" I asked.

"I'm not sure, but I was hoping you could find out."

I steepled my fingers. "I want to help you, Bellanca. I really do, but my plate is kind of full right now."

Bellanca leaned forward in her chair, her expression hopeful. "Please, Mr. Jones."

I knew I should've refused. I should've stuck to my guns—told her that I had more important things to do than to hunt down her idiot husband. But looking into those pretty brown eyes, I found it impossible to say no.

"Tell you what," I said. "I'll keep an eye out for him, no charge."

Bellanca's face brightened. "You will?"

"Yeah."

"I don't know what to say other than thank you," she said, looking like she wanted to reach across the desk and hug me. I wouldn't have complained.

44

HERC AND I WERE EATING AT MINO'S—A BAR AND GRILL ON the boardwalk. An assortment of sports memorabilia adorned the wood-paneled walls. Baseball games played on each of the restaurant's six flat-screen TVs. Most of the lunch crowd had already eaten and gone back to work. The only people left were a few construction workers and an older couple. They all seemed too busy with their own conversations to notice what Herc and I were talking about.

Herc almost choked. "You interrogated Hades?"

He was having an Italian beef sandwich heaped with hot giardiniera. The smell made me wish I had gotten one for myself instead of settling on the bacon club.

"Yep," I said.

"And you're still alive?"

"I'm here, aren't I?"

Herc shook his head, grinning. "You're either the bravest man I've ever met, or the dumbest."

"Maybe I'm both."

"Did you learn anything?"

"Other than the fact that your uncle's a deranged lunatic?"

Herc chuckled and bit into his sandwich. Au jus dribbled down the front of his white button-up.

"Damn it!" He scowled down at the shirt. "This shirt cost twelve credits."

"Big spender."

"Shut up." Herc grabbed a napkin from the dispenser and blotted the meat juice.

"Hera tried to have me killed again," I said.

"Again?"

I nodded. "She and Hades forced me to fight for my life in an underground arena."

"You're kidding?"

"Afraid not," I said, scraping the excess mayo off my sandwich with a plastic knife.

"Did you find out why she's after you? Is it because you're friends with me?"

"No. She thinks I'll compromise the investigation. That's what Hades said anyway."

"Sounds fishy."

"I thought so too."

Herc finished cleaning his shirt. He balled up the napkin and tossed it over his shoulder. It landed in the trash can near the exit. Show-off.

"You think she and Hades might be in cahoots?" he asked.

"It's possible. I don't think either one of them would cry over my grave. Hades has always been obsessed with death. And Hera once threw Hephaestus off Mount Olympus just because she thought he was ugly."

"Not a very motherly thing to do."

"Not at all."

Herc took another bite of his sandwich. "Does my dad know about this?" he asked, his mouth full.

"I don't think so."

"You gonna tell him?"

I cocked an eyebrow. "Are you crazy? Hera will skin me alive."

Herc laughed. "You're probably right about that."

"Besides, Hera shouldn't be a problem anymore. Emphasis on *shouldn't*."

"Why do you say that?"

"She and Hades had a little wager going on. She promised Hades that she'd leave me alone, provided I survived the arena. Let's hope she keeps her word."

Herc covered his mouth to burp. "What're you going to do next?"

"I still need to speak with Dionysus. He's been missing since the time of Eileithyia's murder. No one seems to know where he is."

"That's pretty suspicious."

"No kidding."

"How'll you find him?" Herc asked.

"I'm hoping he'll eventually show up."

"What if he doesn't?"

I bit into my sandwich. Despite the soggy tomatoes and overcooked bacon, it still tasted good. I waited until I had swallowed before answering, unlike a certain Demigod.

"Then I'll have to keep asking around," I said.

45

AFTER LUNCH, I SWUNG BY MY OFFICE. HERMES'S INFORMA-
tion was still on my desk. A stack of documents sat next to
it—alibi letters from Hades's personal staff and from the
construction workers who built his indoor arena. Some were
typed, others handwritten. I read each of them, all the while
taking notes on my laptop. Then I cross-referenced the information, looking for inconsistencies. The stories were all
consistent. I wasn't surprised. Hades as the killer would have
been too obvious.

I still didn't rule out the possibility that the statements
were false. Hades was the God of the Underworld. He could
easily have coerced his workers into giving false information.
To be safe, I called each one of his alibis. They all seemed legit.

It was just as well though. I needed to keep moving
forward.

With Hades out of the way, I had two suspects left. Hera's
ugly history with Hephaestus made her a person of interest.
The idea of a direct confrontation with her scared me half to
death. She had already tried to kill me multiple times. And
though she had lost the bet with Hades, I had doubts she would
keep her promise to leave me alone. If I was going to question
her, I'd have to come up with a plan.

In the meantime, I still had Dionysus to deal with. Finding him wouldn't be easy. But I knew someone who might be able to help.

As I stood and stretched my arms, my cell phone rang. It was Jackass.

"What do you want?" I asked.

"Just checking your progress," Hermes said.

"The case is coming along fine."

"Good to hear."

"I don't appreciate your goons stalking Alexis."

"Just think of it as an incentive," Hermes said. "To keep you on your toes."

"Tell them to back off."

"And what if I don't?"

I opened my mouth to answer but no words came out.

"You're in no position to make demands, Mr. Jones," Hermes said coolly. "You want us out of your life? Then give us some results."

"I'm working as fast as I can."

"Work faster."

"How can I? With all these damn games of yours?" I yelled into the phone.

Hermes didn't respond. He had hung up.

"Son of a bitch!" I shouted, and knocked over the chair in front of my desk.

46

I WOKE UP EARLY THE NEXT MORNING. I WAS STILL PISSED AT Hermes, but I knew better than to let anger interfere with my work. Anger leads to mistakes. And mistakes lead to people dying.

I started the day with a long, hot shower. Then I got dressed. I had just pulled on my jeans when I heard a knock at the door. I looked through the peephole and saw Chrysus standing out in the hallway.

I yanked the door open. "Hi."

Chrysus's eyes trailed down before snapping back up. Abruptly, I realized I wasn't wearing a shirt. I wondered if she was looking at my abs or the black and blue bruises painted across my torso.

She wore a white blouse and a black pencil skirt. The first few buttons of her shirt were undone, showing off some nice cleavage. Her blond hair was in a bun, and she held a large metal briefcase.

She smiled politely. "Good morning, Mr. Jones."

She had a gorgeous smile and beautifully shaped lips. She cleared her throat and said, "Aren't you going to invite me in?" I realized I'd been staring at her lips.

I blinked. "Yes, of course. Come in."

233

She moved past me through the doorway. Her perfume smelled delicious, like citrus and honeysuckle.

I gestured toward the couch. "Have a seat."

"Thank you." Chrysus put the briefcase on the coffee table and sat down. She crossed her legs. Her fair skin gleamed in the morning light.

"Can I get you something to drink?" I asked.

"That would be nice."

I grabbed Chrysus a bottle of water from the fridge and sat down across from her on the loveseat. I noticed her briefcase had a handprint scanner built into its exterior.

"Is that the Aegis?" I asked.

"It is." Chrysus placed her hand on the scanner.

It glowed with an intense green light. With a beeping sound, the case popped open to reveal a sleeveless gold breastplate. A gorgon's face was inscribed on the metal. Its eyes were made of emeralds.

Chrysus picked up the Aegis as though it were a newborn baby and passed it to me. It was lighter than it looked, almost insubstantial. Soft fur lined the inside. Magical or not, it was a beautiful piece of workmanship.

"You say this thing will make me invulnerable?" I asked.

"So long as you're wearing it."

"A little piece of immortality."

Chrysus smiled. She took a data pad and stylus out of her purse and handed them to me. "I need your signature, to confirm that you received the Aegis."

"Sure." I signed next to the X and returned the pad and stylus to her.

"Thank you." Chrysus put the items back in her purse. She stood and grabbed the briefcase.

"Leaving already?"

"I'm afraid so."

I set the Aegis on the coffee table and walked her to the door. "It was nice seeing you again. And thanks for the Aegis. I'm sure it'll come in handy."

"I hope you don't have to use it," Chrysus said as she stepped out into the hall.

An idea came to me as I watched her move toward the elevator. Maybe I didn't have to confront Hera about the murders after all. Chrysus could give me the information I needed. Her job put her in frequent contact with the First Family. She must have overheard something.

I ran after her. "Chrysus."

She stopped and turned around. "Yes, Mr. Jones?"

"Can I ask you something?"

"Certainly."

"Are you free on Saturday night?"

"Why do you ask?"

"I was just wondering if you'd like to have dinner with me."

Chrysus's eyes widened. "Dinner?"

"We could have drinks instead."

She let out a nervous giggle. "Mr. Jones, are you asking me out on a date?"

"Only if you say yes." I smiled, and hoped it made me look appealing.

Chrysus tilted her chin slightly. "And if I refuse?"

I shrugged. "We'll say I had a temporary lapse in sanity, and forget this ever happened."

Chrysus laughed again. "I appreciate the offer, Mr. Jones, but why me?"

"You intrigue me."

"I *intrigue* you?"

"Yes, as cheesy as that sounds. I want to learn more about you. I want to know what's behind the glasses, what's under the fancy skirt suits." I paused. "Okay, that came out wrong."

Chrysus shook her head, smiling.

"Let me start over," I said. "What I'm trying to say is this. I think you're very attractive and very intelligent, and it would be my pleasure to take you out Saturday night, if you're not busy of course."

Chrysus looked at me for a long moment before speaking. "All right, Mr. Jones. One date seems harmless enough."

I grinned like an idiot. "Great. You won't regret it. And call me Plato."

47

THAT EVENING I CONTINUED MY SEARCH FOR DIONYSUS. HE wasn't at his penthouse, and the employees at Elysium still hadn't heard from him.

With Alexis's life at stake, I no longer had the luxury of waiting for him to show up. I needed to locate him. That's where my old pal Argus came into the picture. An ex-mob enforcer turned OBI informant, he had a talent for finding people who didn't want to be found.

Argus owned a bar called Chimera's Crossing. It was in the historic district of downtown, crammed between a barbershop and a party supply store. The red-brick building had been painted over several times. Splashes of white, tan, and gray covered some portions of the brick. Neon beer signs glowed in the tinted windows.

Inside, the place was dark, dirty, and claustrophobic. A typical hole in the wall. The floors were concrete, the walls maroon, and stained glass lanterns hung over tables that were pressed airlessly together. The smell of stale beer mingled with harsh cigarette smoke.

Two old men in flannel shirts and suspenders sat at a table near the window, threatening to knock each other's block off. I recognized a baseball argument when I saw one.

Clad in a short-sleeve tan shirt and faded jeans, Argus was wiping down the bar with a dingy towel. A black apron tied around his waist had the bar's name stitched onto it in yellow thread.

Argus was a giant. Literally. He stood over ten feet tall, with a bald head, beefy arms, and a round belly. A hundred tiny, yellow eyes were packed into the middle of his face, each one independently mobile.

Given that most giants grew in excess of twenty feet tall, Argus was on the small side. But it wasn't unusual for a full-grown adult to have spontaneous growth spurts every now and then, so there was no telling how big he'd end up being.

I slid onto the barstool in front of him. He stopped cleaning, threw the towel onto his shoulder, and gave a half-smile.

"Well, look at what the wind just blew in." His voice was deep and thick.

"Argus," I said with a nod.

"What can I get you, Plato?"

"Scotch on the rocks."

He grabbed a glass from under the bar with his forefinger and thumb, filled it with ice and scotch, and slid it to me. As far as city-dwelling giants went, Argus and his family were the only ones I'd ever met. Because of their size, giants often have trouble getting around. And there aren't many places that cater to them. They tend to live in the country, where there are plenty of wide open spaces.

"Thanks." I sipped my drink. It burned all the way down. The harshness made me long for the vintage scotch I'd sampled at Hermes's office.

"No problem." Argus grabbed the towel off of his shoulder and resumed cleaning the bar.

I got straight to the point. "I need help."

"I've been telling you that for years."

"Very funny."

"So, what can I do for you?"

"I want information on Dionysus."

Argus's eyes focused on me. All one hundred of them. "The God?"

I nodded. "He's been missing for the past month. I'd like to find him."

"Mind me asking why you want him found?"

"Yes."

Argus smiled. "Fair enough."

"It's nothing personal," I assured him.

"I know." Argus scrubbed a stubborn stain on the bar.

"Can you find him?"

"Of course. Won't be cheap, though."

"Money's not a problem," I said.

"What kind of timeframe are we working with?"

"A small one. Virtually microscopic."

Argus threw the towel back onto his shoulder and took a cigar out of his shirt pocket. It was the size of a rolled up newspaper. He sparked it with a candle lighter. Smoke billowed, thick and choking. "Anything else I can do for you?" he asked.

"Yeah." I waved my hand to clear the smoke. "I want to know what he's been up to this past month."

"General or under the table?"

"Both."

"Gotcha." Argus bent and tapped his cigar against the edge of a large, metal wastebasket—his version of an ashtray. "You know, there've been a lot of government-types running around town lately, shaking people down, asking them all sorts of questions. Word on the street is that something big went down on Olympus. And the Gods are working overtime to keep it covered up."

That bothered me. So far, the Gods had done a fair job of covering up the murders. But information was gradually trickling down the pipeline. Eventually, the public would discover the truth. Then things would get real ugly real fast.

"Don't believe everything you hear," I said.

"I don't." Argus puffed his cigar. "But I take it all under consideration."

I took another sip of scotch. "When should I expect a call from you?"

"In a week or two."

"Can you give me something sooner?"

"I'll do what I can." Argus finished his cigar in one long pull, then dropped the butt into the wastebasket. He pulled a fresh one out of his pocket and lit it. The end glowed bright orange in the dim light.

"You sure you won't tell me what's going on?" he asked.

"I would if I could."

Argus grinned. "You law-types and your secrets."

I swallowed the rest of my scotch and reached for my wallet.

Argus shook his head. "It's on the house."

"Thanks."

"I don't know what kind of mess you've gotten yourself into, but try not to get killed, alright?"

"Why, Argus, I didn't know you cared."

"I don't," Argus said. "It's just that dead men can't pay their bills."

48

On Saturday night, I drove to Chrysus's place. She lived in a two-story mansion on the north side of town. A Spanish-style villa with beige walls and sunbaked roof shingles. It was stunning, but looked too much like a summer resort for my taste.

I parked in the driveway, next to an Escalade truck. Its midnight paint and chrome rims gleamed under the light of a nearby lamppost. There's something incredibly sexy about a woman who drives a truck. I can't really say why.

I got out of my car. Two chimera statues—creatures with the head of a lion, the body of a goat, and the tail of a snake—flanked the staircase leading up to the front door. I rang the bell. Chrysus answered, wearing a tight black dress and heels. Her blond hair fell past her shoulders, and her glasses were absent. I didn't think she could make herself look more beautiful, but she had managed to pull it off.

"Hello, Mr. Jones."

"Hi," I said, much too enthusiastically. "You look great."

Chrysus smiled. "Thank you."

"Ready to go?"

"Almost. Come in and have a seat. I shouldn't be too long."

I stepped through the door and into a long corridor flanked by marble pillars wrapped in ivy. Real ivy, not that fake, plastic alternative. Paintings of scenic vistas ornamented the walls, and gold lanterns hung from the ceiling.

The hall led straight back into the living room, which was decorated with light-blue walls and bronze floral patterns. The furniture was white. A grand piano occupied the far-left corner near the window. There were scuffmarks on the floor from where it had been carelessly dragged across the hardwood.

I sat down on the couch. "Nice place."

"Thank you," Chrysus said. "Would you like something to drink?"

"Nah."

"I'll be right back."

While Chrysus was gone, I stood and strolled around the living room. Everything was clean and expensive-looking. There wasn't so much as a speck of dust anywhere.

But as nice as the mansion was, it didn't have that lived-in feeling that made a house feel like a home. I supposed that made sense. Chrysus was Zeus's personal assistant and director of the Treasury. Her duties probably kept her away from home.

Chrysus returned after several minutes, and I led her outside. I couldn't help but feel a little embarrassed about my car. The flaking paint had gotten worse in the past few days, and the passenger-side door now creaked when opened. It was like the old girl was punishing me for trying to replace her.

I was worried that Chrysus would see my car and call off the date. Or at the very least, offer to drive in the Escalade. But to my surprise, she got right on in. No strange looks. No hesitation. Point for her.

"Where are we going?" she asked.

"I figured we'd go to a movie, then get a bite to eat."

"Dinner and a movie," she said, smiling. "A classic formula."

I couldn't tell if she was pleased or making fun of me. I chose the former.

"What kind of movies do you like?" I asked.

"Comedies."

"Romantic ones?"

"No."

I smiled. "We're going to get along just fine, you and me."

Chrysus and I didn't talk much on the way to the theater. I wanted to question her about Hera, but it was too soon for that. First I had to gain her trust. Make sure she was comfortable being around me. Then I'd see what I could get out of her.

It was time to lay on the old Jones family charm.

"Thanks for coming out," I said.

"You're welcome, Mr. Jones."

"Plato," I corrected her.

"I apologize."

"It's okay."

"You'll have to excuse me for not being more sociable," Chrysus said, keeping her eyes straight ahead. "I don't get out much."

"Work?"

She nodded.

"I know how that is," I said. "No matter how much you do, there's always more to be done."

"That's the truth."

I got onto the freeway, drove for several miles, and took exit twelve onto Cold Water Road. From there it was a straight shot to Laurel's Crossing, a popular shopping center.

The theater was at the far end of the center. A yellow neon sign that read GOLD BOW CINEMAS glowed above the main entrance.

Tonight the parking lot was packed—as it was every Saturday night. The line to the ticket booth extended out into the street. Kids ran wild all over the place, mobs of them, with no parents in sight.

Must be a new vampire flick premiering tonight.

As Chrysus and I waited in line, a group of preteens came to stand behind us. They chattered like parrots on caffeine pills. With them was a little girl in a blue-and-white dress. She couldn't have been any older than five or six. Her pale blond hair was in pigtails, and blue stickiness covered her mouth—she must have just eaten some candy.

One of the kids, a boy, bent down and whispered into her ear. I heard what he said. He told her to kick me. I hoped the little girl would be too timid to comply. But seconds later, her tiny foot struck me in the calf.

The kids all burst into laughter. My anger was hot and immediate. The immature part of my brain urged me to turn around and get cantankerous on their little asses. Under other circumstances, I might have given in. But something told me that Chrysus wouldn't condone my yelling at children, so I collared my emotions. Kept it cool.

The little girl kicked me a second time. I forced myself to do nothing. The kids laughed louder. I wanted to hang my head in shame, getting bullied by a prepubescent girl with pigtails. I had officially hit a new low. As we moved up in line, the kicking continued.

Now don't get me wrong. I like kids. I like them a lot. Heck, I'd even like to have a few of my own one day. What I don't like is parents who drop off their in kids public places—movie theaters, malls, bookstores—and expect society to fill the role of babysitter.

When Chrysus and I reached the ticket booth, I felt as though a weight had been lifted off me. I bought two tickets for the new Steve Carell movie. After we secured our seats, I went to the concession and picked up two large drinks and a large popcorn.

On the way back to the auditorium, we passed the little girl and her mob of deviants. The largest of them, a boy with a blond fauxhawk, held an extra-large cherry slushy. He was the first to spot me and began snickering. The others joined in. I *accidentally* bumped into slushy boy, causing him to spill his drink all over the little girl. She pouted and ran off, her entourage chasing after her.

That'll teach you to respect your elders, I thought.

Feeling vindicated, I returned to the auditorium and took my seat. As Chrysus and I sat in the darkness, waiting for the movie to start, I couldn't help noticing how stiff her posture was, and how daintily she ate her popcorn, meticulously picking out one kernel at a time, putting it in her mouth, and then wiping her fingertips on a napkin.

Was she always like this? Was this dry, bureaucratic persona the real her, or just a byproduct of working in a world of procedures and red tape?

Maybe there was another side to her. A fun, wild side she kept hidden from most people. I hoped so. It was disappointing to think that someone so pretty could be such a square.

I guess it didn't matter either way. My goal was to get information on Hera, not start a relationship.

After the movie, we drove to Claudia's Famous Steaks. The waiter seated us at a cozy corner booth. Chrysus had a plate of chicken parmesan. I ordered the top sirloin with fries. One bite and I could see why Claudia's steaks were so famous.

"Did you enjoy the movie?" I asked.

"Very much."

"That's good."

We ate in silence for a while. Chrysus cut a chunk of her chicken into bite-size portions and moved them to the side of her plate. Whenever she ate a piece, she followed it up with a bit of pasta, twirled neatly around her fork. Then she gingerly wiped her mouth with her napkin. Watching her, I could only imagine what my mother would say: "I like this one. She's so refined. You should marry her."

I pictured myself dying of embarrassment.

Chrysus sipped her champagne and wiped her mouth. Despite her red lipstick, she left no marks on the glass, or on the napkin. Impressive.

"Tell me," I said, cutting into my steak. "How long have you worked for Zeus?"

"Since he formed the council."

"That's a long time."

"For a mortal, perhaps," Chrysus said with a smile.

I ate a piece of meat. "How is Hera holding up? I can't imagine she's doing well considering everything that's happened."

"The First Lady is . . . upset by the recent losses."

"Understandably."

"President Zeus is helping her cope." Chrysus sighed then. "I can only imagine what she must be going through."

"Has the OBI made any progress?"

"Not much. Their forces are divided between hunting down the killer and protecting the First Family. After Eileithyia's murder, Zeus and Hera confined themselves to their complex on Mount Olympus. A team of agents watches over them day and night."

"They've been at home for the past month?" I asked.

"Yes."

I nodded, not at all surprised. Despite Hera's attempts on my life, I had reservations about her actually being the killer. Her hatred toward Hephaestus was evident. But she had nothing against Eileithyia. It made little sense that she'd kill both of them. All the same, I wasn't convinced that she and Zeus were totally innocent. Somehow, the two of them were at the root of this whole mess. Of that I was certain.

The waitress came by our table and refilled our drinks. I waited until she left before speaking. "Can you think of anyone who'd want to hurt Zeus and Hera?"

"I'm afraid you'll have to be more specific," Chrysus said. "The First Family has many enemies."

"Do you know of any that live in New Olympia?"

Chrysus pursed her lips. Then she said, "Callisto is the only one that comes to mind."

I recognized the name. Callisto was a nymph—a minor nature goddess—who had an affair with Zeus thousands of years ago. When Hera found out, she punished Callisto by turning her into a bear.

Images of Hephaestus's mangled body flashed in my head like snapshots. His injuries suggested he'd been attacked by a large animal. Could it have been a bear? The possibility was worth looking into.

"Thanks for the info," I said.

"Anything to help."

After dinner, I drove Chrysus home and walked her to her front door. For almost a minute we stared at each other, not saying a word. She was smiling. Her blue eyes sparkled in the night. I couldn't tell whether she wanted me to kiss her or not. I knew *I* wanted to. But I wasn't willing to risk it. Not yet anyway.

"Thank you for a wonderful time, Plato," Chrysus said.

"My pleasure."

She bit her bottom lip.

"Something wrong?" I asked.

"No, I just—" She shook her head.

"Hmm?"

She laughed softly. "This is a little embarrassing, but would you like to do this again sometime?"

"Excuse me?"

"Would you like to go out again?"

I hesitated, taken by surprise. During our date, I never got the sense that she was having a good time. Showed how little I knew about women.

"You're not interested," Chrysus said. "I understand."

"No, it's not that," I objected. "I'm just surprised."

"Why?"

"I didn't think you had a good time."

"I see." Chrysus shifted toward the door, her cheeks reddening.

"But to answer your question, yes, I would like to go out again."

She beamed at me.

"I'll call you sometime," I said.

"I look forward to it. Good night, Plato."

"Good night."

Chrysus stepped inside the mansion and closed the door. I walked back to my car. In terms of personality, she wasn't really my type. Too stuffy and guarded. But she was hot enough to justify a second date.

49

MY CELL PHONE RANG IN THE MIDDLE OF THE NIGHT, JERKING me out of my sleep. It was Hermes.

"Hello?" I said, yawning.

"Jones, we have a problem."

"What kind of problem?"

"A big one. Do you know where Enyo's house is?"

My heart gave a jolt. I didn't have to ask what was going on. "Yeah, I know where it is."

"Meet me there immediately."

"On my way."

I ended the call and rolled out of bed. I wrestled on a T-shirt and jeans. Before leaving my apartment complex, I bought a Coke from the vending machine outside the laundry room. I needed the sugar and caffeine.

At Enyo's mansion, four black sedans idled in the driveway. Hermes stood near the front door. I parked behind one of the sedans and got out.

Hermes came forward to meet me, frowning. "What took you so long?"

"I got here as fast as I could."

"Typical mortal. Full of excuses."

I was too tired to offer a witty rejoinder. "I need to see the body."

Hermes nodded. "Come with me."

The inside of the mansion reminded me of a mountain cabin. The walls, floors, and furnishings were all made of polished wood. A chimera-skin rug hung above the fireplace. I wondered if Enyo herself had slain the beast and skinned it. We went into the kitchen, where five OBI agents were snapping pictures and taking notes. The air reeked of decay, and was alive with swarms of flies.

Enyo's torso lay beside the island in the middle of the kitchen, rotting and covered in flies. The other half of her body was missing. Blood pooled beneath the body, but not as much blood as there should have been.

I knelt beside the torso and shooed the flies away. What remained of Enyo's corpse was clad in a black leather corset and a spiked collar. Dominatrix gear. Four large puncture wounds spotted her face. Her right eye had been gouged out. Maggots squirmed and wiggled inside the wounds.

Hermes remained near the entrance to the kitchen, leaning against the doorframe.

"She's been dead at least a week," he informed me.

"Who found the body?"

"One of our agents."

"Why was he in the area?"

"We received an anonymous call. The caller stated Enyo's address, then hung up. The voice was altered, but we suspect it was the killer."

"Did you gather any more info from the call?" I asked.

"No."

"Were you able to trace it?"

"There wasn't enough time."

I finished examining Enyo and stood up. "Where's the rest of the body?"

"Missing," Hermes said. "We're still looking for it."

I borrowed a pair of examiner's gloves from one of the agents and started looking for clues. The cabinet beneath the sink was slightly ajar. Cleaning supplies littered the inside: bleach, dish detergent, wood polisher, and so on. Most of the bottles had been knocked over. I checked the other cabinets. Their contents were neatly arranged.

I removed my gloves, dropped them into the trash can, and walked over to Hermes.

"What you do make of this?" he asked.

"Enyo had a friend over," I said. "A friend with benefits, given the clothes she's wearing. Now, let's assume this friend of hers is our killer. He and Enyo have just finished having sex. Enyo goes to the kitchen for a snack. Her friend follows and *bam*, he attacks her from behind, somehow killing her. After she's dead, he wipes away his fingerprints. Then he leaves."

"What about the other half of the body?" Hermes asked.

"If he and Enyo were having sex prior to the murder, there'd be DNA evidence inside her."

"So the killer gets rid of it."

I nodded. "And since the killer probably isn't human, there's a chance the missing half was eaten."

Hermes balked at the notion. "Monstrous!"

"Very."

We moved aside as the OBI's medical examiner entered the kitchen. She wore a black short-sleeve shirt and rubber gloves. Her curly brown hair was some of the shiniest I had ever seen, and her face could have graced the cover of beauty magazines. If only she didn't have goat legs. I made a mental note to mention her to Geno.

"Can I ask you a question?" I asked Hermes.

"What is it?"

"A while back, I asked if there was anyone or anything strong enough to kill a God. You said you didn't know. Does that answer still stand?"

Hermes's eyes grew cold. "Are you calling me a liar, Mr. Jones?"

"Not necessarily."
"Then why bring this up again?"
"It never hurts to double-check."
"I wouldn't be so sure about that," Hermes said.

50

THE NEXT MORNING, I SAT IN MY OFFICE, THINKING.

With Enyo dead, I now had a new suspect in the form of Collin Stone. Until I had a chance to speak with him, I planned to keep his existence a secret from the OBI. Though relationships between Gods and mortals were fairly common, some of the bigwigs on Olympus, like Hera and Hermes, weren't too fond of them. Whether Collin was guilty or not wouldn't matter to them. They'd find a way to pin the crime on him. Probably have him executed within the month. I refused to let that happen.

If Collin was in fact the culprit, how did he manage to kill Enyo and the other two victims? He was, after all, only human. Or at least I thought he was. There are plenty of supernatural creatures that appear to be human: sirens, vampires, shapeshifters. Any one of them could easily kill the average human. But none are powerful enough to go toe-to-toe with a God, let alone kill one. Maybe Collin was a new type of creature, one that no one had ever heard of. And I had to confront him. Lucky me.

I called Bellanca to see if Collin had tried to contact her again. She answered on the second ring.

"Hello?"

"Hi, Bellanca. It's Plato Jones."

Her voice instantly perked up. "Oh hi, Plato. How are you?"

"I'm fine. How about yourself?"

"I'm okay. Have you found Collin?"

"Not yet. I just wanted to know how things were going on your end. Has Collin tried to contact you again?"

"No, I haven't heard anything from him."

Damn. On to plan B. "I'd like to talk to his parents if possible," I said. "Do you have their number?"

"I do." Bellanca gave me the phone number.

I jotted it down on a sticky note. "Thanks."

"Is there anything else you need? I want to help however I can."

"No, that's it for now," I said. "I'll call you if there're any new developments."

"Bye, Plato. And thanks again for helping me out. You're a good guy."

"Don't mention it. Take care now." I ended the call and tried Collin's parents. Maybe I'd have more luck with them. Their number was international. San Francisco, California. It went straight to the answering machine.

"This is Alice Stone," said a woman's prerecorded voice. "We're unable to take your call right now, but if you leave your name, number, and a brief message, we'll make sure to get back to you."

Another dead end. I hung up after the beep, leaned back in my chair, and pondered my next move. For several minutes I was shooting blanks. Then I remembered my last trip to the Ammo Crate. Uncle Magus mentioned that a man had ordered fifty boxes of osmium bullets. Unusual, to say the least. Could that man have been Collin? It was unlikely, but still worth a look.

Around lunchtime, I drove to the Ammo Crate. Magus was behind the counter, doing some paperwork. His blue-and-green polo looked new, as did his checkered sun visor.

"You're looking sharp," I said.

"PJ," he said, shuffling his stacks of papers. "Back so soon?"

"Yep. Can I ask a favor?"

"Of course." Magus put aside his pen and calculator and looked up, smiling. "You need to place another order?"

"No, nothing like that. Actually, I'm looking for someone. He might be a customer of yours."

"One of my customers?"

I nodded.

"What does he look like?"

I handed him the picture of Collin that Bellanca had given me. He squinted as he examined it.

"This is an older picture of him," I said. "Now he has a scar on his right cheek."

Magus passed the picture back to me. "Yeah, I've seen him. He's the one who ordered all those osmium bullets."

Jackpot! "Do you have his contact information on file?"

Magus typed something into the computer and turned the monitor toward me.

Travis Martin was the name Collin had provided. I was betting the address was fake too. The phone number was probably real though. If it wasn't, Magus would have no way of contacting him once his order arrived. I took out my cell and added the number to my list of contacts.

"His order hasn't arrived yet, has it?" I asked.

"No. Large orders like his take longer to fill."

"I need you to call me the moment it gets in. Preferably before Mr. Martin comes to pick it up."

"Sure. But why are you after one of my customers?"

"Sorry, that information's classified."

"If you told me you'd have to kill me, huh?"

I grinned. "Afraid so."

"Figures." Magus smirked.

"Thanks, Unc."

"Yeah, yeah."

I was about to leave when I remembered something. "Oh, before I forget. Guess who's back on the dating scene."

Magus's eyes widened. "You've found someone?"

"Maybe."

He leaned forward and propped his elbows on the counter. "Tell me about her."

"Well, let's see. She's beautiful. Smart. Poised. Not much of a personality. But the looks more than make up for it."

"Sounds promising. Does she have any single relatives? A lonely aunt perhaps? One with nice breasts and a little waist."

"In other words, boobs on a stick."

Magus shrugged.

"You're a dirty old man, Uncle Magus."

"I know."

51

THE FOLLOWING MORNING, I DECIDED IT WAS TIME TO SPEAK
with Callisto. At 10:15 a.m. I sat at my kitchen table and called
the records office on Olympus. The clerk gave me some basic
information on Callisto, as well as her last known address.

Even with the Aegis, I disliked the idea of being face to
face with a bear, especially if said bear wasn't very friendly.
I'd feel more comfortable with backup. I knew Herc would be
up for it. He didn't act like it most of the time, but he was a
warrior at his core. Always down to bust some skulls should
the need ever arise. I was about to call him, but he beat me
to the punch.

"What's up?" I said.

"I'm pissed, Jonesy." Herc's voice sounded more strained
than usual.

"Again? What is it now?"

"I found someone snooping outside my house late last
night."

"Paparazzi?"

"No."

"You sure?"

"Positive," Herc said. "I was taking out the trash when I
heard a rustling sound coming from the side of the house. I

went to check it out and found someone all in black sneaking through the bushes. When he saw me, he took off. I chased after the guy, but it was too dark."

"You lost track of him?"

"Yeah," Herc said ruefully. "Bastard was fast. Inhumanly fast."

A chill raised the hair on the back of my neck. "You think it was the killer?"

"I do."

"Where's Hebe?" I asked. "Is she alright?"

"She's fine. I sent her to stay with Dad and Hera until this whole thing blows over."

"Good. Listen, Herc. I need your help with something."

"What's up?"

"I plan to interrogate a potentially dangerous subject, and I may need backup."

"Count me in," Herc said without hesitation. "I've been dying to see some action. So, who are we going after?"

"Her name's Callisto. You heard of her?"

"The bear woman? Yeah, I've heard of her. Never met her though."

"From what I understand, she has a grudge against Hera," I said. "If she turns out to be the killer, I doubt she'll surrender quietly."

Herc cracked his knuckles. "Suits me just fine."

52

Years ago, Callisto started calling herself a supreme goddess. She thought that being a bear had somehow put her on par with the Olympians. I'm not sure how she came to that conclusion, but it got her into some serious trouble.

Callisto broke the news of her newfound ascension to the entire world via public-access television. She went on to become a televangelist. Her goal was to spread the word of the Bear Goddess, convince people to worship her instead of the Olympians. Before long, she gained a small following of wackos.

Naturally, the Olympians didn't appreciate what she was doing and warned her to stop. When she refused, they tried to have her assassinated. Allegedly. The attempt failed, but Callisto was so shaken up she cancelled her show and skipped town, along with several members of her congregation. The Bear Cult survived, but its existence faded from most people's memories.

I pulled into the parking lot of the Temple of the Bear. It was located on the western edge of Boreasville, far removed from New Olympia. The temple acted as both a home and a place of worship for Callisto and her followers.

The pyramid-shaped structure sat in a clearing in the middle of the woods, surrounded by ancient trees. It had no windows and only one door. Its snow-white exterior shone blindingly bright in the sunshine. The temple stood in stark contrast against the smooth black asphalt. A nondescript white van was parked at the far end of the lot. There were no other cars around.

Herc stared up at the temple. "Creepy."

"You got that right," I said.

"You think they'll let us in?"

"I doubt it."

"You got a plan?"

"Nope."

We got out of the car and walked to the main entrance. Broad steps led up to massive double doors. A thin rope hung beside the entrance. I gave it a tug. A bell rang inside the building.

A large man in a white T-shirt and sweatpants answered the door, a walkie-talkie in his hand. He had short brown hair, thick eyebrows, and a bushy beard. His close-set beady eyes gave us the once-over. Suspicion rolled off him in waves.

"Who are you?" he demanded, his voice harsh and raspy. "State your business." He must've smoked a lot. I wondered if he had ever set his beard on fire.

"My name is Plato Jones." I inclined my head toward Herc. "This is my associate, Hercules, son of Zeus."

Herc held up his hand. "Hey."

"I'm a private investigator." I flashed my badge. "I'd like to speak with Callisto, if that's possible."

"The Goddess does not wish to be disturbed," the bearded man rasped.

I tried again. "I just want to ask her a few questions."

"I repeat: the Goddess does not wish to be disturbed."

I smiled politely. "It'll only take a few minutes. Then we'll be on our way."

"No."

"Don't be a jerk, pal," Herc cut in.

"Get out of here." The bearded man slammed the door in our faces.

"That went well," I said.

"Want me to smash the door in?" Herc asked.

"That won't be necessary." I rang the bell again.

The same man answered the door. His small eyes narrowed.

"Quick question," I said to him. "Can you tell me when Callisto will be accepting guests?"

"Never," he said.

"You sure about that?"

"I told you to go away."

"I'm afraid I can't do that. You see, I really need to speak with Callisto. It'll just take a second. Promise."

The man mumbled something into his walkie-talkie, and then put it in a swivel holster on his belt. Seconds later, four equally large men appeared behind him. All were dressed in white tees and sweat pants. The bearded man stepped outside, and the others followed.

"Look, we don't want any trouble." I held up my hands.

"Then leave. Now," the bearded man said.

"Not until you let me see Callisto."

"Have it your way." The guy glanced at his buddies and nodded. The five of them rushed us.

Herc stood his ground near the steps, while I retreated to the parking lot. I fought better when I had room to maneuver. The bearded man chased after me. The other four goons tried their luck with Herc. My opponent had about fifty pounds on me, but I could tell by the way he moved that he wasn't much of a fighter. Poor fool had no idea what he was getting into. I tried one last time to reason with him.

"You don't want to do this," I said.

He threw a wide hook. I dodged the blow and countered with a knife-hand strike to the throat. He made a croaking sound and stumbled backward, clutching his neck. It only took him a second to recover, and when he did, he came at me swinging.

His blows were wild and slow, easy to avoid. When he reared back for a haymaker, I saw an opportunity to end the fight. I stomped on his foot. The tactic surprised him, caused him to hesitate. I struck him just below the nose with my palm. He crumpled to the pavement, groaning, his hands over his face.

A man in white went sailing past me. He struck the ground and rolled several feet before coming to a stop. I jerked my head toward the temple entrance.

Herc stood near the base of the stairs. Two men lay unconscious at his feet. A third dangled in Herc's grip, held in the air by his neck.

"You okay, Jonesy?" Herc asked. He hadn't even broken a sweat.

"Just fine," I panted. "How about you?"

"I'm great."

I looked around at the injured men and shook my head. "I wish we could have avoided all this."

"Hey, shit happens."

"Will you keep an eye on these guys while I talk to Callisto?"

"No problem." Herc dropped the man, who fell to the ground gasping and coughing. "Shout if you need help."

"Will do," I promised. "Just try not to kill anyone while I'm gone."

53

I STEPPED THROUGH THE DOORWAY. A BREEZE OF COOL AIR hit me. It was just what I needed after the fight in the parking lot.

A red carpet ran through the middle of the worship hall toward the pulpit. White pews flanked either side of it. A gold altar sparkled at the head of the worship hall. Behind it hung a stained glass mural of a brown bear standing atop a mountain I assumed to be Olympus. The artificial lighting gave the place an eerie blue tint. Everything was silent except the hum of the air conditioner.

A doorway to the right of the altar led me into a maze of corridors with unmarked white doors. I was hesitant to open them for fear of running into more fanatics. Or a bear's gaping mouth.

I soon came to a door with a gold doorknocker on it. The knocker was shaped like the head of a bear. I sensed a theme.

I rapped the knocker. The sound echoed throughout the hall, and I instinctively glanced over my shoulder. A latch released with a soft click. Then a small voice came from the other side of the door.

"Enter."

I opened the door and stepped into an office or, should I say, the template for an office. The walls and floor were white and featureless. A small desk stood near the east wall, and the room had no other furniture. A computer sat on top of the desk—one of those all-in-one desktops—along with a white phone. At the back of the room were large double doors, framed in a gold border with intricate carvings. The doors were outlined in blue masking tape, and the faint smell of paint lingered. I assumed Callisto and her followers were in the process of redecorating.

A girl who looked about twelve or thirteen sat behind the desk. She was bony and freckled. Her blond hair hung in a long ponytail. Her green eyes sparkled. Like the men outside, she too was dressed in all white.

She gasped and shot out of her chair, her eyes wide. "Wh-who are you?"

When she'd released the door latch, she had probably been expecting someone else. The bearded man or one of his goons perhaps.

I offered her a friendly smile. "Don't be alarmed. I'm not here to cause trouble. My name is Plato Jones. I'm a private investigator. I'd like to speak with Callisto."

The girl shook her head briskly. "The mistress is not to be disturbed."

I wondered why Callisto even bothered to have an office if she never received visitors. I nodded and said, "Okay. Can I set up an appointment for later?"

"No. You have to leave, now."

"I will. I promise. But first I need to speak with Callisto."

Before the girl could respond, the phone on her desk rang. She answered it, keeping her eyes on me.

"Mistress?" She paused, listening. "Yes, right away."

The girl pressed a button under her desk, and the double doors slowly swung open. She smiled at me. The fear was gone from her eyes, as if it had never been there.

"The Goddess will see you now."

"Thanks." I went through the doors.

Beyond was an indoor garden, complete with trees, bushes, and rock sculptures. Everywhere I looked, there was another explosion of multicolored flowers. I heard birdsong and a babbling brook, but I saw no birds, and no running water. I supposed the noises came from speakers hidden throughout the garden.

Callisto was the eight-hundred-pound bear in the room. She lounged atop a large stone altar in the center of the garden. Touches of white spotted her otherwise brown fur. A transparent white cloak draped her body, and a queen's ransom of gold and diamond jewelry gleamed on her neck and legs.

Two men in white loincloths stood before the altar, holding AK-47s. Both were skinny and pale, with no visible body hair. Their eyes were large and vacant.

There was something very wrong about this scene. I pretended not to know what that something was.

With a rustle of fur and a clink of jewelry, Callisto sat up.

"Hello," was the only thing I could think to say.

When Callisto spoke, her mouth moved just like a human's. "Greetings, friend. Welcome to my home."

Her voice was low and gentle, like a grandmother's. But it didn't put me at ease. In spite of how nice the voice sounded, it still came from a creature that could have broken me in half with one swipe of its paw. Why did I leave Herc outside?

I nodded in greeting. "My name is Plato Jones. I'm a private investigator. I need to ask you a few questions, if that's alright."

"Certainly."

I glanced at the two bodyguards . . . playboys . . . or whatever they were.

"In private," I said.

Callisto glanced at the men. At once, they shouldered their guns and marched from the garden into the office I'd just left.

"Thanks."

"You're very welcome," Callisto said. "Before we get started, I would like to apologize for what happened out front. My children were merely trying to protect me."

"You know about that?"

She smiled. The way her bottom lip hung made the gesture look a tad dopey. But her eyes shone with intelligence. "I know everything that goes on in my home."

"In that case, let *me* apologize for beating the tar out of them."

Callisto nodded. "Ever since the OBI came here, my children have been on edge."

"The OBI's been here?"

"Yes. Like you, they came to interrogate me about the recent murders."

"How did that go?"

"Badly, I'm afraid. Because of my history with the First Family, they were convinced that I was guilty. They took my children hostage. Threatened to hurt them if I did not confess."

"I take it you didn't comply."

Callisto shook her head. The jewelry around her neck glittered and jingled. "I cannot tell a lie, Mr. Jones, even to protect my family. It would go against everything I stand for."

A bear with a sense of honor. Now I'd seen everything.

"I can't imagine the OBI took kindly to that," I said.

Callisto frowned. "Three of my children were beaten—almost to death. It pained me to see them suffer, but I stuck to my convictions. When the agents finally realized I wasn't going to budge, they gave up and left."

"I'm sorry to hear that," I said truthfully. "The OBI has a habit of pushing people around."

"I told them I was no longer angry with Hera for what she did to me. And that my children and I wished only to live in peace. But they called me a liar. Do you believe as they do, Mr. Jones? That I am a killer?"

"Until I have all the facts, no one is guilty," I said. *Or innocent.*

"You are either very wise or very naïve."

"We'll go with the first one."

Callisto laughed. It sounded odd coming from a bear. "What would you like to know, Mr. Jones?"

"I'd like to know what you've been up to for the past month."

"I haven't been up to anything. I've been here the entire time."

"The *entire* time?"

Callisto nodded. "I have not ventured outside these walls in twenty years."

I cocked my brows. "Why?"

"My children will not permit me to leave. They wish to protect me from the outside world, from those who would do me harm."

"Hera and the other Gods, you mean?"

"I have forgiven Hera for turning me into a beast, because it led me to my family. But I doubt the hatred she has toward me has diminished."

"Yeah, Hera doesn't strike me as the forgiving type," I said. "Can you prove you were here at the time of the murders?"

Callisto nodded. "To ensure my safety, my children keep me under constant surveillance. If you like, I can provide you with surveillance footage from the last twenty years."

I raised my hand. "Just the footage from last month will be fine."

"Very well."

"Let's assume for a second that this footage proves your innocence. Do you know of anyone who has a grudge against the First Family?"

"Oh yes. Zeus and Hera have garnered many enemies over the centuries."

"Any of these enemies live in New Olympia?"

Callisto glanced at the ceiling, apparently thinking. "Lamia is the only one I know of. Centuries ago, she had an affair with Zeus and bore him children. When Hera discovered the truth, she was enraged. She had the children murdered. Grief drove Lamia insane, and she began killing random children."

"And eating them?" I asked.

"No," Callisto said. "That part of the story was invented by parents to scare their children into behaving. You had better be good, or Lamia will come and gobble you up." She chuckled.

Listening to her story made me think of the painting I'd seen in Hades's office. The one of a woman eating a baby.

"Where I can find her?" I asked.

"I don't know. I haven't seen her in over forty years."

I spent the next two days at my apartment, examining the footage Callisto had given me. I watched it in fast-forward on my Blu-ray player.

Every day was basically the same. Callisto awoke in the garden. Her disciples served her breakfast on a gold platter— a lamb or pig carcass. Once she was done eating, she gave an oration in the worship hall. Services lasted hours, and involved a lot of chanting and swaying back and forth on the part of the audience. At the conclusion of each service, Callisto returned to the garden, where her followers served her dinner—another carcass.

After dinner, Callisto and her two bodyguards engaged in various . . . activities. We'll call them exercises. Highly disturbing exercises. Then she would climb onto her altar and sleep for the rest of the day. Rinse and repeat.

As far as I could tell, the footage hadn't been doctored. There were no weird skips. No missing portions. Callisto was in the clear, for the moment. It irritated me to lose yet another suspect. But my visit to the Temple of the Bear hadn't been a total bust. It gave me a new name to add to my list of suspects.

Of all the would-be killers out there, Lamia probably had the best motivation. Her children had been murdered by Hera. It only made sense that she'd react in kind.

I called the records office on Olympus for information on Lamia. As I waited for the clerk to pull up her file, I thought about how I'd finally gotten the break I had been waiting for. The one that was going to bust this case wide open.

Then I found out that Lamia had killed herself ten years ago.

54

F RIDAY EVENING, I WAS DRIVING HOME FROM THE OFFICE when Chrysus called.

"Plato, I hope I haven't caught you at a bad time."

"Not at all." I held my cell phone between my ear and shoulder as I made a turn. "How are you?"

"Good. Very good. I won't take up much of your time. I just wanted to know if you were still interested in that second date."

I tried to keep the smile out of my voice. "I am. When are you available?"

"Tonight, if that's all right."

"Tonight's perfect. What time would you like me to pick you up?"

"Eight?"

"Eight it is."

"See you then, Plato."

I ended the call and rushed to my apartment to get cleaned up. I took a quick shower, toweled off, and rummaged through my closet for something to wear.

A lot of guys have trouble picking out date clothes. For me it's a fairly easy procedure. When in doubt, go simple. A nice button-up, slacks, and dress shoes usually get the job done.

271

After I'd dressed, I sprayed myself with cologne and was out the door. En route to Chrysus's place, I stopped by a grocery store and picked up a dozen red roses. A little spoiling never hurt.

I arrived at Chrysus's house and rang the doorbell. She answered the door in a red mini-dress and matching heels. Blond hair billowed around her shoulders, and her makeup was bright. We smiled at the same time.

"You look great," I said.

"So do you."

I handed her the roses. "These are for you."

Chrysus's smile widened. She sniffed them. "Thank you. They're lovely."

"They match your outfit."

"Yes, they do. So, where are you taking me?"

"Diamond Earl's. I figured it'd be a nice departure from the old dinner-and-a-movie format. You heard of it?"

Chrysus shook her head. "I can't say that I have."

"In that case, you're in for a surprise."

We drove across town to the boardwalk. Diamond Earl's was part restaurant, part video arcade. It was a popular haunt for professionals looking to cut loose after a hard week. Laughter filled the place, and digitized sound effects spewed from the arcade machines. Disco balls revolved overhead, giving off a kaleidoscope of colors. Bringing a classy woman like Chrysus to a place like this was a big risk, but a necessary one. She might consider me immature after this date, but I needed to know if she had a fun side under all that stuffiness.

The hostess seated us in a booth near the bar. Around us, men and women were getting wasted and pumping tokens into arcade machines. Several groups of small children were sprinkled into the mix. They ran wild, laughing and screaming and clutching streamers of prize tickets. Some genius parents thought it was a good idea to bring their kids along to spoil the vibe. I supposed it didn't really matter. Later, I'd be too slammed to notice them.

A waitress took our drink orders—a cute brunette with full cheeks and large brown eyes. I asked for a gin and tonic. Chrysus got a Manhattan.

"Nice place, huh?" I asked.

Chrysus looked around. "It's . . . interesting."

"You ever been anywhere like this before?"

That moment, a group of children rushed past our table. One of them bumped her chair.

Chrysus gave a stiff smile. "Never."

"You don't like it." It was a statement, not a question.

She smiled apologetically. "It's not that. It's just that this is all so unfamiliar. I feel out of my element."

I grinned. "That'll change after a few rounds. Trust me."

"I'll take your word for it."

The waitress returned with our drinks and set them on the table. "You two ready to order?"

I looked to Chrysus. She shrugged.

"Yeah, I think we're ready," I told the waitress.

She took out her notepad. Chrysus ordered the grilled salmon pasta. I wanted a steak, though I'd already eaten too much red meat this week. But what the heck? You only live once—most of us, anyway.

The waitress wrote down our orders and hurried off.

I tried my gin and tonic. Nice and strong, just how I liked them. A few more would get me where I needed to be.

"Thanks for coming out," I said to Chrysus.

"You don't have to thank me." She shook her head. "I'm the one who proposed the second date, remember?"

"Yeah, I remember. I'm still in shock over that, by the way. It's not every day that a gorgeous woman asks me out. It's usually the other way around."

She smiled.

"Why don't you tell me a little about yourself?" I suggested. "What do you like to do?"

"Besides work?"

"Yes, besides that."

Chrysus narrowed her eyes, as though considering. "I like lots of things. But if I had to choose, I'd say I'm most partial to fishing."

I cocked my brows, impressed. *A woman who fishes and drives a truck. I must be in Elysium.* "Oh really?"

She nodded. "I enjoy the serenity. In the city everything is so frantic, so chaotic. No one ever sits still. It's nice to get away from all that and go back to a simpler time. But I'm rambling." She sipped her drink. "Let's talk about you now. What's your favorite hobby?"

"I collect comic books."

The corners of Chrysus's mouth twitched upward. "Aren't you a little old to be reading comics?"

"For your information, I don't *read* comics. I collect them. Reading them decreases their value."

"It still sounds a bit childish to me."

"It's not childish," I argued. "I'll have you know that comics are big business."

"If you say so." She giggled.

"Can I ask you something?"

"Of course."

"Are you a Goddess?"

"Actually, I'm a spirit," Chrysus said. "This body of mine is a vessel."

"So you're a ghost, then?"

"Not exactly. A ghost is a spirit of the dead. I am very much alive."

"How'd you get the body?"

"Hephaestus made it for me, long ago."

I leaned back, my mind blown. "He *made* a body for you? Is it organic?"

"Yes."

I tried to respond but the words stuck in my throat. Since the Gods seldom flaunted their abilities, it was sometimes easy to forget how amazing they were.

"This body was designed to be faster and stronger than a human," Chrysus continued. "And it never ages."

I stared at her, unable to wrap my mind around this. "Hephaestus was a true genius."

"Yes, he was."

I took a large swig of my drink. I needed it. "What would happen to you if your body were destroyed? Would you be destroyed along with it? Or would you just float around until you found another?"

Chrysus's blue eyes brightened when she laughed. "I would float around. Have you ever seen that speck of light in the corner of your eye? That would be me."

"So you're immortal?"

"I suppose so, but not invincible. My body can be trapped or injured, and I wouldn't be able to escape—just like anyone else. But we're talking about me again. I'd like to know more about you. Your file says that you're divorced."

"You read my file?"

"Yes. I like to know what kind of people I'm associating with before I go out with them. I hope you're not insulted."

"It'll take more than that to insult me," I assured her. "But yeah, I'm divorced."

"What happened?"

"Work happened." I finished off the last of my drink in one gulp. "My obligations to the OBI kept me away from home for most of the year. Alexis wanted a man who could spend more time with her. So she divorced me and found herself one."

Chrysus reached across the table and patted my hand. "I'm sorry to hear that."

I shook my head. "It's ancient history."

The waitress appeared to tell us our orders were almost ready. I requested another gin and tonic. Chrysus asked for an apple martini. The waitress ran off and came back shortly with our drinks. After she had gone, Chrysus asked, "Was it an ugly divorce?"

"Not really. I let her have the house and the cars. We split the money equally. I used my half to start my agency. I'm not sure what she used hers for."

"Do you still love her?"

I swirled my drink. The ice clinked against the sides of the glass. "Yeah, I guess I do. In a way. But it doesn't matter in the grand scheme of things. You can love someone with all your heart, but if you're not meant to be together, then you just won't be. No use lamenting over it. You know what I mean?"

"I believe so."

"How about you?" I said. "Were you ever married?"

"Yes. A long time ago."

"Was your husband a spirit?"

"No, he was mortal, a human," Chrysus said. "He died of old age."

"I'm sorry."

"Don't be. It is, as you say, ancient history."

I sipped my drink. "Do you date a lot?"

Chrysus laughed softly. "No. Like you, I also have trouble finding a balance between work and relationships. Some men don't appreciate a career-driven woman."

"You think you'll ever settle down again?"

"Eventually. And you?"

"Eventually."

She grinned.

I raised my glass. "Here's to eventuality."

55

CHRYSUS AND I ORDERED MORE DRINKS. DON'T ASK ME HOW many. All I knew is that by ten o'clock my head was in the clouds, and I was seeing double. Chrysus wasn't faring any better.

Apparently, her body wasn't as resistant to alcohol as Gods and Demigods. A flush colored her cheeks, and she'd become more talkative. We played skee-ball, pool, and a few rounds of air hockey before calling it a night. I would've done the gentlemanly thing by allowing her to win, but there was no need. She spanked me in everything.

"Are you ready to depart, milady?" I asked.

"I believe so."

We left Diamond Earl's and went back to Chrysus's mansion. I walked her to the door.

"Thank you for a wonderful time," she said, her voice mildly slurred.

"You're very welcome."

"We'll have to do it again sometime."

"The sooner the better."

We stood on the doorstep, looking into each other's eyes, not saying a word. Chrysus glanced at the door. "Would you like to come in?"

"Sure," I said, before even thinking about it.

Chrysus led me into the living room. I settled onto the couch while she took her bouquet of roses to the kitchen. She came back and sat beside me.

"Would you like to watch some television?" she asked.

Not really. "Okay."

Chrysus grabbed the remote from the coffee table and turned on the TV. There was a cooking show on. We watched in silence until the commercial break, at which point our gazes drifted toward each other. As soon as our eyes met, it was on. I leaned forward and kissed her. She kissed me back. Her lips were soft, her tongue a silky wetness in my mouth.

I slid my arm around her waist and pulled her closer. I kissed her on the neck and trailed my tongue upward to her earlobes. Chrysus moaned deep in her throat, squirming against me.

"We shouldn't do this." She started to unbutton my shirt.

"Why not?"

Chrysus removed my shirt and tossed it aside. She ran her tongue along my chest and traced circles around my nipples. I pulled her onto my lap so she straddled me. My hands squeezed her ass.

She kissed me hard and then broke away, breathless. "Gods, it's been a long time," she whispered.

I pulled down her dress straps, to reveal breasts that were large and round and perfect. I buried my face in them. Chrysus gasped.

My cell phone rang. We both froze. I felt the white-hot urge to curse. But more than that, I wanted to kill the caller, whoever it was.

"Are you going to get that?" Chrysus asked, still out of breath.

I lifted her off me and took out my cell phone. I glanced at the caller ID, expecting to see Hermes's number. But the caller was unknown. I hesitated to answer. It was probably a wrong number.

"Hello?"

"Is this Plato Jones?" The voice on the other end belonged to a man. It sounded vaguely familiar, but I couldn't place it.

"Yes," I said uncertainly. "Who is this?"

"Someone who wants to help you."

"With what?"

"What do you think?"

"I think I don't have time for this."

"Don't play dumb," the voice said. "I know you're hunting a God-killer."

My heart all but stopped. I stood up.

"Surprised?" the voice asked.

"Are you . . . ?"

"The killer? Well that depends on which murder you're talking about. If your referring to the murders of Eileithyia, Hephaestus, and Enyo, the answer is no."

"Then who are you?"

"I can be your best friend or your worst enemy," the voice said. "The choice is yours. See you soon."

The line went dead.

Chrysus was standing up now. She had restored her dress straps. Her cheeks, neck, and chest were flushed, and her blond hair stood out at odd angles.

"What was that about?" she asked.

I stuck my phone in my pants pocket. "I wish I knew."

We avoided eye contact. Silence filled the space between us—the kind that descends when a mood is broken beyond repair. There was nothing left to do but go home and take a cold shower.

"I should probably go," I said.

Chrysus returned a quick nod. "I think that would be wise."

"We should go out again, sometime."

"I'd like that."

"How about next Friday?"

Chrysus smiled regretfully. "I would love to, but I have plans."

"Work?"

"Afraid so."

I tried not to look upset, despite my frustration. "Some other time, then."

I put my shirt back on and Chrysus walked me to the door. After an awkward good-night kiss, I got in my car.

Driving home, all I could think of was how close I came to getting Chrysus out of that dress and onto the living room floor. I still smelled her perfume on my skin. Damn that caller, whoever he was. Next time, I'd have to put my phone on silent.

56

My hangover was ruthless. Nausea, headache, sensitivity to light—the whole nine yards. But somehow I managed to make it through work.

I got home just as the streetlamps began to light up. As I reached into my pocket for my keys, I noticed my door was slightly ajar. The knob hung askew, broken. My senses went on high alert. A burglar. Wonderful. Just wonderful.

I drew my gun and flattened against the wall next to the door. Three break-ins in less than two years. That had to have been some kind of record for this part of town. The first thief got away with my laptop and MP3 player. The second didn't fare as lucky. He ended up in the ER with a bullet in his kneecap. Served him right.

No sounds issued from inside the apartment. Maybe the thief had gone. Or maybe he was lying in wait. Unfortunately, there was only one way to know for sure.

I counted to three and shoved open the door. I aimed my gun at a shadowy figure on the couch.

"Don't move!" I shouted.

The figure raised his hands. "Oh no. You've caught me. Whatever will I do?"

I kept my gun trained on him as I hit the lights. "Ares?"

"Welcome home."

I put away my gun. Ares lowered his hands.

"So you're Plato Jones, huh?" he said. "I expected you to be taller."

"You owe me a new doorknob."

"You weren't home when I got here. I didn't feel like waiting outside." He glanced around the room. "Your place is a dump."

I closed the door and placed a chair in front of it. Though in truth, it might have been safer to leave it open. The God of War didn't look particularly threatening, but that was just an illusion. He was tall and athletically built—like a professional swimmer—with crimson eyes and a charming smile. His leather jacket, white T-shirt, and jeans added to the cool vibe. Lines of red streaked his shoulder-length black hair.

"What are you doing in town?" I asked. "I thought you and your band were on tour."

Ares grinned his famous rock-star grin. I'd seen it on TV a few times before. "You follow my band?"

I shook my head. "Saw you on TMZ."

Ares nodded. "Got any beer?"

"What? You didn't ransack the fridge while I was out?"

He returned a sly grin. "I didn't find any."

"I'm all out. Sorry."

"That's too bad."

"You're telling me." I walked past him and sat on my recliner.

"I heard you've been screwing Aphrodite."

"You heard wrong."

"I guess so," Ares said. "You're still sane, after all. At least as far as I can tell."

"Is there a reason you're here?" I asked outright. I was out of patience with the Gods.

"Actually there is. You met with my father. He persuaded you to investigate the recent murders."

"Persuaded. That's funny."

Ares got up and sauntered around the apartment. "I've come to help you."

"Help me?" Just then, something clicked in my head. "Wait a minute. You're the one who called me last night."

Ares took a bow. "Guilty as charged."

"Thanks to you I missed out on what might have been the most exciting *bust* of my career."

"I'd like to apologize."

"Doesn't help. But thanks, I guess."

"I said I'd *like* to apologize." Ares smiled. "Not that I was going to."

I sighed. "You mentioned something about helping me."

"Indeed I did. I want to join your investigation."

"No way," I said, shaking my head.

Ares stopped walking around the room and turned toward me. An amused grin played on his face. "Excuse me?"

I went into the kitchen. I wanted to put as much distance between us as possible. "Look, I appreciate the offer," I called across the kitchen bar, which opened into the living room, "but the answer is no."

"You seem to be confused. This isn't a request."

Instinctively, I checked the refrigerator for beer. Still out of stock. "Call it whatever you'd like. The answer is still the same. You can't join me on this case."

Ares's eyes shone with laughter. "You're a bold little mortal, aren't you?"

"All I'm saying is that a case this sensitive requires a gentle approach."

"I can be gentle."

I smirked. "Somehow I doubt that. I've heard stories about the things you've done."

"Oh really?"

"Does the word Troy ring a bell?"

Ares winced. "A bit of a low blow, don't you think?"

"Maybe."

"Troy was a long time ago. I've changed since then. I'm a new man, so to speak."

I believed him to an extent. He was a far cry from the psychopath I had read about in history books, but that wasn't saying much. He was still bat-shit crazy, and letting him tag along would be an invitation for disaster.

"Sorry," I said. "It's still a no."

Ares came into the kitchen and stopped a few inches away from me. He was no longer smiling. His crimson eyes stared me in the face. I fought the urge to look away.

"I need to find the person who killed my siblings," he said in a low, even tone. "I need to make them pay."

"I understand where you're coming from, but there are certain procedures that have to be followed when conducting an investigation."

Ares smiled. It was one of those dazzlingly white Hollywood smiles. But there was something slightly feral about it. "From what I've heard, you were never one to play by the rules," he said.

"People say a lot of things about me."

"Are you sure you won't change your mind?"

"Absolutely."

He eyed me up and down, as if measuring my capability. "If you find this God-killer, how exactly do you plan to take him down?"

"I haven't figured that out yet."

"I could help you."

"True."

"But you don't want my help?"

I smiled. "Bingo."

Ares examined me the way someone looks at a mosquito seconds before squashing it. Then he laughed and raised his hands in surrender. "Fine, you win. I'll let you do things your way, for now. But if you don't find this killer soon, I launch my own investigation."

The notion sent a chill down my spine. Ares would rip the city apart to find the killer, and leave a trail of bodies a mile long. I couldn't allow that.

"How much time do I have?" I asked.

Ares shrugged. "I haven't decided yet. But don't worry. I'll give you a heads-up."

"I suppose I should thank you."

"That would be wise."

"In that case, thanks."

Ares nodded and turned to leave.

"Ares," I said.

He glanced over his shoulder. "Yeah?"

"Watch your back out there. The killer might come after you at some point."

Ares's grin broadened into something sinister. "I hope he does. It'll save me the trouble of hunting him down."

57

AT 1:34 P.M. I GOT A CALL FROM UNCLE MAGUS. TRAVIS MARtin's, a.k.a. Collin Stone's, order had arrived. I drove to the Ammo Crate and parked across the street. A half hour later, a blue Saab pulled onto the curb in front of the store. Collin stepped out. He must have gotten rid of the BMW so as not to draw attention to himself.

His brown sweatshirt, shades, and cap hid most of his features. I wouldn't have recognized him if I weren't looking for him. I watched him enter the store. Then I crossed the street and ducked into the alleyway between the Ammo Crate and the store next door. There, I waited and watched. No need to get Uncle Magus involved any more than I already had.

Collin came back outside carrying a huge cardboard box. I drew my gun and held it under my shirt. Collin set the box on top of his car and took his keys out of his pocket. As he unlocked the door, I sneaked up behind him and pressed the gun barrel into the small of his back. He froze.

"Hello, Travis," I said.

Collin turned his head just enough to glance at me from the corner of his eye. "Jones?"

"That's right."

"What do you want?"

"I want you to get in the car and take us somewhere private."

"And if I say no?"

"I put a bullet in you."

His eyes narrowed. "You're bluffing."

"Maybe. You want to risk finding out?"

Collin didn't answer. I pressed the gun harder into his back. He flinched.

"Don't be stupid," I warned.

He cursed under his breath. "Fine."

He unlocked the doors and loaded the box of osmium rounds into the passenger seat. I made sure we got into the car at the same time, so he wouldn't try to bail. I aimed my gun at the back of Collin's seat as he started the engine.

"Drive," I said.

Collin pulled into traffic. He drove us to a rundown motel near the waterfront. The one-story complex featured blue vinyl siding and gray window and door casings. A sign on the edge of the property read SEAMAN'S RETREAT in faded white scroll. Beside the words was a picture of a mermaid wearing a bikini top.

Collin pulled into the space in front of room twenty-six. Besides his, there were only two other cars in the lot. One of them was on flats and looked as if it hadn't run in years.

"Out," I said. "Leave the ammo."

Collin complied. The cramped motel room smelled of cigarette smoke. Stains covered the brown carpet, which was littered with tiny bits of trash. There were no sheets on the bed. Burn marks and dark-brown stains spotted the king-sized mattress.

I stood on the opposite side of the room, near the bathroom, wishing I had a bottle of hand sanitizer, as Collin locked the door.

He turned around with his hands up. "What now?"

I pointed at the bed with my gun. "Have a seat."

Collin placed his keys on the nightstand and sat on the edge of the bed. The old mattress groaned under his weight.

"Lose the cap and sunglasses," I said. "I need to look into your eyes while we talk."

"Why?"

"So I'll know if you're lying to me."

That was partially true. I also needed to know if—and when—he was going to transform into some kind of beastie.

Collin did as he was told. His eyes were bloodshot, as if he hadn't slept in days. There was anger in them. Fear as well. But more anger than fear. He was definitely human. If not, he probably would have turned by now.

I went to the door and leaned against it. "Alright, Collin, let's talk."

"About what?"

"About Enyo."

Collin gave me a defiant look. "Screw you, asshole."

So much for the civil approach. I lowered my gun and fired a shot into the floor beside his foot.

He recoiled, scooting further onto the bed and tucking his knees into his chest. "Gods!"

"The next one won't miss."

Collin eased his feet back on the floor, his hands up. His breath came in sharp gasps. "Okay, okay! What do you want to know?"

"I want to know what happened between you and Enyo."

"Nothing happened."

I smirked. "Come on, Collin. Do you take me for an idiot?"

"I didn't murder her," he insisted.

"Who said anything about a murder?"

"Shit," Collin hissed through clenched teeth.

"Calm down. I'm not accusing you of anything, Collin. But you know something. You knew Enyo, and now you're hiding out here. So I just want to ask some questions. That's all."

He stared at me for a moment. "Fine."

"Recently, you and Enyo had an argument," I said. "She chased you out of her house and down the street. What was that about?"

"It was about the torture parties."

"What are torture parties?"

"Secret get-togethers for immortals, where they mutilate one another."

"Why do they do that?" I asked.

"For fun."

"Was Enyo into these parties?"

Collin nodded. "Yeah, and she wanted me to be into them too."

"But you weren't, right?"

Collin nodded again. "She convinced me to go to one with her. It was the sickest thing I ever saw. It's where I got this scar on my face." He paused.

"Go on."

"After the party, I told Enyo I'd never go to another one. And I didn't want her going to them either. She said okay, and for the next few weeks everything was fine. Then one day, out of the blue, she tells me that she never stopped going to the parties, and that she was breaking up with me. We argued and things got out of hand. I told her that my wife was a better lay than she'd ever be."

I sucked air through my teeth.

"She didn't appreciate being compared to a mortal," Collin continued. "She came at me like a madwoman. I had to run for my life."

"What happened after that?"

"I gave her a few days to cool off. Then I went to her place and begged her to take me back. She did, and we had sex. After we finished, Enyo went downstairs to get something to drink. I stayed in the bedroom. The doorbell rang. About a minute later, I heard a scream. Then crashing noises. I rushed down to the kitchen and found Enyo dead. Her body had been torn in half."

"Was there anyone else there?" I asked.

"No."

"What did you do?"

Collin let out a shuddering breath. "I knew the Gods would pin Enyo's death on me, so I tried to get rid of any evidence that might place me at the scene. I wiped down everything I had touched. And . . ."

Again, he paused.

"You've come this far," I told him. "Might as well go all the way."

Collin lowered his gaze to the floor. "Enyo and I had unprotected sex the night she died. There was DNA evidence inside her. I had to get rid of it. I . . . took her bottom half and buried it in the woods."

I shook my head. Sometimes I hate being right. "And you bought the osmium rounds to protect yourself against the Gods, if they come after you."

"Yes."

"I'd like to know more about these torture parties. Where are they held?"

"In different locations. Depends on who's throwing them. The one I attended was on a yacht. Things got out of hand, and the immortals ended up setting the thing on fire. Most of the guests jumped overboard, but a couple of crazy bastards thought it'd be fun to go down with the ship."

"Who was throwing the party?" I asked.

"Dionysus, I think."

"Did you meet him?"

"Yeah. He was the one who suggested setting the yacht on fire."

It seemed that Dionysus had a secret life. If I could infiltrate one of these torture parties, there was a chance he and I might run into each other.

"How would someone go about getting invited to a torture party?" I asked.

"The parties are primarily immortal-only. But mortals can be brought along as guests."

"Good to know."

"Are you going to turn me in to the authorities?"

I shook my head. "No."

Collin sighed, and some of the tension drained from his expression. He bowed his head. "Thank you."

"Don't thank me yet. If I find out you're lying, you'll hear from me again."

"What should I do in the meantime?"

"Keep a low profile, but don't leave town. And under no circumstance are you tell anyone about the murder. Also, you might want to find a new hideout—one that doesn't resemble a trap house."

Collin returned a jerky nod. "Got it."

"Now that we understand each other, I'll be on my way." I lowered the gun and opened the door. Before stepping through, I smiled and said, "Oh, before I forget. I don't want you contacting Bellanca until this whole fiasco is over. She's been through enough."

Collin said nothing.

I took a step back into the room. "Are we clear?"

"Yeah," he sneered.

58

HERC AND I WERE HAVING DRINKS AT THE NIGHT OWL AT three in the afternoon. The booths and close-set tables were all vacant. Besides us, only two other customers occupied the place. They were seated at the bar, laughing and talking. Although I heard their voices, their words didn't carry over to us, which meant they probably couldn't hear what I was saying either.

"Lemme get this straight," Herc said, holding up his hand. "Ares showed up at your apartment?"

"Broke in, actually," I corrected him.

"What did he want?"

"Your dear brother wanted me to let him in on the investigation."

"A partnership?"

"I guess."

"How'd he know you were looking into the murders?"

I shrugged. "Zeus or Hera probably told him, not that it really matters."

"What'd you tell him?"

"No."

Herc nodded approvingly. "Good. The last thing you need is his help. That psycho's as likely to murder you as the killer."

"He still might be a problem."

"What do you mean?"

"He promised not to interfere with the investigation, but only temporarily. If I don't solve this case soon, things could get messy."

"You want me to take care of him?" Herc offered.

"No need. He hasn't done anything yet."

"If you say so. But if he gives you any trouble, just let me know. I'll straighten him out . . . or I'll try to."

I tipped my beer bottle toward him. "Duly noted."

"How close are you to finding the killer?"

"Not as close as I'd like to be. Sometimes I feel like I'm going in circles."

"You must have something to go on."

I drank some beer. "I do, actually. You familiar with torture parties?"

"I've heard of them."

"Ever been to one?"

"Nope. Not planning to either. Too much craziness for my taste." Herc narrowed his eyes. "You're not thinking of going to one, are you?"

"Maybe."

Herc leaned back in his seat, shaking his head. "Gods, Jonesy."

"It might bring me one step closer to the killer," I argued.

"And one step closer to getting killed. Do you realize how dangerous those parties are?"

"Thanks for the concern, Mom. But don't worry. The Aegis will protect me."

"What if someone rips it off of you?" he asked.

I hadn't considered that. "I'll improvise."

Herc sighed. "You're not going to change your mind about this, are you?"

"Sorry."

"In that case, let me come with you."

I shook my head. "I'd love to, but the party is immortals-only. Last I checked, Demigods didn't count as immortals."

Herc went silent and stared down at his beer.

"Don't worry, I'll be fine," I assured him.

Herc nodded, but I could tell he wasn't convinced. "If the party's immortals-only, how are you going to get in?"

"I haven't figured that part out yet."

59

ARGUS CALLED ME AND SAID HE HAD SOME INFORMATION ON Dionysus. We agreed to meet at Griffin Park that afternoon. The weather couldn't have been better. Sunny without a cloud in the sky. Everywhere I looked there were children at play, moms chatting on benches, joggers running along flagstone footpaths, couples having picnics, and people walking dogs.

Argus sat on a stone bench near the swings; his massive body took up the entire bench.

His twins, Amos and Agatha, played nearby. Both children stood over six feet tall, and were carbon copies of their dad—except that Agatha had more hair on her head. When Argus spotted me, he told his kids he'd be right back and then walked over to me.

"Plato," Argus said.

"Argus."

I looked past him at Amos and Agatha, who were playing tag with a group of human children. Both siblings were taller than me and towered over their current playmates.

"Kids seem to be having fun," I said. "How old are they now?"

"Ten."

"They grow up so fast."

Argus laughed. "Tell me about it."

"Let's go somewhere private."

We walked to a gazebo near the lake, where there weren't as many people around. I sat on one of the wooden tables. Argus remained standing.

"It seems your pal Dionysus has some interesting tastes," he said. "Tastes he prefers to hide from the public eye."

"Does it have anything to with torture parties?"

Argus blinked all of his eyes at once. "Yeah, how'd you know?"

I smiled. "Lucky guess."

"*Right.* Anyway, my sources tell me that Dionysus has been at a torture party for the past month."

"The entire month?"

Argus nodded.

"How long do these torture parties usually last?" I asked.

"Anywhere from a few days to a year."

"That's a hell of a party. Who's throwing it?"

Argus smacked a mosquito on the nape of his neck. "Prometheus."

My eyes flashed wide. "The Titan?"

"That'd be the one."

Wow, I thought. *An Olympian partying with a Titan.* I could hardly believe it. The Titans were a race of deities that once ruled the world. Their reign came to a violent end when the Olympians overthrew them. Defeated and shamed, most of the Titans sank into obscurity. To this day, there's still a lot of bad blood between the two races. Every few centuries, a Titan would pop up and attempt revenge on the Olympians.

Prometheus was a Titan. Once upon a time, he stole fire from Zeus and gave it to us puny mortals, who, until then, had sat around in the dark, grunting and scratching our nether regions.

Zeus punished Prometheus by having him tied to a rock while an eagle ate his liver. But here's the kicker: the liver would regenerate overnight, only to be eaten again the next day.

In time, Zeus decided Prometheus had learned his lesson and let him go. You'd think Prometheus would still be pissed about what happened. I know I would. His carousing with Gods suggested otherwise. It seemed he had made peace with Olympus. But in my line of work, things were rarely what they appeared to be.

"You know anything about his personal life?" I asked.

"I've got a little information." Argus reached into his shirt pocket and withdrew one of his giant cigars. "I'd be willing to part with it for the right price."

"Put it on my tab."

Argus lit his cigar and took a pull. "Like I said, I don't have much info on him, but what I do have is pretty juicy. It turns out that Prometheus has a secret lover. An Olympian."

My mind went blank for a second. I stared at Argus, my mouth hanging open. "An Olympian?"

"Yep."

"Which one?"

"Enyo."

60

Two dozen paparazzi were gathered outside Cherine's, a French restaurant on the Siren Strip. I shoved past them to reach the entrance, where a minotaur doorman prevented anyone from entering.

I showed the minotaur my ID card.

He examined it, nodded, and opened the door. I stepped inside and was greeted by the maître d'. He was short and wrinkled as an old bed sheet, with thin gray hair and a pair of small-rimmed glasses.

"Mr. Jones?"

"Yes, sir."

The maître d' smiled. "Please, come with me."

I followed him through the empty restaurant to a table by the window. Aphrodite sat there with her legs crossed, sipping a flute of champagne. Her white tube top and blue-green skirt showed off her athletic figure. Strands of jewelry glittered on her neck. Her skin glowed like polished bronze in the intimate lighting. She smiled at me.

"Hello, Mr. Jones."

"Hi." I sat down. "You look great."

"Thank you."

On the other side of the window, the paparazzi snapped photo after photo of us. The glass must have been soundproof because I couldn't hear the sounds of the camera shutters. But I saw the bulbs flash. I wasn't comfortable conducting business in front of an audience.

"Do you want to move to a more private table?" I asked.

"No, this is fine."

"You sure?"

Aphrodite glared at me with a look that said politely: *Don't make me repeat myself.*

I dropped the subject. "Alright then."

The maître d' handed us our menus and scuttled off. A waiter arrived seconds later to take our drink orders. He was tall, lean, and balding.

Aphrodite ordered another glass of champagne. I asked for water.

"Thanks for meeting me on such short notice," I said, after the waiter had gone.

"How could I refuse?" Aphrodite gazed at me with those big sea-green eyes. "I had such a nice time on our last date."

"You considered that a date?"

"Yes. Didn't you?"

Before I had a chance to respond, the waiter returned with our drinks. "Are you ready to order?"

"Give us a few minutes," Aphrodite said.

As she examined me, I could sense her energy. It was more curious than anything else. It danced over me like ghostly fingers, feeling, exploring, but not getting too invasive.

"You still haven't answered my question," Aphrodite said, tapping my shoe with hers under the table. She gave me a coy smile. "Was our last encounter a date, or am I mistaken?"

I shrugged. "It's whatever you want it to be."

"Good answer." She sipped her champagne.

"I have a favor to ask." I knew there would be a price to pay. The Gods never did anything for free.

"Certainly. What can I do for you?"

Looking at her in that tight little tank top, I could think of a few things. But only one of those things would leave me with my sanity intact.

"Are you familiar with torture parties?" I asked.

Aphrodite didn't answer right away. "I've heard of them," she said after a moment. "Why do you ask?"

"I think there's a connection between the parties and the murders. I need to get into one, but the only way I can do that is in the company of an immortal."

"And you need me to be your date?"

"More or less."

She smiled, her eyes shining mischievously. It made me nervous, and a bit excited.

When the waiter came back, Aphrodite ordered the seafood niçoise. I got the stuffed mushrooms. The waiter jotted down the orders and left.

Aphrodite continued to smile at me. "I'm flattered that you came to me with this."

"It was either you or Hermes. You're a lot prettier."

Aphrodite giggled, covering her mouth. "Has anyone ever told you that you're quite the charmer, Mr. Jones?"

"You'd be the first."

"Somehow I doubt that."

"So, will you do this for me?"

"Of course."

"Thanks."

"You're quite welcome. I do, however, have one concession."

"What kind of concession?" I asked, and took a sip of water.

"Oh, it's nothing difficult, I assure you," Aphrodite said with a wave of her hand. "I'd like you to make love to me."

I nearly choked. "What?"

She held up her index finger. "One time, that's all." She sipped her champagne and awaited my answer, her expression calm and self-assured. My entire body felt tight.

I knew it. I knew something like this would happen sooner or later.

"When?" I asked.

"Now."

"Where?" I shot a glance at the paparazzi, snapping their photos from the other side of the window.

"Right here, right now. On the floor or on the table, whichever you'd prefer."

"In front of the paparazzi?"

"Yes."

I started undressing her in my mind. Warmth rushed to my crotch.

"Why do want to have sex with me?" I asked.

"Simple. Because I want to. And so do you."

"How would you know what I want?"

Aphrodite grinned. "I'm the Goddess of Love. I know what all men want."

I guess she had me there. "What about my sanity?"

"If your will is strong, you'll keep it. If not . . ." She let the statement hang.

Beads of sweat popped up on my forehead.

Oh boy.

"Do we have a deal?" Aphrodite asked.

I took a long look at her. *She seems harmless enough.* Maybe the stories about people going crazy over her were just exaggerations. Lies concocted by the media. I guess I could give her what she wanted . . .

"No!" I shook my head as if just breaking out of a trance. "I'm sorry, but I can't risk it."

Aphrodite frowned. I'm sure she wasn't used to people turning her down—especially for sex.

"That's unfortunate," she said.

"Is there anything else you want?"

She stared at me, her large eyes reflecting the camera flashes nearby.

"Perhaps." She sipped her champagne. "If you won't give me what I want, then at least give me the next best thing."

I narrowed my eyes. "And what is that?"

"A kiss."

"Is that all?"

"That's all."

I figured she was trying to set me up. I had refused her request for sex, and she thought she could change my mind with a kiss. She was probably right. I knew that saying no would have been the smartest thing to do. But I needed to get into Prometheus's torture party, and Aphrodite was my ticket. Besides, who'd pass up the chance to kiss Aphrodite?

"Alright, I'll do it," I said.

Aphrodite smiled. She stood up. I did the same. Outside, the paparazzi moved closer to the window.

I was strangely aware of my heartbeat. Aware of my breathing. I drew a deep breath, let it out slowly, and then stepped toward Aphrodite. In her eyes, my reflection stared back at me. I looked as nervous as I felt.

"Kiss me," she whispered.

I leaned forward. Aphrodite closed her eyes and parted her lips. *I can't believe I'm doing this. I must be going insane.*

My lips hesitated near hers. Blood pounded in my head. She smelled amazing. Like flowers and candy and desire all rolled into one. Her scent filled my lungs.

Her lips were soft, her kiss slow and deep. I tensed up as she put her arms over my shoulders. Our tongues brushed, exploring each other's mouths. My pulse raced. Adrenaline flooded my body. I felt light-headed. Drunk. The only thing I could think about was bending Aphrodite over the table and yanking up her skirt.

I grabbed her by the waist and pulled her closer. Her small breasts pressed against my chest. The heat from our bodies mingled. She sucked my bottom lip into her mouth, gently biting it.

My control began to unravel. Aphrodite's voice resonated in my brain. "Make love to me."

N-no. No!

Her voice grew louder, issuing from the darkest, most primitive corners of my subconscious. "Don't fight it."

Get out of my head!

"You want this."

Get out! I tore away from her, and she let me. Dizzy and breathless, I planted my hand on the table to keep from stumbling off balance.

Aphrodite's breathing was quick, her lips flushed and shining with wetness. Her lust reached out to me, beckoning me back to her arms, an almost tangible presence.

"Okay, that's enough!" I shouted, my voice cracking.

"As you wish," Aphrodite said. And just like that, the energy receded.

I lowered myself into my chair, trembling. I felt faint. My heart crashed against the inside of my ribcage.

Outside, the photographers had worked themselves into a frenzy, taking shots and rapping on the glass.

Aphrodite sat down, calm and poised. "That was fun. You're quite the kisser, Mr. Jones."

"You're not too bad either." It was the truth, and an understatement.

"I'm surprised though. Most humans would have given in to temptation. But you did not. You must be remarkably strong-willed."

If she'd known how close I came to losing control, she might have thought differently. One more second and I would've cracked.

"Maybe," I allowed. "But something tells me you were holding back. If you'd wanted, you could have forced my will, turned me into one of your thralls." I made it sound like a question.

Aphrodite gave me a smile that said everything and nothing.

"Now that I've lived up to my part of the bargain, will you do the same?" I asked.

"I will."

"Thank you."

She looked at me and giggled.

"What so funny?" I asked.

She shook her head. "Nothing, nothing at all."

Gods are strange.

61

ON THE WAY HOME FROM WORK, I PICKED UP AN ORDER OF pepper steak and fried rice from my favorite Chinese restaurant. Only seconds after I sat down at the table in my apartment, Alexis called me.

"You filthy dog," she hissed.

"Hello to you too."

"I knew you were lying. I just knew it."

"Lying about what?"

"You know what."

I ate a forkful of rice. "No. I don't."

"Stop playing dumb," Alexis said. "I saw the pictures."

"What pictures?"

"The ones of you and that . . . that tramp."

"Oh, you mean Aphrodite."

"That's exactly who I mean. I'm disappointed in you, Plato. Whoring yourself out just to get back at me. What do you have to say for yourself?"

"It's not what you think."

"You honestly expect me to believe that?" she asked.

"Well, yeah."

"Have you had sex with her?"

"Why do you want to know?"

"As your ex-wife, I have a right to know."

I chuckled. "Do you realize how absurd that sounds?"

"I don't give a damn how it sounds," Alexis said. "I want to know. Have you had sex with her?"

I speared a piece of onion with my fork and crunched into it. "I'm not answering that."

"Why not?"

"Because that information is confidential."

"Are you saying it's none of my business?"

"More or less."

Alexis gave a scornful laugh. "You're a piece of work, Plato Jones."

"And a mighty fine one at that," I said.

Incredible. She was getting married and she still thought she had the right to dictate my love life. Or fantasy love life.

"I can't talk to you right now," she said. "I'm too angry. I'll call back later."

"Bye, Alexis."

She hung up and I resumed eating. Less than a minute later, my phone beeped. Someone had sent me a text. I assumed it was from Alexis. Probably some expletive-filled rant on how I should be ashamed of myself for lying about my alleged relationship with Aphrodite.

I checked my cell. The message wasn't from Alexis. It was from Ares. There was only a single line of text:

"Time is running out."

62

At 10:00 p.m., I waited on the bridge at Griffin Park. Fifteen minutes later, Aphrodite showed up with a pair of minotaur bodyguards. A black Cleopatra wig with gold clasps hid her auburn hair. Jewels embellished her gold brassiere and thong. A transparent white train was attached to the back of the panties. Somehow she made the outfit look classy.

Her perfume smelled of pomegranates and something else I couldn't put my finger on. But I liked it.

"Nice getup," I said. "Makes me wish I'd dressed as Mark Antony."

Aphrodite smiled.

"Thanks for showing up," I said.

"Anything to help."

"You ready?"

"Yes."

She dismissed her bodyguards and followed me to my car. I opened the passenger-side door, and she slid in. She regarded the interior with apt curiosity. I couldn't tell if that was a good or bad thing.

I pulled out of the parking lot. "Sorry about my piece-of-junk car."

"There's no need to apologize," Aphrodite said. "I like it."

I blinked. "Come again?"

"It has a certain charm to it. Like a three-legged dog. Or an old beat-up hat you refuse to throw away. It fits you perfectly."

"Thanks." My brow furrowed. "I think."

I took the first ramp onto the highway. Prometheus lived in Phane City. Argus had given me Prometheus's phone number and directions to his main estate, which saved me the trouble of calling the records office. The downside—it was a two-hour drive. A long time to spend with someone who wanted to jump my bones and turn me into a sex slave. It was worse than it sounded.

"You like music?" I asked.

"Who doesn't?"

"Good point." I turned on the radio. The Olympus Top 40 was playing.

For the first twenty miles we sat quietly, listening to music. Now and again, I glanced at Aphrodite. She had on lots of black eyeliner. It made her large eyes look even larger.

"Who are you looking for at the party?" she asked.

"Dionysus and Prometheus."

"Do you think one of them could be the killer?"

"It's possible," I said.

"I know Dionysus very well."

"I'm sure you do."

Aphrodite smiled coyly. "He's killed before, but for good reason. He just doesn't seem like a cold-hearted murderer."

"Most of the Gods don't," I said.

"True."

"What can you tell me about Prometheus?"

"He's . . . strange. Of all the Titans, he bears the least amount of hatred toward Olympians."

"Why is that?"

"Oh, I couldn't begin to tell you the reason," Aphrodite said. "He's just strange."

"Would you be surprised if he turned out to be the killer?"

"A little, I suppose. He seems more interested in torturing people than killing them."

Great. So at least I'll still be alive after he rips off my fingernails one by one. "I'll keep that in mind," I said.

We were silent for some time. Then out of the blue, Aphrodite said, "I understand you're dating the treasurer."

"Who? Chrysus?"

She nodded. "She's very beautiful."

"Chrysus and I aren't dating."

"Oh?"

I could tell she didn't believe me. "Really," I insisted. "We're just friends."

"But you want to be more than that." There was a hint of jealousy in her voice. And beneath that, a dash of intrigue.

"You think so?" I asked, challenging her insight.

"I do."

"Is that your Godly perception at work?"

Aphrodite gave me a small, secretive grin. "Just a woman's intuition."

I took the Phane City exit. It veered right and emptied us onto a strip lined with shopping centers. The buildings all looked shiny and new. But the cobblestone streets were more suited for horse-drawn buggies than cars. My Thunderbird bounced along the thoroughfare.

Past the shopping centers was a long road that led to the outskirts of town. The area beyond was flat and rural. Farms, ranches, and vineyards were scattered throughout vast stretches of countryside.

Prometheus's mansion was at the end of a private road. A four-story palace with lots of windows and marble pillars.

In the middle of the driveway stood a fifteen-foot statue of Prometheus holding a torch. The fact that the statue was life-size almost made me piss my pants. Its shadow loomed across my vehicle as we parked. Even scarier was the thought of having to arrest him if he turned out to be the killer.

There were at least fifty cars in the front parking lot, with a line of more cars leading around the side of the mansion. I was betting more were parked around back.

I could never figure out why Gods drove cars. They could run like the wind, covering dozen of miles in mere minutes. Some could even fly. I guessed—to them—cars were novelty items.

"What do you want me to do once we get inside?" Aphrodite asked.

"Just stick with me please. If something goes down, I might need you for backup."

"I'm not much of a fighter, but all right."

I turned off the car and we stepped out. Nervous butterflies hatched in my stomach. Marilyn Manson's "Mutilation Is the Most Sincere Form of Flattery" poured from the mansion's windows.

"Shall we?" I offered Aphrodite my arm.

She took it. "Let's."

The front doors were around twenty feet tall, and half as wide. They had to be, to accommodate a Titan.

In the shadows near the door, a couple gyrated against each other, partially nude. As we approached, their heated moans floated toward us. They were having sex.

The woman was a nymph, shaped like a human but with transparent skin. A pale, blue liquid suspended her organs inside her torso. The man was rail-thin and covered with piercings. Silver spikes formed his mohawk. As far as I could tell, he was human.

"I hope that nymph doesn't spring a leak," I whispered to Aphrodite.

"I don't think she'd mind," Aphrodite said.

I rang the doorbell. Prometheus himself answered. His long black hair fell down to his shirtless, bare shoulders. Leather pants were slung low over his hips.

Tattoos covered his muscular body. There were so many of them; it was hard to tell where one image ended and another began. I was able to make out a skull and crossbones, a smiley face, a dragon, and what looked like a dog riding a submarine sandwich. Tattooed in black across his forehead was an eagle with its wings outstretched.

Standing so close to Prometheus made my nose burn and my eyes water. He smelled like he'd just jumped into a pool of aftershave, cologne, and bleach. I figured he was trying to cover up the smell of his innards, which were spilling from a huge wound in his stomach. Cords of intestines hung almost to the floor, crusted with dried blood. He could've stuffed them back into his belly before answering the door. That would have been the polite thing to do.

Prometheus's blue eyes latched onto Aphrodite. His jaw dropped and he swayed in place, clutching his chest as though he were having a heart attack.

"Whoa, man, have the planets aligned and created an alternate reality? Or is the Goddess of Love actually standing on my doorstep?" His deep voice had its own built-in echo.

Aphrodite smiled cordially. "Hello, Prometheus."

"Hey, yourself." Prometheus took a step back. His intestines quivered, shedding flakes of dried blood. He looked Aphrodite over and shook his head. "You look great. Fan-fucking-tastic."

"Thank you."

"Are you here for the festivities?"

"I wouldn't be here if I wasn't."

Prometheus nodded. He looked at me and grinned. A silver ring flashed in his bottom lip.

"I see you've brought a pet," he said to Aphrodite.

"This is Plato," she said.

"Nice to meet you, Plato."

I held up my hand. "Same here."

"Is Dionysus around?" Aphrodite asked.

"Inside." He stepped aside and allowed us to enter.

Aphrodite wasn't lying when she said Prometheus was a strange character. The guy was a contradiction made flesh. He looked like a biker, talked like a stoner, and smelled like a chemical plant.

Genius was not a word that came to mind. But he was acknowledged as one of the most brilliant minds in existence. And he had managed to pull off one of the biggest heists of all time—stealing fire from Olympus. An idiot couldn't have accomplished that. No, he was smarter than he let on.

A lot smarter.

63

THE FOYER WAS ROUGHLY THE SIZE OF A FOOTBALL FIELD, packed with half-naked bodies writhing to the beat of the music.

I couldn't take one step without witnessing a crime against nature. Guests were cutting each other, dismembering each other, burning each other, breaking each other's bones, and of course, having interspecies sex. Lots and lots of interspecies sex. Overhead, a number of people hung from the ceiling by meat hooks. Their sliced-open bodies dripped blood onto the crowd. Shockingly, all of them were still alive.

"I have to go check on the other guests," Prometheus said. "Enjoy yourselves."

And he walked away, towering over everyone.

"Thanks," I called after him.

"Now what?" Aphrodite asked.

"Now we find Dionysus."

"What about Prometheus?"

"I'll catch up with him later. He's not going anywhere. This is his party, after all."

Aphrodite and I threaded our way through the crowd, looking for Dionysus. We found him lying at the base of the grand staircase, making out with two naked women. One was a blonde, the other a brunette. Either could have been a supermodel.

He held a golden chalice in his right hand. Red wine sloshed over the brim, spilling down the women's bodies and splashing onto the floor. I had heard about Dionysus's chalice. No matter how much wine he drank, it was always full. I could've used one of those, only with beer.

"Hello, Dionysus," Aphrodite said, frowning at his display.

Dionysus glanced at her and blinked. "Aphrodite?"

"Having fun?"

Dionysus pushed the two women away and stood up. He looked like a cover model from a cheesy romance novel. Tall with chiseled features and curly black hair cut short. He wore a pair of blue jeans and no shirt. His dark eyes sparkled merrily.

"It's good to see you." Dionysus tried to hug Aphrodite. She backed away.

"Is something the matter?" he asked.

Aphrodite glanced at the women, who were at Dionysus's side, rubbing his arms and chest.

He got the hint. "Give us a moment, ladies."

"Aww," they said in unison.

"Go."

"Oh, alright," the blonde pouted, and both women left.

Dionysus watched them vanish into the press of bodies, and then returned his attention to Aphrodite. "Mortals can be so childish sometimes."

Aphrodite crossed her arms "The same can be said about certain Gods."

He chuckled. "I didn't know you were a fan of torture parties."

"I'm not."

"Then what are you doing here?"

"A friend of mine would like to speak with you."

"A friend?"

Aphrodite inclined her head toward me.

"Plato Jones," I said.

Dionysus and I shook hands. He had a firm handshake. Any firmer and he might have broken my hand.

"Nice to meet you, Mr. Jones," Dionysus said.

"Same here."

"What would you like to speak with me about?"

"Something important. Can we step outside for a minute?"

"I don't see why not."

The three of us went outside to my car. There was no one else around, so we could talk freely without being overheard. I leaned against the driver-side door. Aphrodite stood beside me, glaring at Dionysus.

"Thanks for cooperating," I said.

"You're welcome, Mr. Jones, but what is this all about?" Dionysus asked.

"I'm a private investigator. Zeus hired me to investigate a recent string of murders in New Olympia."

"They must not be very high-profile if Zeus is hiring mortals to look into them."

"Plato was once a member of the OBI," Aphrodite informed him. "He was the best. That's why the president wanted him on the case."

"If you say so." Dionysus didn't sound impressed. "Who were the victims?"

"Eileithyia, Hephaestus, and Enyo," I said.

Dionysus cocked his eyebrows. "The Gods?"

"Yes."

He laughed. "You're joking."

"Afraid not."

He continued to laugh, so hard that he doubled over and clutched his side. He glanced at Aphrodite. "Is he serious?" he asked, through spurts of laughter.

Her head sank and she said nothing.

Dionysus's laughter faded. "You *are* serious."

"Unfortunately," I said.

The sparkle in his eyes dimmed for an instant. He took a sip of wine. Red liquid swirled upward in the chalice to replace what he'd just taken.

"I'm sorry to have to break this to you," I said.

"It's okay," he said casually.

The reaction caught me by surprise. I mean, I wasn't expecting him to cry his eyes out or anything. But I did anticipate some show of regret. Instead, I got nothing.

"You're not upset?" I asked outright.

Dionysus shrugged. I didn't know what to make of the gesture.

I glanced at Aphrodite, hoping she could she could shed some light on Dionysus's lack of reaction. She was too busy making bedroom eyes at him to notice me. Apparently, she had forgiven him for the two bimbos near the staircase.

I turned my attention back to Dionysus. "I'm trying to find the person responsible for the murders, but I'm short on information. I'd like to ask you a few questions if you don't mind."

Dionysus swallowed another mouthful of wine. "Ask away."

"Thanks. First question. Is it true you've been at this party for the last month?"

"Yes."

"Have you left at all?"

"No." He grinned. "It's a killer party."

"Is there someone who can verify that?"

Dionysus tilted his head toward the mansion. "Ask anyone, they'll tell you. Especially any of the women."

"Okay, next question," I said. "Do you know anyone who'd want to hurt Eileithyia and the others?"

"The Gods have many enemies."

"What about Prometheus? Is he your enemy?"

Dionysus chuckled. "He's a lot of things, that one. But he's no killer."

"Last question. Is there anything that can kill a God? Anything at all?"

Dionysus shook his head, his lips pursed. "No, nothing."

"You sure?"

"Yes," he said. There was an undercurrent of annoyance in his voice. I kept forgetting how sensitive the Gods were about repeating themselves.

"Alright," I said.

"Is that all?"

"For now."

Dionysus nodded. He glanced at the sky. It was a starry night. A haze of pale light encircled the moon.

"Nice night," he commented.

"It is," Aphrodite agreed.

Dionysus shifted his gaze to her, grinning deviously. "You remember what we used to do on nights like these?"

"How could I forget?" Aphrodite replied, matching his expression.

"It's been a long time, hasn't it?"

"Too long." She moved closer to him until they stood only inches apart. "We should find a quiet spot and get reacquainted."

"Here is fine."

Aphrodite turned to me. "Plato, would you care to join us?"

I smiled graciously. "I think I'll pass."

"That's too bad. Do you want to watch instead?"

I took a few steps back, my hands raised. "No, I'm going back inside to talk to Prometheus."

Aphrodite nodded, looking marginally disappointed. "I'll look after Dionysus while you're gone."

"I'm sure you will."

Dionysus chuckled.

"Have fun, you two." I turned and started back to the mansion.

I kept my eyes straight ahead, ignoring the compulsion to look back. Though Aphrodite and I weren't romantically involved, I still hated the idea of her having sex with other guys. I couldn't—or wouldn't—have sex with her. But I didn't want other people to have sex with her either.

What bothered me even more was the thought of leaving her alone with a suspect. Everyone had their own methods of coping with tragedy, but Dionysus's lack of compassion bugged me. It bugged me a lot.

All the same, I couldn't stop Aphrodite from doing what she wanted to do. And I knew better than to try.

I was almost to the front door when screams of passion rose up behind me. I almost wished they'd been screams of terror. Then I could have run to Aphrodite's rescue with guns blazing.

I would have gotten my ass handed to me, but at least I would've looked heroic doing it.

64

I scanned the crowd for Prometheus. Given that he was fifteen feet tall, spotting him should have been easy. But the big guy was MIA.

Instead of blindly searching the mansion for him, I decided to ask around. I looked for the most normal-looking person in the room, which—with all the freaks and sadists running around—was easier said than done. The closest thing I found was a pale-skinned woman near the buffet area.

The tight blue dress she wore emphasized some fairly impressive curves. Honey-colored hair cascaded to the middle of her back, and her large eyes shone a bright shade of green. She held a Styrofoam cup in her hand.

I approached her. "Excuse me."

When our eyes met, she gasped and dropped her drink. Dark-red liquid splashed onto my shoes. I told myself it was punch.

"Sorry," I said. "I didn't mean to startle you."

The woman didn't respond. She just stared at me. Her eyes were larger up close, and there was something extremely creepy about them. They reminded me of the eyes on a porcelain doll. Glassy and lifeless.

"Have you seen Prometheus?" I asked.

The woman slowly backed away from me. She turned and ran, disappearing into the crowd.

Okay, that was weird.

I grabbed a napkin off the buffet table and wiped the red stuff off my shoes. Then I searched the crowd for the second-most normal-looking person at the party. A satyr with long white hair and a beard leaned against the staircase railing. His white dress shirt was unbuttoned all the way, and the sleeves were rolled up to his elbows. A black necktie was wrapped around his head like a bandanna.

"Excuse me," I said.

The satyr glowered at me. His pupils were dilated, and his hands trembled. I glanced at his arms. I could have played connect the dots with all the track marks.

"Wh-what? What? What do ya want?" the satyr stammered, scratching the side of his neck.

"Have you seen Prometheus?"

"Who?"

"Prometheus," I said. "You know. Big guy, covered in tats, guts hanging out. The one who owns this house."

"Oh! *That* Prometheus. Yeah, I've seen him."

"Where is he?"

"On the third floor. Second door on the right."

"Thanks."

The satyr grinned, revealing a set of crooked and yellow teeth. "No problem."

I stepped past him and went upstairs, to the third floor. A dark corridor stretched before me. A crimson runner covered the hardwood floor, thick and plush. Generic paintings of mountains and seascapes hung on the walls, illuminated by bronze sconces. I stopped at the second door on the right and knocked. The noise resounded throughout the hallway. No one answered. I knocked again.

"Prometheus?"

Still nothing.

I tried the knob, and it turned easily in my hand. Unlocked. I eased the door open. It clicked shut behind me.

Inside were a bed, a dresser, and a nightstand—all super-size like their owner. A leather sex swing hung over the bed. Prometheus wasn't here, which meant one of two things: either the satyr had made a mistake, or he was a lying sack of crap. I suspected option number two.

I was about to leave when I heard a rustling sound. I froze, my hand poised near the doorknob. I turned around, slowly. A low hiss filled the room as a gorgon with green and silver scales emerged from the other side of the bed.

I shut my eyes before she could fix her gaze on me. I wasn't sure if the Aegis would protect me from getting stoned, and didn't intend to find out. I turned the doorknob and yanked. It wouldn't budge. Someone had locked me in.

The gorgon shrieked. The noise rang in my ears, masking the sound of her approach. Clawed hands caught my arm and waist in a crushing grip. I shouted for help as she lifted me into the air and tossed me across the room. I crashed on the bed and rolled over the edge onto the floor.

Heart thumping, I scrambled to my feet and drew my gun. I could hear the gorgon slithering around. But she moved so fast, I couldn't pinpoint her location in the room with my eyes still squeezed shut. I fired three blind shots. I must have missed because she didn't grunt or cry out in pain.

There was another shriek. Something, probably the gorgon's tail, wrapped around my ankles and swept me off my feet. When I tried to rise, the creature scrambled on top of me. She pinned my wrists to the floor with clawed hands. I struggled but couldn't break her hold.

The gorgon hissed. Her breath stank like rotten meat, scalding against my face.

"Get off me!" I yelled.

I heard the door boom open, and the gorgon abruptly released me. Next came the sounds of a struggle, followed by a loud crash. Then everything went silent.

"You okay, man?" a voice asked.

I dared to open my eyes, and sat upright.

Prometheus stood near the dresser. The gorgon was on the opposite side of the room. She had been knocked halfway through the wall. Her now-still tail drooped, while the other half of her body hung through the wall into the hallway.

"I'm fine, thanks." I got up and put my gun away.

"Plato, was it?"

"Yeah."

"What are you doing up here? The party's downstairs."

"I was looking for you, actually. We need to talk."

65

PROMETHEUS LED ME TO A SMOKING LOUNGE FARTHER DOWN the hall. The room was dim and circular. Thick red curtains covered the walls, and a giant hookah sat in the middle of the floor, surrounded by pillows as wide as car hoods. Tobacco smoke scented the air. The wacky variety.

"Thanks again for helping me out," I said, climbing onto one of the pillows.

"No problem." Prometheus gathered his intestines, stuffed them into the gash in his stomach, and dropped down across from me. The floor shuddered beneath him.

"I'm lucky you came along when you did."

"Luck had nothing to with it, my friend." Prometheus pointed at the ceiling. "It was the stars."

"Excuse me?"

"The stars. They're the architects of fate. They dictate our every action. It is because of their power that we even exist."

"So the stars led you to that room?"

"Of course."

I nodded slowly. *Okay. Moving on . . .*

"I'm a private investigator." I showed him my ID. "Zeus hired me to look into a series of crimes that recently occurred in New Olympia. If you don't mind, I'd like to ask you some questions."

"Go ahead."

"Are you acquainted with the Goddess Enyo?"

"I am."

"How well do you know her?"

"Very well." Prometheus had one of those if-you-know-what-I-mean grins on his face.

"You were romantically involved?"

"Yes."

"Exclusive?" I asked.

"No, but she wanted to be."

"Did you feel the same way?"

"In a way," Prometheus began, "but we're too different to ever work. It'd be like two galaxies trying to occupy the same space. The universe would never allow such a union."

"You told her no, then?"

"Yes."

"I can't imagine Enyo took the rejection very well," I said.

"She threw me out a window."

"Harsh. And then?"

"She went home."

"Did you hear from her again?"

Prometheus nodded. "She called a few days later, begging me to be with her. She'd even gone so far as to break up with her other lovers."

So that's why she broke up with Collin. "What did you tell her?"

"To forget about me. To move on."

"Did she take your advice?"

"I don't know. She hung up on me. That was the last time she and I spoke." Prometheus paused and squinted at me. "Is she in some kind of trouble?"

"You could say that," was all I was willing to tell him for now. I'd never been a fan of putting all my cards on the table at once. To me, conducting an interrogation was a lot like painting. It required patience and finesse. One brushstroke at a time, until the picture began to take form.

Prometheus gave a half-smile. "She's dead, isn't she?"

My eyebrows shot upward. *So much for strategy! But does this mean he's the killer?* "Yes, she is."

Prometheus nodded, his expression calm.

"You don't seem very upset," I said.

"I'm not."

"That's a little insensitive, don't you think?"

"To the unenlightened mind, perhaps." Prometheus rested his hands behind his head. "I believe everything happens for a reason."

"Let me guess. Her death was written in the stars."

He pointed at me. "Exactly!"

"Did the stars also tell you to kill her?"

"Oh no."

"If they had, would you have done it?"

"Well, yeah."

"How?"

Prometheus shrugged. "I guess I'd used the Claw of Erebus. That is, if I could get my hands on it."

Hearing the name Erebus took me back to freshman history in high school. Supposedly, Erebus was an ancient deity, the primordial darkness from which all life was created. For as long as anyone could remember, scholars and scientists had been debating its existence. The Gods were squarely on the "no comment" side of the argument. I was on the fence about the issue.

"What's the Claw of Erebus?" I asked.

"A weapon fashioned from the darkness of creation."

"I don't understand."

"That's not surprising. The Olympians keep its existence a secret. But don't worry, I'll set you straight."

"I appreciate that."

"So here's the deal," Prometheus said. "Think of Erebus as a big hunk of modeling clay. This clay was used to shape the world and everything in it: oceans, mountains, birds, mortals, Titans, everything. But as with most modeling projects, there were a few bits of clay left over. Little pieces of unfathomable power."

"And someone thought it'd be a good idea to collect those pieces and forge them into a weapon," I said.

"Able to destroy anything," Prometheus said. "Even a God."

"What happened to the claw?"

"Last I heard, the Olympians had it. I imagine they still do."

I rubbed my chin and considered this. If everything Prometheus said was true, I now had a potential murder weapon. How did the killer manage to get his or her hands on it? And why didn't the Olympians tell me about it from the beginning? Someone had some explaining to do.

I stood up. "Thanks for your time, Prometheus."

"No problem."

"Do me a favor and keep this whole murder thing between me and you, okay?"

Prometheus gave me a thumbs-up. "Sure thing."

As I started to leave, I remembered Nicolas's description of the missing gorgon.

"One more thing," I said.

"Hmm?"

"What was up with the gorgon in the bedroom?"

"Oh, that?" Prometheus laughed. "A friend of mine brought it over. She's a gorgon charmer."

"Gorgon charmer?"

Prometheus nodded. "Like a snake charmer, only with gorgons."

"How does she charm them without getting turned to stone?"

"She's half-gorgon, so she's immune to their stares. And she can charm them into doing what she wants."

"What?" I raised an eyebrow.

"It's true," Prometheus assured me. "Her mom is Medusa."

I could tell by the look in his eyes that he was telling the truth. I wished he'd been lying. Half-gorgon. I had no idea gorgons could mate with other species, and frankly, I would've been happier having never known. The thought of lying down with one of those ugly, smelly things was the stuff of nightmares. And Medusa had been the ugliest and smelliest of all.

Who in his right mind would have sex with something like that? You couldn't even look at her without turning to stone. And not in a good way.

"Why did she bring the gorgon over?" I asked.

"Some of the guests thought it'd be fun to get turned to stone."

"Who's this friend of yours?"

"Why do you want to know?"

"Because that gorgon is stolen property."

"Are you serious?" he asked.

"As a heart attack."

Prometheus frowned.

"What's your friend's name?" I asked.

He shook his head. "Sorry man, but I'm no snitch."

"Gorgon theft is a federal offense, you know. If someone was to, I don't know, tip off the OBI, you could get into serious trouble . . . with Zeus."

Prometheus's attitude instantly shifted gears. He raised his hands, grinning nervously. "Whoa, no need for that, friend. I'll tell you what you want to know."

"Smart move."

"She goes by Mia. But her real name is Lamia."

"Lamia?" I stared at Prometheus in confusion. "I thought she was dead."

Prometheus smirked, his lip ring flashing in the dim light. "That's what the *official* records say."

"I don't get it."

Prometheus gestured for me to sit back down. "I assume you already know about Lamia's affair with Zeus."

I nodded. "Hera punished her by killing her children."

"Yeah, but that's not all she did. Hera painted Lamia as a psychopathic child-killer, made it impossible for her to lead a normal life."

"Wait, so the whole story about Lamia killing children is a lie?"

Prometheus nodded. "Lamia, poor thing, tried to clear her name. But no one would believe her. Who's going to take the word of a cold-blooded child-killer over the Queen of the Gods?"

"You believed her," I said.

Prometheus chuckled, without humor. "I know how Hera can be sometimes."

"You and me both."

"Anyway, she faked her death to get Hera off her back."

"Do you know where I can find her?"

"She was here earlier, but I think she bailed."

"What does she look like?" I asked.

Prometheus shrugged. "Depends on how she's feeling."

"What does that mean?"

"Lamia's a shape-shifter. She inherited that power from her father."

I assumed he was talking about Poseidon, the God of the Sea. As far I knew, he was Lamia's biological father. Her mother—I'd thought—was Lybie, an ancient queen of Libya. But according to Prometheus, Medusa was the real mother, which meant that she and Poseidon . . . Yuck.

"A shape-shifter who can hypnotize gorgons and is immune to their stares," I said. "Your friend's pretty well-rounded."

"No doubt."

"What did she look like tonight?"

"Like a human female. Pale skin. Light-brown hair. Nice ass. That's the form I'm most familiar with. I think it's her real one."

"Does she have any distinguishing features?"

"Yeah. She's got these freaky eyes. I mean real freaky. Like space age, flying saucer shit."

I leaned forward. "Her eyes, are they green?"

"Yeah."

The woman near the buffet. The one who ran away from me. Could that have been Lamia?

"And you say she left?" I asked urgently.

Prometheus nodded.

"Is there a way I can get in contact with her?" I asked.

"Not that I know of. She kinda comes and goes, you know."

I got up. "Thanks for your help."

"Anytime."

I went back downstairs and started asking random people if they knew where Lamia—a.k.a. Mia—had gone. No one knew. Or if they did, they weren't telling. After an hour of searching, I gave up. As I walked toward the door on my way out, a voice called out to me.

"Did you have fun?"

It was the satyr with the necktie around his head.

"Did you know there was a gorgon upstairs?" I asked.

He smiled, looking pleased with himself. "Uh-huh."

"And you sent me up there?"

"Yeah, pretty funny joke, huh?"

I punched him in the jaw. He fell unconscious onto the floor.

"Hilarious." I turned and left the mansion.

66

BY THE TIME I REACHED MY CAR, APHRODITE AND DIONYSUS were gone. I didn't bother looking for them. I was too pissed off to deal with them right now.

The Gods had been lying to me this entire time. They told me there was nothing they knew of that could kill a God. And now I found out there was, the Gods knew about it, *and* the killer had possession of it. I always knew the Gods were assholes. They just kept coming up with more and more ways to prove it.

As angry as I was, I could still see the intelligence behind the lies. If I were the omnipotent ruler of mankind, I probably wouldn't want my subjects to know my one fatal weakness. Still, that didn't justify what they'd done. Cowardice is cowardice, no matter how you slice it.

When I arrived home, I called the records department on Olympus for information on the Claw of Erebus. They said exactly what I knew they'd say: "I'm sorry, Mr. Jones, but no such weapon exists." Surprise, surprise.

I ended the call and considered my next move. If the Gods had the claw, they'd likely keep it in the secret vault on Olympus, under twenty-four-hour guard. Chrysus was the director of the Treasury. In the morning, I would try to finagle some answers out of her. She'd probably play dumb, but it was worth a shot.

Having done all I could do for one day, I dragged myself to my room and crashed onto the bed. I finally had a break in the case. I just hoped Ares wouldn't screw everything up.

In the wee hours of the morning, I was awakened by the sound of my cell phone ringing. Rubbing the sleep from my eyes, I grabbed it from the nightstand.

"Hello?" I grumbled.

"Plato?" a woman's voice said.

I sat up and pressed my back against the cool wood of the headboard. "Aphrodite?"

"Yes, it's me," she said. "I apologize for calling so early, but I was concerned."

"Concerned about what?"

"About you, of course. You disappeared last night."

"Oh yeah." I held back a yawn. "Sorry about that. Something urgent came up."

"That's all right."

"Did you have trouble getting home last night?"

"No," Aphrodite said. "Dionysus gave me a ride."

I'll bet he did.

"Prometheus told me you were almost mauled to death by a gorgon. Is that true?"

"Yeah, I was attacked."

"You poor thing," she cooed. "Are you feeling alright?"

"I'm fine."

"Are you sure? I can bring over some hot soup. Or a nice pie."

I could've gone for some pie. But not Aphrodite's. Hers tended to drive people crazy.

"I appreciate the offer," I said, "but I'm okay, really."

"All right." She sounded disappointed. "So did Prometheus give you any useful information?"

"Maybe."

"Nothing you're willing to discuss?"

"Afraid not," I said. "Sorry."

"I understand."

"Thanks for helping me out last night."

"Anytime."

"I'll talk to you later."

"I look forward to it."

I ended the call and put my cell phone back on the nightstand. The numbers on my digital clock glowed neon red in the dimness. It was five until four. I tried to go back to sleep, but the conversation with Aphrodite had left me wide awake, and sexually frustrated. I rolled out of bed, went to the living room, and watched TV until the sun came up.

At eight in the morning, I called the Department of the Treasury and asked for Chrysus. The receptionist told me Chrysus was filing some reports for Zeus, and that I should call back later. I was in no mood to play phone tag, but I left her a message anyway.

At half past one, I was about to give the Treasury another ring, when my cell rang. It was Chrysus. Finally.

"Hey, beautiful," I said.

"Hello, Plato."

"Did you get my message?"

"I did. Is there something you wanted?"

"Yeah. I need to ask you a question. Are you alone right now?"

"Hold on one moment." Chrysus was quiet for a time, but I could hear her heels clack against the floor. When she spoke again, there was an echo. I assumed she was in the restroom.

"What's going on?" she asked.

"I'd like some information on an item in the vault."

"Which one?"

"The Claw of Erebus."

Chrysus went silent. After a few seconds she said, "What's the Claw of Erebus?"

"You know, weapon of unimaginable power. The only thing that can kill a God."

"I'm afraid I've never heard of such a thing."

"You sure about that?" I asked.

"Absolutely."

"Okay," I said. There was no point in pressing the matter. She wasn't going to talk.

"This Claw of Erebus," Chrysus said, "who told you about it?"

"About what? It doesn't exist. Right?"

There was another stretch of silence on the other end.

"You still there?" I asked.

"One second."

I heard the sound of a toilet being flushed. Moments later, Chrysus said, "I apologize. Someone came into the bathroom. They're gone now."

"Chrysus, are you sure there's not something you want to tell me?"

"I wish I could tell you what you want to hear, but I'm afraid that's just not possible. Listen, I have to get back to work. We'll talk later."

"Okay, bye," I said.

My search for the Claw of Erebus had only just begun, and already I had hit a brick wall. I didn't stress about it too much. The Claw was only one piece of a much larger puzzle. If I found the killer, I'd inevitably find the murder weapon. Whether or not the smoking gun turned out to be the Claw, I'd just have to wait and see.

67

WITH THE CLAW OF EREBUS TEMPORARILY OUT OF THE picture, I shifted my attention to Lamia. Her history with Zeus and Hera made her a huge suspect. As did the fact that she had faked her own death. Prometheus believed she did it to escape Hera's wrath, but I suspected there was more to it than that.

Every year, dozens of criminals staged their own deaths. Dropping off the grid gave them more freedom to move around. They could commit crimes without having to worry about the cops coming after them. Maybe that was what Lamia was doing.

I called Prometheus and asked if he'd seen her. I had a feeling he was going to say no, and I was right. The only other thing I could think to do was speak with Poseidon. Being Lamia's father, he might have some useful information.

I called the offices on Olympus and set up a meeting with him. The next morning, I drove to the harbor. Two men in white suits waited for me in the parking lot. One of them held a sign with my name on it. I flashed them my ID, and they motioned for me to follow them.

They led me to a luxury speedboat moored to the dock. It was blue with white leather seats. The wood-grain dash panel and silver instruments gleamed in the sunlight. A bottle of champagne sat in a bucket of ice next to one of the passenger seats. I knew where I was going to sit.

We sailed east, slicing through the waters of the Aegean. Poseidon's yacht bobbed in the distance. It was massive, more along the lines of a cruise ship. The hull was pearl white, and the prow was shaped like a horse's head. Dozens of windows spotted the exterior. I didn't even want to think about how much a vessel like that might cost.

We boarded the yacht. The suits escorted me to the bow, where Poseidon was oil-painting. With his short black hair and light blue eyes, he looked almost identical to Zeus. Only he was taller and brawnier and had a fuller beard. He sported a navy polo, white slacks, and no shoes.

I had first met Poseidon while working for the OBI. I felt about as safe around him as I did with Ares. He had a notoriously bad temper, and almost anything could set him off. Bad news for people living near the coast.

I knew nothing of his relationship with Lamia. It seemed like he and Zeus were battling for the title of biggest deadbeat dad on Olympus.

"Good morning," I said.

"Hold on, old boy." Poseidon continued to paint.

He was doing a self-portrait in which he stood naked atop Mt. Olympus, holding his trademark golden trident overhead. It looked photorealistic, even up close. Several strokes later, he put down his brush and pallet and turned toward me. He smiled. That was a good thing . . . I hoped.

"What do you think of my latest work?" He gestured at the painting. His voice was deep and even. Sophistication clung to his every word.

"It's great."

His smile waned.

I laughed anxiously. "Did I say great? I meant perfect."

Poseidon nodded. "I love painting. I can't think of many things more fulfilling. Do you paint, Mr. Jones?"

"I took a few classes in high school. I was good. But not as good as you."

"Naturally."

"Thanks for seeing me on such short notice."

"Don't mention it, old boy. Now then, you wanted to talk about the murders, yes?"

"I just have a few questions."

Poseidon motioned for me to follow him. He led me up to the observation deck. The space doubled as a formal dining area, with warm lighting, upholstered furniture, and three fully stocked bars. The hardwood paneling and floor appeared freshly polished. Heavy red curtains covered the windows.

We sat down at one of the many dinner tables lined up in two rows on the deck.

"Tell me, old boy," Poseidon began, "do you like the ship?"

"Yeah, it's really something else."

He smiled approvingly. "I designed it myself, you know."

I pursed my lips and nodded, acting more impressed than I really was. "Wow, that's really amazing."

A female servant came over to the table. She was tall with straight brown hair and large, come-hither eyes. Her tight white polo, white pants, and black apron showed off a slender figure. To Poseidon she said, "What can I get for you, Captain?"

"Vodka martini."

The servant nodded, then shifted her attention to me. "And you, sir?"

I raised my hand. "Nothing for me."

"Oh, come on, old boy," Poseidon urged. "Don't be a stick in the mud. Have a drink."

"I'm still buzzed from the boat ride over. Thanks for the champagne, by the way."

Poseidon smiled. He glanced at the servant. "Just the martini, my dear. And be quick about it."

"Yes, Captain," she said. As she turned to leave, Poseidon gave her a playful smack on the rear. She let out a squeal and hurried along.

Poseidon took a metal cigarette case and a lighter out of his back pocket. "Smoke?"

"No thanks."

"You're a bit of a mossback, aren't you, old boy?"

I had no idea what that even meant. But I wasn't about to disagree with him. "I guess I am."

Poseidon slipped a cigarette out of the case. He lit it, took a drag, and blew out the smoke. "So what would you like to ask me?"

Before I could respond, the servant came back with Poseidon's martini. Her timing couldn't have been better. It gave me a chance to think about the best way to bring up Lamia. I couldn't just come out and say, "Hey, let's talk about your formerly deceased daughter."

Well I could, but I'd probably end up being the ship's new figurehead.

Once the servant left, I said, "Thanks again for being so gracious. This case has been pretty tough. But I think I'm finally on the verge of a breakthrough. Right now, I'm trying to fill in some missing pieces."

"I'll help however I can," Poseidon said.

"First, let me ask you. Is there anything that can kill a God? A weapon of unimaginable power maybe? Created at the dawn of time? Any of that ring a bell?"

The mood in the room shifted. But Poseidon's calm expression remained unchanged.

"I'm afraid it doesn't," he said.

I didn't bother asking him if he was sure. I had learned my lesson about asking Gods to repeat themselves. I certainly wasn't going to make that mistake on Poseidon's boat, in the middle of the sea.

"Okay, next question," I said "Do you know of anyone who has it out for Zeus and Hera?"

Poseidon took a pull from his cigarette and seemed to consider the question. "There are the Titans. That bunch has always hated us. But they're too cowardly to come after us directly."

"Does anyone else come to mind?" I asked.

"Not really."

I nodded. "When was the last time you spoke to Lamia?"

Poseidon froze, his cigarette less than an inch from his lips. His face was unreadable. Carved marble. He took another drag and tapped his cigarette on the edge of the ashtray. Red-orange cinders fell into the crystal bowl. "Why do you ask?"

"I heard a rumor about her."

"What kind of rumor?"

"That she may be involved in the murders."

Poseidon's blue eyes fixed on my face. "Lamia is dead."

"Sources tell me differently."

"What do you mean?"

Poseidon's gaze weighed upon me. My palms moistened with sweat. Every animal instinct in my brain shouted at me not to proceed. To drop the subject. But I was already in too deep. I had to keep going.

"She faked her death," I said. "Lamia is still alive, and I need to find her. I was hoping you could help me do that."

"Lamia is dead," Poseidon repeated.

His huge frame seemed to grow even larger. My muscles tensed. My jaw tightened as I spoke. "I've seen her with my own eyes."

He rose to his feet and said, in a monotone, "I think it's time for you to leave, old boy."

That was my cue to exit, or possibly get thrown into the sea. I chose the exit. "Right. Thanks for your time."

As I left, Poseidon sat back down and continued to smoke his cigarette. That went well.

I stepped out onto the deck and was nearly knocked over by a violent gust of wind. It threw me against the railing, which bit into my back as I collided with it. The water had become choppy, and dark clouds churned overhead. They rumbled with thunder, threatening to burst.

68

THE STORM THAT RAGED ACROSS THE CITY SOON AFTER I LEFT the boat was one of the worst I'd seen in recent months. Rain and sleet fell in thick sheets, creating a near-total whiteout.

I drove fifteen miles under the speed limit with my high beams on, using the taillights of other cars as beacons to guide me down the road. If I was lucky, I'd make it home without wrapping my car around a light post.

I was still pretty shaken up after the meeting with Poseidon. I probably should have apologized to him before leaving the yacht. The last thing I needed was another enemy on Olympus. Hera was one too many.

Our conversation hadn't given me much in the way of clues. But it did let me know one thing: Poseidon had strong feelings for Lamia. The only question was whether those feelings were positive or negative. Did he care about her, and feel that I was defiling her memory? Or did he despise her to the point where the mere mention of her sent him into a rage?

I was leaning more toward the first possibility. It was no secret that Poseidon and Hera weren't the best of friends. But no one really knew why. Maybe it was her charming personality. Or maybe Poseidon blamed Hera for the death of his daughter. Maybe he killed the other Gods to get back at her.

Maybe he knew Lamia was alive. And the two of them were secretly working together, trying to get back at Hera for slaying Lamia's children.

Any way I looked at it, Poseidon had reason to seek revenge against Hera. Regardless, I had doubts about his being the killer. When it came to revenge, Poseidon took a more direct approach—or so I'd heard. He confronted his enemies in public and beat them to a pulp. He didn't give a damn about witnesses. In fact, Poseidon enjoyed having an audience. The killer, on the other hand, seemed to favor the shadows.

Despite his reputation, I wasn't ready to drop Poseidon as a suspect. People could change after all. Just look at Herc and—to a lesser extent—Ares.

I arrived home at a few minutes after three. I was soaked to the bone and shivering. All I wanted was a long, hot shower. I wished Chrysus could join me, but hey, we couldn't always get everything we wanted.

I kicked off my shoes and headed to the bathroom. I flipped the light switch and there, standing in front of me, was a figure in black sweats. A white ski mask covered his—or her—face.

My heart jumped into my throat. "Who are you?"

The figure said nothing, but raised a pistol with a silencer.

Before I could react, the intruder fired two shots. The impact was like getting hit full force with a sledgehammer. I fell backward onto the floor. I couldn't breathe. My pulse raced out of control. I pressed trembling hands against my chest. Warm blood spilled over my fingers. The world dimmed. I didn't feel any pain. Only intense pressure.

Then I felt nothing at all.

69

I AWOKE—WHICH WAS A WELCOME SURPRISE, CONSIDERING I'd been plugged in the chest. I was alive as far as I could tell, and in no pain. Both pluses in my book.

I swallowed and looked around. I was lying in the tub in my bathroom, stripped down to my boxers. Pinkish water sloshed about me as I sat up and inspected my chest. No bullet wounds. The skin was unmarred.

What in Hades is going on?

A dark-haired man appeared in the doorway. "Welcome back."

"Ares?"

"The one and only." He bowed low, making a dramatic sweep with his arm.

"What are you doing here?"

"I came to see if you had changed your mind about working together," Ares said. "Saving your life—I did that on the fly."

I looked at my chest again. Touched the spots where the rounds had entered. "Thanks, but how exactly did you save me?"

He winked. "I'm a God, remember? Now, are you going to tell me what happened or not?"

"Someone broke in and shot me."

"Did you get a good look at him?"

I shook my head. "His face was covered."

Ares smirked. "Mortals are so worthless."

"I was wearing the Aegis," I said as I climbed out of the tub. "It should have protected me."

"You mean that thing?" Ares glanced at the gold breastplate lying near the toilet. There were two bullet holes in the metal. "Sorry to break it to you, but that's not the Aegis. It's a replica. The real article is indestructible."

I knelt in front of the Aegis. Blood had dripped down its front from the holes. My blood. Why would Zeus screw me over like this?

"Can you do me a favor?" I asked.

"I just saved your life, and you're already asking for more favors?"

"This is important."

"Fine. What do you want?"

"I need you to call the records office on Olympus and check the statuses of Athena's Aegis and the Claw of Erebus."

Ares raised an eyebrow. "What's a Claw of Erebus?"

"Cut the act. I know the Claw exists and so do you. It's the only thing that can kill a God."

Ares didn't respond. He crossed his arms and leaned against the doorframe.

"This is ridiculous," I griped. "Look. The Claw is the murder weapon, alright?"

Ares narrowed his eyes. "How do you know?"

"I just do. You're going to have to trust me on this."

"I hope you're right about this, Jones," Ares said. "For your sake."

He pulled his cell phone from his jacket pocket and walked out of the bathroom, shutting the door behind him. He came back a few minutes later.

"What did they say?" I asked.

"They said the Aegis is currently checked out by one Plato Jones." He pointed at me. "That's you."

Wiseass. "And the Claw?"

"The Claw is in the vault."

"Are the artifacts ever taken out of the Treasury, for cleaning or restoration?"

"Yeah," Ares said. "About once a year, around this time."

"So they were both removed from the vault recently—before I got the Aegis?"

"Most likely."

My Aegis was a fake, which meant the Claw in the vault could be a fake too. Who could have switched them? I clapped my hands. "That's it!"

"What?"

"I know who the killer is." I ran past Ares and out of the bathroom. I grabbed my cell phone off the kitchen bar and dialed Hermes's number. He answered on the third ring.

"What is it, Jones?"

"Send every OBI agent you've got to Chrysus's house," I said. "I'll meet them there."

Ares snatched the phone out of my hand. To Hermes he said, "Correction. *We'll* meet them there."

70

ARES AND I JUMPED INTO MY CAR AND HIT THE FREEWAY. I was opposed to his coming along. But I knew it would be in my best interest to just let him have his way. Moreover, I'd probably need the extra muscle.

"The Treasury director," Ares said in disbelief. *"She's* the killer?"

"Not exactly," I said. "The killer is Lamia, a shape-shifter. She wants revenge against Hera for the murder of her children."

"That's impossible. Lamia's dead."

"Only on paper."

"Did you see her?"

I nodded.

"How do you know she's the killer?" Ares asked.

"Because the clues all point to her. Not too long ago, a gorgon went missing from a ranch in Boreasville. Evidence suggested the creature had escaped on its own. But that wasn't the case. Lamia had charmed the gorgon. Forced it to follow her off the property. She also charmed the other gorgons in the enclosure, so they wouldn't make a fuss and alert the owner. When Lamia and the gorgon reached the street, she loaded it into the back of her truck and drove off."

"Why'd she steal a gorgon?"

"So she could turn the real Chrysus into stone and assume her identity. Chrysus is a spirit. Simply killing her wasn't an option. She would have just found another body to inhabit, and then told Zeus what was going on. Lamia's only course of action was to imprison Chrysus, hence turning her into stone."

"And she did all of this, why?"

"To gain access to the secret vault. Lamia got Hephaestus to make replicas of the Claw of Erebus and Athena's Aegis. Then she switched them with the real ones while they were being cleaned. She used the Claw to murder the Gods. The Aegis assured the victims wouldn't be able to turn the tables on her."

Ares frowned. "Why would Hephaestus help the killer?"

"Revenge, most likely," I surmised. "He wanted to get back at Hera for throwing him from Mount Olympus, and for favoring her other children over him. He wanted her to suffer as he had suffered. But after Eileithyia was killed, he suddenly grew a conscience. He wrote a letter to Aphrodite, basically confessing his involvement in the murder. Lamia was afraid he'd rat her out, so she took care of him. Then she continued her killing spree."

Ares nodded slowly. "You never mentioned where you saw her."

"We ran into each other at one of Prometheus's torture parties. The next thing I know I'm getting shot in the chest. She knew I was getting close to the truth. I can't wait to see the look on her face when we show up on her doorstep."

Ares grinned darkly. "Neither can I."

71

THE SUN HAD BEGUN TO RISE BY THE TIME WE REACHED Chrysus's mansion. Her Escalade truck was parked in the driveway. There were no other cars around.

"Damn," I griped. "The OBI hasn't gotten here yet."

"Screw 'em," Ares said. "Let's get in there and take care of business ourselves."

"No. We need to wait for backup."

"Revenge waits for no one." Ares got out of the car and approached the front door of the mansion.

I went after him. I knew it was a stupid thing to do. But I couldn't in good conscience let him face Lamia alone—especially if she had the Claw of Erebus.

Ares kicked in the door, knocking it off its hinges. It flew across the room and slammed against the opposite wall. Inside, the lights were off. The silence was absolute. Adrenaline raged through my body, shattered my breathing, quickened my pulse. In the living room we found what looked like a castoff skin. It looked a lot like Chrysus.

Gazing at the empty husk, I had no choice but to face the terrible truth: I had been dating the infamous God-killer. I had bought her roses. Kissed her. Almost had sex with her. And she was half gorgon.

My stomach churned. The realization left me feeling sick and humiliated. The clues had been staring me in the face this whole time, but I had been so infatuated with Chrysus/Lamia, that I ignored them. I let them slip past my notice. Some detective I was.

Ares turned in place, looking around the room. "Lamia! Come out and face me!"

I shushed him. "Haven't you heard of the element of surprise?"

"Only cowards fight from the shadows. Lamia!" The volume of his voice rose so loud that it pounded against my eardrums. "Lamia!"

My frustration level went through the roof. I fought to suppress it. Fought the urge to lash out at Ares. To tell him to shut his damn mouth before he got me killed. I needed to stay cool and focused, especially now that Lamia knew we were here.

"We should check the rest of the house," Ares said.

"Yeah." I spoke through gritted teeth. I restrained myself from saying something he'd make me regret.

As we started to leave the room, my attention was inexplicably drawn to the scuffmarks near the piano, as if someone had whispered, "Hey, buddy, look over there," into my ear.

"Hold on." I knelt and examined the marks. Tiny wood shavings curled upward from the damaged floor. The curls led away from the piano rather than toward it—which meant the scuffs had been made when the piano was moved *away* from its current position.

"What are you looking at?" Ares asked.

I stood up. "I think these marks will lead us to the real Chrysus."

We followed the marks into the kitchen. The flowers I had given Chrysus sat in a vase in the middle of the kitchen table.

Glancing at them, I wondered if she had actually liked me, or if it was all an act. Did I even want to know?

The marks led us to a door at the back of the kitchen. It was locked. I took out my lock-pick, but Ares pushed me aside and kicked the door open.

"Ta-da!" he said.

Darkness loomed through the doorway. A narrow staircase led down to the cellar. Ares went in front, down the stairs. I drew my gun and followed him, my eyes trained on the space behind us. Moving through the shadows, weapon in hand, I felt like Beowulf going to face the dragon. I guess that meant Ares was Wiglaf.

The stairwell opened into a spacious cellar with cobblestone walls and hardwood floors. Built-in wine shelves lined the walls, each one fully stocked with bottles. A wrought iron chandelier burned overhead.

The scuffmarks ended at the far left corner of the cellar, where we found Chrysus's petrified form. She was looking over her shoulder in surprise, as if the gorgon had sneaked up on her. Even her short bathrobe had been turned to stone.

"It looks like you've found my little secret," a mousy voice said from behind us.

We spun around.

Lamia stood at the base of the stairs, wearing Athena's Aegis over black sweats. Her saucer-like emerald eyes glittered. On her right hand was a huge, plate armor gauntlet. Wisps of shadow drifted from the gauntlet, like blood in water. A foot-long claw made of black metal tipped each finger.

The Claw of Erebus.

"You!" Ares shouted.

"Ah, Ares," Lamia said. "I have to thank you for coming here. You saved me the trouble of tracking you down."

Ares rushed her, his body a blur of motion. He slammed his shoulder into her chest. With a deafening boom, Lamia flew across the cellar. Her back struck the wall with enough force to make the entire room shake. Wine bottles tumbled off the shelves and smashed to the floor.

"Get up," Ares growled.

Lamia began to laugh. "Is that the best you can do?" She pulled herself off the floor. There wasn't a scratch on her. The Aegis twinkled even in the dim light of the cellar.

Ares went after her again. Lamia swiped at him with the Claw. Ares caught her arm and twisted it sharply. There was an audible snap. She howled in pain.

Still holding Lamia's arm, Ares swung her into a wine shelf, and then flung her into another. Wood cracked and glass shattered. Wine spilled across the stone floor, black as oil under the light of the chandelier.

Lamia braced her left hand against the wall and got up. Her right arm dangled at her side, bones poking through the flesh. She hunched over, breathing heavily, her hair plastered to her face with the wine running down her cheeks.

Ares yanked off his leather jacket and threw it to the floor. "Don't quit on me now. We're just getting started."

Lamia straightened. Her pained expression vanished, replaced by a smile. Her arm jerked back and forth at crazy angles as the bones snapped into place.

"Much better," she said, bending her arm at the elbow.

Ares cursed and charged forward.

Lamia drew a handgun from an ankle holster and fired three rounds at Ares. The bullets must have been osmium, because he fell to one knee, clutching his chest.

"Shit!" I emptied my clip into Lamia.

She jerked with every shot but didn't fall down. She looked at me and smiled. Her wounds had already begun to close.

"Don't do that again," she said sweetly, then returned her attention to Ares.

She unloaded her gun into him, threw the weapon aside, and then kicked him in the face. He tumbled across the floor into a clumsy sprawl, his white T-shirt soaked with blood. She sat astride him and stabbed him repeatedly in the chest with the Claw. Blood flew, dark and viscous, splattering against the walls and floor.

I loaded another magazine into my gun and fired.

Lamia recoiled. She rose off Ares, a hole in the middle of her forehead. There was a whooshing sound, like rushing wind, and she was right there in front of me. I shot her twice more, in the neck and shoulder. The bullets barely fazed her. She slapped the gun out of my hand. I backed away with both my hands held up.

Lamia stalked after me, her eyes wide and unblinking, her face spattered with blood.

When I felt the chilled stone wall against my back, I knew I was screwed.

"I like you, Plato," Lamia said. "That's the only reason you're still alive."

"You tried to kill me earlier, remember?"

"I didn't want to. But you were becoming too meddlesome."

"Comes with the territory."

"I still think about that night in the living room. I wish we could've finished what we started. We still can."

"I think I'll pass." I glanced at my gun, which lay about ten feet away in a puddle of wine. If I moved fast enough, maybe I could . . .

"Don't even think about it," Lamia warned. "I'll rip you in half before you take the first step."

"You have to stop this, Lamia."

"Why should I? Hera—that bitch—she took everything away from me. Everything!"

"Killing her children won't bring yours back," I reasoned.

"Maybe not, but it brings me happiness."

"You don't look very happy."

A tear rolled out of Lamia's eye, streaking through the blood and wine on her cheek.

"Please, Lamia, give up."

Lamia gave a trembling smile. More tears fell from her eyes. "Don't try to save me, Plato," she said. "I'm beyond saving."

"I can't let you continue to do this."

"But I can't let you stop me."

Lamia raised the Claw. I braced for death. This wasn't how things were supposed to end. The dashing, streetwise detective never gets killed—

"Did I say we were done?" a voice asked.

Lamia glanced over her shoulder. Ares was standing behind her, his face and clothes drenched with blood.

Before Lamia could react, Ares locked his arms around her waist and slammed her onto the floor. While they tussled, I grabbed my gun. When I looked up again, Ares was on top of Lamia. He wrestled the Aegis off her and flung it across the cellar.

Ares pinned Lamia's clawed hand to the floor. She mauled his face with her other hand, her fingernails unable to break his skin. Screaming like an animal, she tucked her knees into her chest and kicked. The attack launched Ares into the air. He crashed into a wine rack and collapsed flat on his face.

Lamia stood up, panting and gnashing her teeth. Her blood-soaked hair hung in ratty strands down the sides of her face. "I'll kill you! I'll kill all the Gods! Every last one of you!"

Ares fought to his hands and knees, coughing up blood. Lamia lurched toward him. I ran between them and shot her in the shoulder. She reeled and came back snarling. The wound didn't heal this time.

"Leave him alone," I said. "Don't make me kill you."

Lamia ignored the warning and lunged at me. I squeezed off another round. It hit her in the chest. She dropped to one knee.

"Please," I begged. "Stop this."

Lamia looked up at me. Her green eyes burned with mindless hatred. There was nothing human in them. This wasn't the woman I'd dated; that had been nothing but an act. She rose and ran at me.

I fired a third time. The shot struck her between the eyes.

Lamia made a croaking sound and came to a sudden stop. She stared at me in bewilderment for what felt like hours, though it couldn't have been more than a few seconds. A wisp of smoke coiled from the hole in her head. She took three wooden steps forward and collapsed.

I fell to my knees, breathless and shaking. My gun slipped from my hand. Lamia was dead. She was dead and I was alive. I had stopped her. I had stopped the God-killer. The moment seemed detached from reality. Cold sweat dripped into my eyes and stung them, reminding me how real all of this was.

I looked at Ares. He was on his feet but slumped against the wall.

"Nice job," he said weakly.

"You okay?"

"I'm alive, aren't I?"

I retrieved my gun and the real Aegis. The gun I returned to its holster. I clutched the Aegis in my hand.

"Can you walk?" I asked. "Or do you want me to carry you upstairs, like a rescued damsel?"

Ares chuckled faintly. "You're lucky I'm so busted up."

"I know. But I couldn't resist. It's not often you get to insult the God of War and live to tell about it."

Ares and I returned upstairs. Ares gripped the railing as he climbed the steps, dragging himself along. As we entered the living room, the roar of car engines came from outside.

"Sounds like the cavalry's here," I said.

Ares smiled. He fell onto the loveseat and closed his eyes. I sat down across from him on the couch. Seconds later a squad of OBI agents in black suits and Kevlar vests stormed the room, their guns drawn.

"Hi, guys," I said. "Welcome to the party."

72

Zeus summoned me to his office. The president was all smiles that morning, sitting at his desk in a snazzy ivory suit. Hera stood beside him in a matching gown, her hand resting on his shoulder. The way she was glaring at me you'd think I was the killer.

"Good morning, Mr. Jones," Zeus said.

"Sir. Ma'am." I came to stand in front of his desk.

"How are you today?"

"I can't complain."

"Would you like something to drink?"

"No thanks."

Zeus nodded. "I read your report. Impressive stuff. I especially liked the part where you and Ares took on Lamia. Very thrilling."

"How is Ares, by the way?" I asked.

"Already back on his feet."

"No thanks to you," Hera added.

Zeus patted her on the hand. "Now, my love, we should be grateful. Mr. Jones has done Olympus a great service."

"Well I suppose he did put down that monster," Hera sneered.

I held my tongue to keep from saying something stupid. Lamia may have been the killer, but she wasn't the only monster in New Olympia. There were two others, and they were right in front of me.

"Now that the case is closed, will you leave my ex-wife alone?" I asked.

"Certainly," Zeus said. "As you mortals say, a deal is a deal."

"Thanks. And what about Chrysus?"

"The stoning will wear off, and she'll come back to work. Is there anything else I can do for you?"

"Maybe," I said. "During the investigation, did your agents encounter a mortal named Collin Stone?"

Zeus checked his computer. "It seems they did. He was arrested last Thursday for tampering with evidence at the site of Enyo's murder. And impeding an OBI investigation. He's currently being detained at OBI headquarters."

"I need you to pardon him."

"For what reason?"

"For Enyo," I said. "He meant a lot to her. She wouldn't want to see him rot in prison for the rest of his life."

Zeus stared at the computer screen, his blue eyes thoughtful.

"Surely you don't mean to grant such a ludicrous request." Hera's grip on his shoulder tightened. "This Collin person knows that Gods can die. And he's already made it clear he doesn't care for us or our laws. Disposing of a Goddess's body! What if he decides to share that information with other mortals? We would have a full-blown rebellion to deal with." She waved a dismissive hand. "I say we execute him and be done with the whole matter."

"Collin won't say anything," I said.

"And how can you be so sure, *mortal*?" Hera raised a perfectly manicured eyebrow.

"Because he promised me."

She laughed, but somehow managed to do it while scowling. "I find that to be less than reassuring."

"If he tells anyone, I'll take the blame."

"An enticing offer, but I'm afraid it's not good enough."

"It's good enough for me," Zeus cut in. "Collin Stone will be released and granted a full pardon."

Hera made a strangled sound. "You can't be serious!"

"I am."

Hera started, "But—"

"The decision has been made," Zeus said.

She stared at him with her mouth hanging open, at a loss for words.

"Thanks again," I said.

"No, Mr. Jones, thank *you*."

I smiled and turned to leave.

"One more thing before you go," Zeus said.

"Sir?"

He took a check out of his suit pocket and handed it to me.

"What's this?" I asked.

"A little bonus."

I glanced at the check. My eyes widened at the sight off all those zeros. I folded it and slipped it into my wallet. I checked the wallet twice to make sure the check was still there before putting it in my pocket.

"I would also like to offer you your old job back," Zeus continued, "with a substantial pay increase."

"Not interested."

"Are you sure?"

"As I'll ever be," I said.

Zeus nodded. "If you change your mind, the offer is still on the table."

"Goodbye, Mr. President. First Lady."

Hera scowled.

Zeus stood from his seat and shook my hand. "Farewell, Mr. Jones. I'm certain our paths will cross again one day."

Not if I can help it.

Chrysus—the real Chrysus—was waiting for me outside Zeus's office. A red blouse peeked out from under her stylish black skirt suit. Her blond hair was down, and she'd added bangs. The glasses were missing. I thought she looked better with them on. Not to say she wasn't still drop-dead gorgeous.

"Hello, Mr. Jones."

"Hi."

We shook hands.

"I want to thank you for helping me," Chrysus said.

"Just doing my job."

"Will you be returning to work with us?"

"Afraid not," I said.

"That's unfortunate. I was looking forward to our getting better acquainted."

"Sorry."

Chrysus smiled politely. Looking at her reminded me of the time Lamia and I had spent together. For a while, I really liked her. In a way, I still liked her. I wonder what that said about me.

"I'd like to repay you for giving me my life back," Chrysus said. "Can I take you out to dinner this weekend?"

"How about lunch instead?" I asked.

"Lunch sounds good. Is there anywhere in particular you'd like to go?"

"Anywhere but Diamond Earl's."

73

A LARGE BOUQUET OF RED ROSES WAITED FOR ME AT THE front desk of my apartment complex. The note on the vase was handwritten in elegant letters with black ink.

> *Plato,*
> *Here's a small token of my gratitude. When next we meet, I'll give you a more suitable reward.*
> *Hope to see you soon,*
> *Aphrodite*

The implication in the note made me a bit nervous, but I appreciated the gesture nonetheless.

I picked up the bouquet and carried it upstairs to my apartment. I set it on the kitchen table, then headed to my bedroom to change into something more comfortable. I flipped on the lights and almost cursed.

"Okay, you've officially pissed me off."

The cat had returned. And he was lounging on my bed.

"You think you're pretty clever, don't you?"

It ignored me and licked its foreleg.

"You little swine!" I dove at the cat.

It sprang over me and bolted into the living room. I gave chase.

The cat ran under the coffee table and leapt onto the windowsill.

Oh no you don't, I thought, *not this time.* I hurdled over the couch and grabbed the intruder as it tried to scramble through the partially opened window. I laughed in triumph, raising the cat overhead like a trophy.

"I got you! I've finally got you!"

Surprisingly, the fiend made no attempt to escape. I wish it had. Seeing it struggle in vain would have made my victory that much more rewarding.

I lowered the cat so our faces were level. "Now who's the smart one?"

The cat meowed. It was a kitten's meow, small and charming.

"Nice try, pal, but you're not going to sweet-talk your way out of this." I looked at the tag on the cat's collar. Its name, Mr. Fancy Pants, was engraved in the aluminum. Below that were the owners' names and address. John and Christina Davies lived in the same apartment complex I did, on the floor above me.

I put the cat under my arm and went to pay Mr. and Mrs. Davies a visit. It was time they took responsibility for Mr. Fancy Pants here.

I went upstairs, knocked on their door, and waited. No one answered. I knocked again, harder. Nothing.

I pressed my ear against the door. No sounds came from inside the apartment.

"Are you looking for John and Christina?" a voice said.

I turned around to see a short, round woman with a white beehive. Her floral muumuu was a seizure-inducing shade of neon blue.

"Yes ma'am," I said.

"Then you're out of luck, I'm afraid. They moved out about two weeks ago."

I wanted to curse. Instead I said, "Thank you."

The woman smiled and went about her business.

Frustrated and disappointed, I returned to my apartment. I put Mr. Fancy Pants on the floor and sat on the couch. The cat jumped onto the loveseat and looked at me, its expression bland as usual.

"What am I going to do with you?" I said. "I'd feel guilty putting you out on the street. And a shelter is out of the question. A mangy beast like you would be euthanized on arrival."

Mr. Fancy Pants blinked but didn't respond.

"I suppose you want me to take you in."

He yawned and stretched out on the loveseat.

"Fine. But you had better watch yourself. One ripped curtain, one scratched-up bedpost, and you're out the window. Got it?"

Mr. Fancy Pants jumped from the loveseat to the couch. He crawled into my lap, curled into a ball, and went to sleep.

"I hate cats."

74

THE NEXT MORNING I SAT IN MY OFFICE, ON THE PHONE WITH Alexis.

"I must be hallucinating," she said. "Did you say you might have a job for Calais's nephew?"

"Sure did."

"What's the catch?"

"No catch."

"Are you sure?" Alexis asked. "There's usually a catch with you."

"No, there isn't."

"Then why are you so eager to put him to work?"

"I could use an extra pair of hands around the office."

Alexis was quiet for a moment. "I guess I believe you," she said. "When should I have him come see you?"

"Tomorrow at one."

"He'll be there."

"Great. I'll talk to you later."

"Later then."

"Oh, and Alexis. Congratulations on your engagement."

There was another stretch of silence on the other end. Then Alexis said, "Thank you, Plato."

"Take care of yourself, kiddo."

"You too." I ended the call and leaned back in my chair.

Emilie poked her head in the door. "Mr. Jones?"

"Yes?"

"Nicolas Parker called the office a few minutes ago," she said. "I told him you were on a very important call."

"What did he want?"

"He wanted to tell you that his missing gorgon has been found. Apparently, a good Samaritan turned it over to the police."

I gave a thumbs-up. "Good for him."

"Also, Mrs. Stone is here to see you."

I quickly stood up and smoothed down the front of my shirt. "Send her in."

Emilie left, and Bellanca came into my office carrying a large fruit basket.

"Hello," she said.

"Hi." I stepped around my desk and took the basket from her. "What's this?"

"A gift."

"Thanks, but for what?"

"For helping Collin."

I put the basket on my desk and gestured for her to sit. Her strapless purple dress ended slightly above mid-thigh. Her curly black hair rested on her shoulders.

"He called last night," Bellanca told me. "He said you helped him out of a bind."

A chill crawled up my spine. Had Collin told her the truth about the Gods?

"Did he say anything else?" I was almost too scared to ask.

"Only that he's sorry for what he put me through, and that I deserve a better man than him."

I let out the breath I'd been holding. "He's right."

Bellanca smiled. "Thank you."

I sensed a nervous energy about her. Her movements, the tone of her voice, all seemed tinged with indecision. I suspected I was giving off a similar vibe. My brief relationship with Lamia was now officially finished, and Alexis and I were long since over. It was probably time to move on. I wondered if Bellanca could feel my energy just as I could feel hers.

"How have you been holding up?" I asked.

"Fine, all things considered."

"You're still going through with the divorce?"

Bellanca ran her fingers through her hair. "I feel like I need to."

"Always go with your instincts."

"It feels strange though, being alone after all these years."

"Consider it a chance to reclaim missed opportunities," I said.

"I just might."

My cell phone rang. I picked it up and checked the caller ID. It was Alexis again.

Bellanca stood up and adjusted the bottom of her dress.

"I should probably be going," she said. "Thanks, Plato, for everything."

"My pleasure."

The phone continued to ring after she left. I stared at it, debating whether or not to answer. Then I looked at the fruit basket and smiled.

"Sorry, Alexis." I put down the still-ringing phone and ran outside.

The nearest parking lot was across the street. Bellanca was at the crosswalk, waiting for the light to change. I tapped her on the shoulder. She turned toward me.

"Hi, again," I said.

"Hello," she said. Her eyes widened expectantly.

"This may seem a little forward, but would you like to have dinner with me?"

Bellanca shrank away from me. Rarely a good sign.

"It's alright if you don't want to," I said, before she could answer.

"No, I'd love to. It's just that . . . Aren't you dating Aphrodite?"

Damn. I had forgotten about that little scandal. There was no time for damage control. I was going to have to wing it and hope for the best.

"She and I went out a couple times, but we were never dating," I said.

"Does she know that?"

"Of course."

"The tabloids say you two are madly in love."

"They also say that Bigfoot and the Loch Ness Monster have a secret love child."

Bellanca grinned.

"I know I'm not looking too hot right now," I confessed, glancing down at my wrinkled blazer and slacks, "but I refuse to pass up a good thing when I see it."

"And you think I'm a good thing?"

"Absolutely."

Bellanca crossed her arms and looked me in the eye, her head tilted to the side.

"One date," she said after a few seconds. "We'll see where things go from there."

75

IT WAS FRIDAY EVENING. THE NIGHT OWL WAS BARREN, BUT that would change in about an hour or two, when the first influx of regulars trickled in.

Herc and I were seated at a table with a bottle of scotch and two lowball glasses. The jazz band was setting up their equipment onstage, while behind the bar, Abas took stemware out of the dishwasher and placed it in a hanging glass rack.

I sipped some scotch and shook my head, smiling. "Man, that's good."

"If you say so," Herc said.

"You don't like it?"

"Tastes like deer piss."

"How do you know what deer piss tastes like?"

"I don't." Herc held his glass of scotch up to the light, frowning at it. "But if I ever tried it, I imagine this is what it would taste like."

I laughed.

"Well, you did it, Jonesy," Herc said. "You saved the day."

"Yeah, I guess I did. But I couldn't have done it without you."

Herc raised his brows. "Really?"

I shook my head. "No."

"Asshole."

We both laughed.

"So what's next?" Herc asked.

"Disneyland, I suppose."

"Think you'll take any more government contracts?"

"Only if the Gods hold a gun to my head."

Herc grinned wryly. "What are the chances of that ever happening?"

I wouldn't put it past them.

We raised our glasses and had a toast. To what, I wasn't entirely sure.

EPILOGUE

THE SUN PEEKED FROM BEHIND A VEIL OF CLOUDS, ITS WARM
light cascading down the peaks and slopes of Mount Olympus.
On the roof of the presidential estate, Zeus and Hera sat at a
luxurious patio table, having a lunch of sautéed Wagyu beef
and bird's nest soup. Far below, New Olympia unfurled like a
map before them. Hera had barely touched her food. She sat
motionless and quiet, staring at the horizon.

"You're angry," Zeus said.

"How very observant of you."

"Is this about Plato Jones?"

"What do you think?" Hera sneered.

"He did a good job."

"Of course *you'd* think so."

"Be nice."

Zeus ate a slice of beef while Hera continued to stare at
the horizon. A chilled breeze swept across the roof. The hiss
of its passage interrupted the silence.

"I understand you tried to assassinate him," Zeus eventually said.

Hera raised an eyebrow. "Who told you that?"

"Hades."

"That bastard. He swore he wouldn't mention that."

"Why did you go through such great lengths to destroy Jones?"

Hera sipped her champagne and said nothing.

"I don't intend to ask again," Zeus said, his tone low and even, as foreboding as the darkness before a storm.

Hera looked at him, her mouth a tight line. Clouds rolled across the sky, covering the sun once again. The air dimmed and grew cooler.

"You know why," Hera responded at last.

Zeus looked down at his plate. "It's not his fault."

"Plato Jones is a perversion of nature." Hera's tone grew louder and angrier with each word. "He and others like him don't deserve to breathe the same air as you and I."

Zeus sighed. "I understand how you feel."

Hera chuckled humorlessly. "Oh, you do, do you?"

"Yes."

"I doubt that."

Zeus shrugged. "Believe what you'd like. But know this: you will not harm Plato Jones."

"And why not?"

"Because I won't allow it. If you so much as scratch him, you'll be vacationing in Tartarus for the next century. Is that understood?"

Hera tilted her chin imperiously. For an instant it seemed she might argue. Then her face broke into a smile. "As you wish, Mr. President."

ABOUT THE AUTHOR

A fan of thrillers, fantasy, and science fiction, Robert B. Warren has been writing stories ever since he could hold a pencil. In 2009, he received a Bachelor of Arts degree in English and creative writing from the University of Alabama—Roll Tide! He currently lives in the South.

More Plato Jones books are coming soon.